best lesbian love stories
2004

best lesbian love stories 2004

edited by
angela brown

alyson books
los angeles

MANUFACTURED IN THE UNITED STATES OF AMERICA.

THIS TRADE PAPERBACK ORIGINAL IS PUBLISHED BY ALYSON PUBLICATIONS, P.O. BOX 4371, LOS ANGELES, CALIFORNIA 90078-4371. DISTRIBUTION IN THE UNITED KINGDOM BY TURNAROUND PUBLISHER SERVICES LTD., UNIT 3, OLYMPIA TRADING ESTATE, COBURG ROAD, WOOD GREEN, LONDON N22 6TZ ENGLAND.

FIRST EDITION: JANUARY 2004

04 05 06 07 08 09 a 10 9 8 7 6 5 4 3 2 1

ISBN 1-55583-825-1

LIBRARY OF CONGRESS CATALOGING-IN-PUBLICATION DATA

Best lesbian love stories 2004 / edited by Angela Brown.—1st ed.
  ISBN 1-55583-825-1
  1. Lesbians—Fiction. 2. Lesbians' writings, American. 3. Love stories, American. I. Brown, Angela, 1970–
PS648.L47B466 2004
813'.085089206643—DC22   2003062818

CREDITS
• COVER PHOTOGRAPHY BY YVETTE GONZALEZ.
• COVER DESIGN BY MATT SAMS.
• LUCY JANE BLEDSOE'S "THE BREATH OF SEALS" FIRST APPEARED ON BLITHE HOUSE QUARTERLY: A SITE FOR GAY SHORT FICTION (WWW.BLITHE.COM), SPRING 2002 .
• AMY HASSINGER'S "LA LLORONA" FIRST APPEARED ON BLITHE HOUSE QUARTERLY: A SITE FOR GAY SHORT FICTION, SPRING 2003.
• JENIE PAK'S "KEEP YOUR FINGERS LOST" FIRST APPEARED ON BLITHE HOUSE QUARTERLY: A SITE FOR GAY SHORT FICTION, FALL 2003.
• GINA SCHIEN'S "AN ORDER, A DISPUTE, A BURNING" FIRST APPEARED ON BLITHE HOUSE QUARTERLY: A SITE FOR GAY SHORT FICTION, FALL 2002.

for my sweet friends
Melissa, Carol, and Jane,
who all, for some weird reason, get me

contents

►introduction◄

"One human can stop another's heart
like a clock held underwater."
—Carol Guess, "Homeschooling"

I've always had a thing for magic: from sleight-of-hand card tricks to rabbits being yanked from big black hats to David Copperfield whisking the Statue of Liberty off into thin air. Magic makes me wonder. It makes me alert. It tickles my brain and my heart. I guess it comes as no surprise to me, then, that I've always equated magic with love: They both evoke the same feelings for me. But when I was rereading this collection, as a whole, from front to back, it blew me away to see how many of the authors in this book incorporate magic—both literally and figuratively—into their plots, characters, and themes.

Take, for instance, Lucy Jane Bledsoe's astounding opening story, "The Breath of Seals," in which the magic and majesty of nature work in concert with the mysteries of love and yearning. Or Amy Hassinger's dazzling and strange "La Llorona," in which the power of the heart and the soul's deepest desires create a magic that is visceral and unsettling.

Jenie Pak, in "Keep Your Fingers Lost," and Tzivia Gover, in "Francesca," summon a dreamlike magic that propels each of their protagonists to question how and where they find love. And Orly Brownstein, in her poem "The Jew in Bright Red" finds magic not just in a Chagall painting, but in the language of her soul, her tribe, the woman she yearns to find, not to complete her but to make her blood pound faster and keep her heart beating.

Yep, face it, love keeps our hearts beating (usually after stopping them for a moment). Remember that line at the end of *The Wizard of Oz* where the "wizard" says to the Tin Man, "A heart is not judged by how much it loves, but by how much it is loved by others"? How harsh is that? In my opinion, it's a big load of malarky (and it's a line straight out of my favorite movie, for crying out loud!). In these stories I hope you'll find words that will urge you to keep loving for the sake of loving, not because you expect something in return; to find love wherever it presents itself; to take giant leaps of faith; to tell someone you love her, even if there's no way in hell you think she'd ever love you back (because you *never* know!); to explore the wonder and love and delight and magic that's all around us.

A big thank-you goes out from me to all the writers in this book for making life—and living—a little more magical.

—Angela Brown

the breath of seals

lucy jane bledsoe

At 5 A.M. Roz shoved a spatula under the first fried egg and began her day. The workers were first in line. Folks who shoveled the snow, fixed the machinery, hauled the garbage and recyclables. They ate eggs, sausage, French toast. A handful of scientists started their days that early too, like Tom, the guy who studied penguin feces, and Stanley, who studied ice cores. Roz guessed Tom was looking for diet clues and Stanley for history-of-the-Earth clues. Either way, their data was no fresher, no more meaningful at 5 in the morning, but they were just that kind of people, and would make the first breakfast shift whether they were in New York City or here at McMurdo Station. They ate bowls of oatmeal or fruit.

The last group, who showed up right when the galley opened, were the folks manifested for a flight to the Pole, recognizable by their inability to eat at all at that hour. They tried a Danish, maybe a banana. These were the people Roz anticipated the most, sifted through, searching every morning for *her*. She'd seen Tamara the cosmologist only once ever, that first week when so many people were in McMurdo before flying off to their field camps or, as in the case of Tamara, to the South Pole. Roz still looked for her every single morning, on the off chance she'd had some reason to return to McMurdo.

It wasn't a crush. Roz was way too raw for that. It was more like Tamara was an important subject for her own research project. Everyone came to Antarctica looking for something, and if they denied that, they were lying. True, probably a good half of the folks here couldn't say what it was they were looking for, including Roz, but she knew she was looking, and Tamara seemed like prime data. Tamara herself was looking for the beginning of the universe. Which made Tamara, to Roz, something akin to *being*—okay, maybe just symbolizing—the beginning of the universe. Certainly nothing about Tamara's physical appearance indicated divinity. She was on the short side, wore her brown hair parted in the middle, let it hang over her ears—which stuck out a bit—and she had a goofy, lopsided smile. Roz thought someone who had looked so deeply into the source of the universe would glow from within, would *look* as if she had seen something wondrous. But it wasn't like that. The truth was—and Roz knew this—Tamara spent her days with data, staring not at the swirling black cosmos studded with pricks of light but at a computer screen. Her data wasn't visceral like penguin feces revealing fish species or ice cores showing cataclysmic events in the history of the Earth—no, Tamara's data was no doubt long lists of numbers, probably unvarying numbers, maybe even just combinations of zeros and ones, as she waited for some ideal combination, some long-hoped-for spike or aberration. In the month Roz had been on the Ice, this she had learned was the greatest paradox about scientists: Though they may be studying the most fascinating instant in the history of the universe, an event an ordinary person like herself could ponder for a long time and not get bored, the actual work of scientists was deadly dull. Not just hours but years and, in some cases, decades of examining minute shreds of potential evidence, billions of pieces of data, waiting, waiting, waiting for that one shred or datum that bursts open a new piece of the puzzle. That took patience in the most extreme. It took tolerance for boredom. But there was one character trait it also took that kept Roz interested, in all scientists but mostly in Tamara, and that was hope. A person couldn't dedicate a life to looking for one piece of a puzzle unless she possessed some uncanny investment in the future, some beautiful vision of the big picture. There was that paradox again: people who focused on a tiny piece of the story their whole lives only because they had a rare ability to imagine the grand epic.

Roz got through her mornings as the grill cook in the galley at McMurdo by posing questions to herself about human nature then trying to answer them by studying the people who came through her line. The Tamara question, about how a person maintained hope on a futile planet, was the apex of her studies. But on some mornings she concentrated only on such trivialities as why some women felt the need to smile even when they really didn't feel like it or why some men thought it was okay to scratch intimate body parts right there in the galley just because it was 5 in the morning.

Tamara didn't come through her line that morning, of course, because she was at the South Pole. But he did. He came through the galley every single morning, like clockwork, painfully gorgeous with his shaggy blond hair and doe eyes, and definitely not scratching rudely. He spent his days out at the airstrip plowing snow, pushing it out of the way, or sometimes into big piles, constructing and destructing. What was his name? John. Or maybe Jim. It was wrong not to remember the name of someone you'd made out with. Roz winced at the thought of it. She winced every morning at the thought of it these three weeks since it'd happened. She'd only been on the Ice for a week at that time; it was her first party. What was his name? Maybe not a J name at all. Ralph. Sam. Maybe it'd been internalized homophobia that had caused her to do it, but she didn't really think so. Nor did she think it had anything to do with Karen, or Karen and Larry for that matter, although Roz admitted taking this job in Antarctica had everything to do with Karen. But what had happened with John-Jim-Ralph-Sam hadn't been a reaction to anything. She had been sincere with him. He had that shaggy blond hair and those eyes. Maybe it'd been the party, which was an exact replica of the parties she'd attended when she was in high school, probably also of the parties her students attended now, and the atmosphere must have drawn her into its reality. There was the rock music at distorting decibels, a cluster of guys near the speakers pretending to play the guitar, a few other guys wandering, looking, sad, dissatisfied with the party, knowing the big guys with imaginary guitars were idiots but wanting anyway to feel what they were feeling. Roz was wandering that night too, wandering, and wondering if the pumped bass beat were a substitute for heartbeat, like people who cut themselves to feel something. Maybe that's why people took jobs in Antarctica, to see if the wildest, coldest, windiest continent on Earth could make them feel something.

Roz didn't leave the party. She had stayed. And oh, what a mistake. Each morning, 5:30, and there he was. All doe eyes, sweet, still after these three weeks, hopeful. Maybe as young as twenty, a full ten years younger than Roz. Shy, painfully shy. Perhaps if he wasn't, perhaps if he could make a bold move and she could reject him, they would be done with it. But he couldn't. He made brief, fleeting eye contact every morning while ordering his eggs.

"Hey, Roz."

"Hi."

The doe eyes intensified from a light coppery color to bronze. He placed his tray squarely on the slide, his hands gripping the edges. Uh-oh. He smiled differently this morning, a smile Roz recognized as a calcification of resolve. He said, "You don't remember my name, do you?"

Roz shook her head.

"It's Josh. My name is Josh."

"Two over-easy, Josh?"

"You going to the party in the Heavy Shop tonight?"

"Maybe."

"I'll stop by your room. We can go over together."

She wasn't prepared for that. After a month of too shy to say more than hi. She had thought the statute of limitations on when after a make-out session you could ask a person for a date had run out. She almost said yes, for lack of knowing what else to say, but she shook her head, then cruelly shifted her eyes to the next in line, shoved her spatula under two sunny-side ups, lifted an eyebrow at her next customer. When Josh moved on, she snuck a glance at his back, thin but standing tall. He'd be okay. What had been wrong with her? Making out with a boy behind a bunch of boxes of tinned peaches! Of course, she'd had a bit of beer. Was that an excuse? She'd been afraid of the lesbians, dancing in a small group, in

the middle of the party. She had needed sweetness, light-
ness, yes, the doe eyes were what she had needed. She had
meant the making-out—it had been something she wanted then, but she didn't mean anything else; she didn't
mean even a moment into the future, just that corner
behind the tins of peaches was all she had meant. The
peaches themselves had been a part of it. If, for instance,
she had found herself with the boy behind cartons of
canned ham hocks, she's sure she would have left.
Peaches and doe eyes. His sincerity was what she had
wanted, and if she were a good person, she would tell
him that.

When Roz's shift ended, she left the galley and
walked up to the post office. Ten degrees today, the sky
clear and creamy-blue. Standing on the hill, in front of
the post office, she held the envelope in her mitten and
looked out across the sea still covered with ice. A few
black curls, like parentheses, clustered around the
cracks. Seals, big Weddell seals, with eyes like Josh's. It
was a card envelope, square, slightly inflexible, rather
than the rectangular soft packet of a letter. That alone
was a disappointment. Cards can be equated with guilt.
A quick greeting, the gist of which is written by
Hallmark. Roz told herself to wait until sometime in the
future to open the card, but what time would that be?
She pulled off a mitten and tore open the envelope flap.
All the white space of the card was covered with Karen's
scrawl, a real letter after all. Roz trailed a mitten-cov-
ered finger over the green ink, touched the overall aes-
thetics of the message, the not quite out-of-control
handwriting, with small portions of text tucked in at
right angles to the main message. Then she flipped the
card over to look at the back, and there she found a couple of sentences of the neater but cramped handwriting,

also in Karen's green ink, borrowed, she supposed, for a moment, to add his charity:

Roz, I can't believe you're actually there, living your adventure. How many people actually follow through on dreams? Good for you! Larry.

Her dream! More like Siberia. How generous he must have felt writing that note. Roz looked across McMurdo at the seals again and let herself wonder how they could feel comfort lying on the ice like that, as if they were basking in warmth. Perhaps this ten degrees above freezing was warmth for them.

Why did she write?

Of course, it was a Christmas card. How could you ignore at Christmastime someone you had loved quite recently? Karen couldn't. She loved Christmas and strove to invest it with what she considered true meaning.

Roz read the card. Newsy. It had been raining on the Oregon coast for three weeks. Did she remember Carleen McBride—what a ridiculous question, as if Roz had been gone years rather than weeks—well, her daddy was lost at sea in one of the storms. It was so awful, Karen wrote, how these things keep happening, but then why wouldn't they; the ocean is so powerful and that doesn't change with time, and yet it seems like we should be able to *prevent* disasters as ancient as a fishing boat getting lost at sea. Was the entire card going to be about Carleen McBride's dad? No, she goes on with a series of questions. What were the people like in Antarctica? What was her job like? Did she have a good boss? Then at the end: I know this is a lot to ask, but maybe you could send back some pictures. It would so thrill the students to see their own Ms. Frick in her new environment.

That last was cruel. Code to slip by Larry, who obviously had read the card before adding his greeting. Ms. Frick. She had also written, Love. Love, Karen.

Karen Fenoglio was the principal of Lincoln City High School, Roz's most recent place of employment. Her husband was a writer—unpublished, but he should know better than to use the word *actually* twice in a two-sentence note. Roz had moved to the Oregon coast about eighteen months ago because she'd gotten a job there, because it was beautiful, and because she had worn out her welcome in Portland. She should have immediately sought out the lesbian community (a lesson she still, apparently, hadn't learned in Antarctica), but she had hoped to medicate herself with a big dose of abstinence, to see how long she could go without drama. Besides, it was time she committed herself to holding on to a job. She spent her first weeks on the coast dedicating herself to becoming a fabulous teacher: She read new, revolutionary books on teaching, she made poster-size copies of the covers of her favorite books and displayed them in her classroom, she had individual conferences with each of her students and many of their parents. Karen Fenoglio was the most demanding principal she'd ever worked for, and because she didn't have anything else to do, Roz strove to meet her high standards. She stayed late many nights. Sometimes the new teacher and principal chatted over the copy machine when they were the only two left in the building. Though Karen's personality approached a kind of athletic severity, she was friendly, and obviously impressed with the long hours put in by the new teacher. Still. There was no excuse for what Roz did.

The coastal storms in Oregon had an insulating effect. That November evening it was dark by 4 o'clock, and the rain lashed about the high school building as if tying it up. Roz wasn't going home only because she didn't want to go out in the weather. She'd corrected all her papers, and so she strolled down to the administration offices. A wedge of light shot out from Karen's cracked door. Roz placed her toes in the point of that wedge and knocked very lightly, then pushed open the door.

"Have a great evening, Dr. Fenoglio."

Everyone called the principal "Karen." Using her title and last name was not required. Doing so now was either subversive or flirtatious. Karen stood up behind her big oak desk. She didn't smile. She answered, "Good night, Ms. Frick."

Ridiculously, that's all it took. From then on, only if they were alone, they spoke their little joke. Not too often and always turning away quickly, as if witnessing the effect it had on the other would be admitting too much. It was so silly, and yet the phrase "Ms. Frick," spoken by Karen, shocked Roz's core. She should have found the lesbian community in Lincoln City.

From there it spiraled quickly into a *Well of Loneliness* thing, only the twenty-first-century version.

Larry never knew they had fucked. Or even kissed. Karen said she had hinted, said she had "let him know the seriousness of the situation."

Karen didn't fire Roz. Even if she had wanted to, how could she have explained the job termination? Instead Roz left. She hadn't been in Lincoln City long enough for anyone to really care why she was leaving so suddenly. The whole affair was very clean and the surgery to remove it fully successful.

Roz propped the Christmas card up on the small desk in her dorm room in McMurdo. Miraculously, she didn't have a roommate. Occasionally a transient scientist, on her way to a field camp or the Pole, was placed in her room for a few nights, though never Tamara. It was the kind of luck she often had, getting a room to herself when everyone else had to share, and she mentioned her fortune to no one in case it was a mistake they didn't even know they had made.

Roz slept for several hours. When she woke up, she lay in bed a while wondering if she should go to the party in the Heavy Shop. Still undecided, she dressed in expedition-weight long underwear, fleece pants and a sweater, her enormous down parka, and a hat and mittens. She placed Karen's card in the pocket of her parka and stepped out of the dorm. It was quite late and she'd slept through dinner. She could get something at midrats, short for midnight rations, later. Now, instead of walking up the hill to the Heavy Shop, she headed down to the continent's edge where the tides had pushed the sea ice up hard against the land, creating pressure ridges, piled-up chunks of ice. She stood there for a minute, her toes pointed due south, and closed her eyes. Roz heard a huff of wind and she tilted back her face to feel it on her cheek, to find out from which direction it came. But the air touching the bit of exposed skin on her face was still. She turned toward Hut Point, and then in the other direction, toward Scott Base, and finally faced north, and still felt no wind. She heard it, though, just barely, like a long sigh, followed by silence, and then another long sigh.

Roz walked around the side of Observation Hill so she could look out at the frozen sea without seeing the ugly buildings of McMurdo. The ice soared toward the horizon in its white glory, eventually meeting the sky, but only eventually. Long fractures in the ice revealed slits of black sea, and scattered around these few cracks were seals, pale ones, spotted ones, black ones. She sat on the rocky soil on the side of Observation Hill and looked at the seals, sky, sea. Black, blue, and white. Roz took the card out of her pocket and held it at arm's length. A red ornament on the front and the word PEACE.

At Christmas, Karen and Larry would go to Portland where Karen's parents and all her brothers and sisters and their children would convene. Larry would be uncomfortable. He'd confided this to Roz near the end, willing to share his vulnerability, as if it were a gift that would benefit Roz. Perhaps he was saying: There are other parts of Karen's life with which I'm uncomfortable, not just you. Or perhaps he was saying: You don't really want her, she comes with a big messy family.

Sitting now on the side of Observation Hill, looking out at the seals, Roz reread Karen's note. It really wasn't a letter, even though the card was full of green handwriting; it was only a note. Karleen McBride's dad's death and questions. That was all. Except for the Ms. Frick. How could her own name scrawled in green ink bring back so much?

Roz's own language arts classroom in Dr. Fenoglio's own school. The *principal,* for crying out loud. Long after the custodian had left for the day. A month after the Ms. Frick and Dr. Fenoglio game had begun. A year ago this month. It must have been 6 in the evening, an absurd hour for a teacher to still be in her classroom, as if she wouldn't rather be reading student essays in her own home, covered by a fleece blanket, sipping hot tea. It was raining again, and outside her classroom windows silver slashes lit the black December night. Karen stepped into the room and shut off the light. Roz embarrassed herself by gasping. Karen laughed.

"Scared ya."

"Well."

"What are you doing here so late, Ms. Frick?"

Karen leaned against Roz's Jack London display and flinched when the head of a pushpin poked her shoulder. She folded her arms and didn't smile. That not smiling of Karen's was like a hand slid under her shirt.

"Reading essays. And you?"

"I'm always here this late."

What she should have done then was remind Karen of her husband. It would have been easy: How does Larry feel about your staying late all the time? Instead Roz stood up and walked toward her. Just beyond Karen was the shade Roz had installed on the door window to prevent kids in the hall from making faces at her students. Administration officials never approved of those kinds of changes she made in her classrooms, the irregular ones, the ones she did without prior approval. But Roz didn't see Karen as the principal anymore. She saw her only as a woman who had come into her classroom and shut off the light. Roz reached past Karen and pulled the blind. Karen put a hand on Roz's hip. Roz couldn't tell if the pressure was away or forward. It didn't matter because Karen kissed her.

The sound of boots crunching on rock brought Roz's attention back to the present.

"I followed you. I'm sorry."

She turned to see Josh traversing the slope. He sat next to her.

"You shouldn't have followed me. That's not right."

"I know."

"Josh, I can't be your girlfriend."

"I know."

"There're so many nice girls here."

"They're all lesbians."

She wanted to ask, *Who's a lesbian?* but it seemed unfair to use his pain to solicit information that she wanted. Roz nodded, intending to keep quiet, but heard herself saying, "All of them?"

"Are you?"

"I'm afraid so."

He nodded an "it figures" nod. Then he asked, "Who are you after?" assuming that everyone is after someone.

"Tamara. The cosmologist." Of course, she lied.

Josh brightened, then coughed out a laugh. "Really? The one who works at the Pole? Is she a lesbian?"

"I doubt it."

"Do you have it bad?"

Yes, Roz had it bad. She wanted to tell him how it felt to come to work in the morning, to face a crowd of oversexed adolescents and try to get them to discuss *Jane Eyre* in the classroom where you'd had sex with the principal the night before.

She handed Josh the card from Karen, and he read it carefully. He relished the story that Roz then told him, and she appreciated that in him.

"So it's not really the cosmologist," he said.

Roz shook her head. "She looks too far. She misses everything." She said that as if she knew her, as if she'd had conversations with her.

It was true, though, what she had just said about Tamara. The beginning of the universe had to have been a cold, desperate place. The Big Bang had to have been cosmically painful, excruciating beyond comprehension. To pin one's hope on the beginning like that was the ultimate need to start over. Not just life, not just this century, but the whole universe! Maybe that wasn't hope at all. Maybe that was desperation.

Roz lay back in the rocky soil, slanted against the side of Observation Hill, and looked out at the creamy sky floating above the faintly luminescent sea ice. Who was to say this very moment, this very moment that held a silence deeper than any she'd ever known, wasn't the beginning of the universe?

The seals, who had been squirming earlier, were nearly still now, as if they had all fallen asleep in unison. Only their blubbery sides rose and fell as they slept. A faint, rhythmic whoosh brushed across the icy stillness; not wind at all, only the breath of seals.

seven-year itch

harlyn aizley

————————→

Dara Lenox has a dirty little secret. It—the secret—unfortunately has nothing to do with Dara's girlfriend, Madison N. Lalonde, and everything to do with Yvonne B. Sexpot, the generously endowed and impossibly straight manicurist at V. Salon, where Dara's great-aunt Eva has her hair done every Friday at 2 o'clock. The dirty little secret is this: Dara wants to fuck Yvonne, even though Yvonne has like sixteen boyfriends, and Dara has, as mentioned above, one long-term, in-house, majorly serious girlfriend. That would be Madison—rail-thin, ultra-vegan—N. Lalonde.

There's nothing nice about this, wanting to bang to high heaven some strange girl with biggies and high heels and plush lips painted a shade of red so deep and rich they make you sweat just to think about them. Especially when you're already involved. And Dara feels awful about it, really terrible. At night when she and Madison are eating sautéed tofu with brown rice and fresh kale steamed with sesame seeds, Dara almost feels guilty. But an hour later, reading with Madison on the sofa, there Dara goes again dreaming of Yvonne, imagining their bodies pressing against each other, heat rising off them in luminescent waves.

"I love you," Madison says one such evening without taking her eyes from her book.

"Me too," Dara mumbles, her mind all wrapped around Yvonne's soft curves. She's not exactly sure what she and Yvonne would talk about, but that hardly matters. *You don't have to have a conversation in your own fantasy!* Dara chastises herself. After spending an afternoon in bed, Dara imagines she and Yvonne would go out for steak and eggs. Maybe they'd even share a cherry Coke.

"Me too what?" Madison asks as she tips her reading glasses above her line of vision.

"Me too, love you," Dara says like a shamed child. All images of Yvonne shatter into a million tiny pieces, floating to the floor of Dara's imagination with a disappointing tinkle, just as they would if this were an animated movie of two lesbians at home in Boston on a Friday evening and one's thought bubble suddenly burst.

It's not that Dara has stopped loving Madison. It's not that she's no longer attracted to her. It's not even that she harbors some unconscious or semiconscious resentment, some long-standing injustice or unresolved rage. It's just that seven and a half years after sharing a Gardenburger and fries at Connie's Boardwalk Veggie Stop Café, Wellfleet, Massachusetts, circa 1996, everything's the same between them. Same jobs, same music playing on their living room stereo, same haircuts, same sex; Madison's even wearing the same clothes.

Then one afternoon Dara's great-aunt Eva phones to say she no longer can drive—backing out of her parking space into a neighbor's garage temporarily cost her her license. "How would you like to take me for my hair on Fridays, honey?"

Dara loves Aunt Eva almost as much as she loved Eva's older sister, Rosie, Dara's grandmother. And she's free on Fridays ever since cutting back her hours teaching. So, "Sure," she tells Aunt Eva. "I'd love to."

That's when everything changes, or threatens to. That's when Dara first enters V. Salon, where old women have been having their hair done every Friday since their grown children were babies; where free coffee and doughnuts and piles of *People Magazine, Us,* and *Vogue* are nonjudgmentally there for the taking; where idle chit-chat about idle husbands—dead and alive—and talk of mah-jongg games, canasta, recipes for kasha and varnischkes, crumb cake and borscht fills the air; where a drop-dead gorgeous manicurist, all curves and splendor in tight-fitting skirts and low-riding necklines, catches Dara's eye. The heart-shaped name tag above her right breast reads YVONNE B. Dara tries not to look at it as she sits each week wondering whether the old women whose fingers Yvonne B. dips into this bowl and that, whose hands she pats dry with a soft pink towel, aren't secretly in love with her.

But each time she winds up looking at the tag, at the breast, at both breasts, at Yvonne, and then all hell breaks loose inside Dara and she starts imagining blowing down the walls of her politically correct life with Madison and putting up a whole new house—one with wall-to-wall carpeting and a wide-screen TV, nonrecyclable containers and slow-cooked red meat. Despite her own leftward politics and bleeding heart, Dara finds herself longing for a world in which people don't need to rally at the State House against war if it's really cold out and some years even can forget to vote. A world she fears Madison—meticulously

17

respectful psychologist, peace activist, and driver of a hybrid car—would never agree, or even know how, to live in. To top it off, each week Yvonne winks conspiratorial little winks at Dara, who sits frozen in libidinous paralysis, pretending to read.

"Life can be simple," Dara says to Madison one afternoon as they select perfectly ripe organic pears and grapes at the food co-op.

"I know," replies Madison. "That's what I love about ours."

"I mean, people don't have to worry about everything all the time."

"Like what?"

"Like war or pesticides or the ozone."

Madison looks puzzled.

"You can come home from work and watch TV. You can eat doughnuts and get a manicure!"

"Doughnuts?"

"I'm just saying, life can be easy."

"What's easy about doughnuts and manicures?"

◆

That evening, back on the sofa, Madison slips her reading glasses on and turns to her book, while Dara flips a page of *The New Yorker* lying on her lap and turns to Yvonne. In this fantasy she and Yvonne are at a carnival, eating cotton candy and stealing heated glances at each other across the merry-go-round until they can't stand it any longer and quickly duck into a five-star hotel and fuck each other's sticky, sugary brains out for the rest of the day and night. When at last they come up for air, they order room service and lie back to watch the next installment of *The Osbournes* or *The Bachelorette*.

"I think I'm anemic," Dara tells her therapist the next morning. It's Thursday, the day before V. Salon Friday. "Or maybe I just need a vacation."

Dara's therapist asks what blood type she is, and soon they're talking about beef and pork, light therapy and vitamin E, and Dara leaves the session more confused than ever. She keeps trying to tell her therapist about Yvonne, about craving a new life of aerosol cans and whiskey sours. Each week she inches closer. But the detours are just too easy to take; her bespectacled feminist therapist, she imagines, is too much like Madison and too far from Yvonne to understand. Besides, Dara thinks, it's only been a month. It's not like she's been harboring adulterous feelings for a year or more.

At school it's Pizza Thursday, and Dara embraces the hordes of unruly sixth-, seventh-, and eighth-graders as welcome distraction from her preoccupation with Yvonne. Fantasizing about Yvonne, though endlessly stimulating, is freaking Dara out, making her feel all strange and evil around Madison and deeply unsettling the thirty-eight-year-old calm she previously had enjoyed. It's like she, herself, is twelve or thirteen and uncomfortably hormonal. Dara forgoes the pizza, thinking maybe the school's spiking it with prepubescence or some other pansexual intoxicant. Besides, being hungry, listening to the rumble of her stomach, Dara thinks might mute the call of her wayward libido.

But on the way home, desperately in need of nourishment and bent out of shape from having spent hours trying to force the face of her resident lover, Madison, into fantasies involving black lace stockings and Yvonne, Dara does the unthinkable: She stops at McDonald's and orders a double cheeseburger at the drive-thru. She can't believe the words coming from her mouth, that it's actually her voice saying "a double cheeseburger with medium fries and a Diet Coke." It's crazy and arousing, and twenty minutes later, for a split second, she can't remember whether the act that has her all red and guilty and afraid like a junkie fallen off the wagon involved eating red meat for the first time in fifteen years or kissing Yvonne.

Thursday evening. Ten hours post-therapy, three hours post-cheeseburger, and nineteen hours pre-Yvonne. Dara continues with her concerted effort not to think about Yvonne, not to imagine the two of them making out on a Hawaiian beach at sunset, groping in the back of Dara's car, or groaning and panting in the linen closet at V. Salon. She even phoned Aunt Eva and recommended they skip this week's salon visit, maybe go to a museum instead.

"Oh, dear, I couldn't do that," Aunt Eva sounded as if Dara had suggested both of them stop bathing for a week. "What would I tell the mah-jongg girls?"

"Well, what if I do your hair?"

"You, dear?"

"Sure. I used to cut my friends' hair in college." Dara imagines washing and setting her great-aunt's fine gray hair in the privacy of Aunt Eva's garden apartment. They'd turn on a soap, maybe bake cookies, then sit down at the dining room table, where Dara would massage Aunt Eva's tired scalp and gently comb its crown of sparse, delicate silver.

"Oh, no, I don't think so. I like going to the salon. But thank you, honey. That's a very kind offer."

In a last-ditch effort to free herself from temptation, Dara holes up in the bathroom and clips her fingernails down to the quick. Better safe than sorry, lest tomorrow she get the bright idea of going over to Yvonne B. and asking her for a manicure while Aunt Eva kibbitzes under the dryer.

"Honey, can I make you a cup of tea?" Madison shouts from the kitchen.

"No, thanks."

"I've got a new Moroccan Mint."

"I'm fine," Dara grunts. She's moved on to her toenails, uncertain as she is whether Yvonne's many talents include pedicures. Dara pauses a moment to imagine slipping her shoes and socks off and reaching her feet into a warm lavender bath, when suddenly the very real possibility of Yvonne touching her feet sends a shiver through her so sharp and deep that she slips with the clippers and lightly nicks her left big toe. It's a slight wound, but it stings and bleeds, and for what seems like no reason other than that—unexpected pain and the sight of her own blood—Dara yelps and then bursts into tears.

Madison knocks lightly on the bathroom door and peeks her head in. "Hey," she says. "What happened?" It's not clear whether she's referring to the blood or the tears.

"It's nothing." Dara holds up her wounded toe for closer examination.

"But you're crying."

"I know."

Madison takes her into her arms and holds her tight. "Oh, honey, you probably don't even need a Band-Aid," she says soothingly.

Dara heaves a sigh then erupts into wrenching sobs. Desperate to push all thoughts of Yvonne from her mind, she runs her hand up and down Madison's back and, starting below Madison's shoulder blades and ending above Madison's waist, counts each of her ribs. She is suddenly grateful for how slender Madison is, that she can count her kind lover's ribs with her fingers, one, two, three, Yvonne, four, five…

"Honey?" Madison asks. "What are you doing to my ribs? I like it. But what exactly are you doing?"

"I'm trying," Dara cries.

"Trying what?"

"To love everything about our life together, to not want any changes. Trying not to imagine you putting on fifteen pounds and watching HBO with me every night."

Madison takes a deep breath, leans back, and disengages herself from Dara. "Is that the easy, simple life you've been pining for? HBO, doughnuts, and what was the other thing? Oh, right, manicures." She lets out a little giggle.

"What's so funny?"

"Nothing. I guess I'm just trying to picture either of us getting a manicure."

Dara steels herself. "I ate a cheeseburger today, a double cheeseburger." She recoils as if waiting for a blow.

"And I had a cigarette," Madison says entirely unperturbed.

"You what?"

"Something about Thursday's caseload always make me want to smoke on the way home."

Dara can't believe her ears. Madison smoking.

"You have a cigarette every Thursday?"

"And a Diet Coke. The cigarettes are in the glove compartment. I can't believe you never found them."

Dara feels dizzy and nauseous, like the sky is falling in around her, only it's images of Madison and Yvonne tumbling down, disintegrating into dust. Maybe she has it all wrong. Maybe Madison is as much a figment of her imagination as Yvonne. Maybe you never really know anything about anybody, even the people you live with. Maybe everyone and everything is just a product of our imaginations, a projection of our own inner prude or whore. Maybe Madison harbors some secret fetish. Maybe Yvonne is really boring in bed or a vegetarian or afraid of carnival rides.

Dara looks at Madison, at her brown eyes sparkling like cinnamon sugar underneath a head full of thick brown curls. Madison, so beautiful and strong, so solid and focused. Who knows what goes on within the privacy of her own mind or car? Cigarettes, Diet Coke, maybe even a sexual fantasy or two or three or four.

"Maybe I should eat a cheeseburger every Thursday," Dara says defiantly, though she doesn't know to whom or what she is making the threat.

"You should, if you want one," Madison says.

"And what about sex toys?"

"What about them?"

"What if I might want to use one sometime?" Dara mumbles. "You know, just to try it."

"Can we pick it out together?"

"I guess."

Madison takes Dara's hand. "Getting a little bored of us, sweetie?"

Dara's tears return. She's crying so hard again, she can't get the words out to answer Madison, who is kneeling before her, holding both of her hands in her own. Instead she just sobs and shakes her head no, yes, no.

"It's okay, you know, impossible to avoid."

Dara can't picture Yvonne now. Can't see her on her knees before her, holding her hands and looking so sweetly familiar as to resemble almost a part of herself, like an arm or a leg she can't imagine living without, even though sometimes it would be nice if said arm or leg were firmer, maybe not so pale in the winter. Madison, who laughs at all her jokes, who held her grandmother Rosie's hand when she died just six months into their relationship. Madison. What was she thinking?

"Maybe I could come with you for a cheeseburger one Thursday afternoon," Madison says.

"You'd eat a cheeseburger?"

"Sure. I mean, not every week, but once in a while, why not?" Madison answers as she gently washes Dara's toe with warm water and soap, dries it with a towel, and applies a Band-Aid. "But McDonald's, not Burger King."

Madison leads Dara by the hand into the living room and props her up on the sofa, wounded toe resting lightly on a pillow. She strokes Dara's cheek with the back of her hand and kisses her lightly on the top of her head, resting her face for a moment in Dara's long blond hair.

"Anything else you need to tell me?" Madison asks.

"No." Dara pulls Madison down beside her. "Never."

Madison lets free a quick breath.

"Why not Burger King?" Dara asks.

"The fries at McDonald's are better."

"Jeez. Who the hell are you?" Dara is only partially kidding.

She holds close this Madison of the weekly cigarette and french-fry expertise. She imagines the two of them feeding each other bites of cheeseburger and fries, taking turns sipping from the same Diet Coke. Maybe they would get something to go and share it in bed, or a hot tub, or the back of Madison's Honda. It's such a relief, like finding out you're not the only kid in town who sucks her thumb. Exciting too, like discovering a secret passageway in your attic. Dara wiggles her wounded toe. Maybe Madison wouldn't even mind a little toenail polish one day: Cherry Red, Orange Sunset, Slutty Vegan.

stuck

shelly rafferty

Surprisingly, the idea of prayer did not immediately occur to the Right Reverend Laurie Cady just after she nail-gunned her hand to her own roof; she had other concerns.

For one thing, she was alone.

For another, she wasn't expecting company any time soon.

The roofline of the parish house at St. Andrew's Episcopal is parallel to the street. She was on the back side, shingling, when the mishap occurred. For the previous few days she'd been watching her Uncle Ray operate the nail gun. Two hours of practice was all she'd had before he declared her fit for duty.

The early summer heat was brutal on the roof. Working in a tank top and jeans, Laurie felt particularly butch in her leather tool belt and boots. She'd tied a navy-blue bandanna around her sweaty forehead, Springsteen-style, and she and Ray were two-thirds done by the time he quit to make his guard shift at the prison.

Before he departed, Ray reloaded the nail gun and left it on the mesh table on the patio. Laurie snagged a bottle of water, took off her tool belt, and followed him into the house. They shook hands. "Thanks for coming, Ray," she told him.

"Whatever happened with that Anchorage thing? You going to take it?"

"Alaska's too far, even for me," Laurie answered softly. "I'm still thinking over my options."

"You've been here a while."

"Almost a year."

Alone on the roof twenty minutes later, Laurie braced herself carefully with one foot below and the other knee cocked. She set the next shingle in the middle of the pitch and leaned in with the nail gun. The upper right corner tacked down with a rapid thunk. A distant, weirdly sweet aroma glazed over the surface of the roof. Laurie lifted her head for just a second. "Barbecue," she murmured, and took aim at the other corner.

There was hardly any blood. "Shit," Laurie muttered. Immediately she dropped the nail gun and dumbly watched it slide down the incline of roof, clank through the rain gutter, and disappear over the edge. She felt for her hammer at her waist, then remembered she'd left the tool belt down below. Double shit.

She fell to her knees and studied her hand.

The nail had penetrated the taut curve of flesh between her left thumb and forefinger, just nicking the knob of thumb bone. Her hand was solidly tacked down; she could barely wiggle her lesser three fingers.

Her neighbors weren't home.

The house sat back too far from the street for any passersby to hear her.

And Alex, in all probability, was working the night shift. Triple shit.

After a few hours, Laurie had nearly succeeded in forgetting the pain. She was lying on her stomach now, the one hand nailed above her, the other under her head. Eventually, she reasoned, someone would come along, if not by tonight, then tomorrow. She wasn't about to try and rip her hand away; the slightest movement shot pain through her head as well as her hand. Church members often stopped by on Sundays anyway, with coffee cakes and baked hams, or special requests for announcements before services began. From the look of things, she wouldn't freeze to death. She was parched and uncomfortable but nowhere near death. She would've killed for a Budweiser.

She gazed off across the slant of the roof into the trees, and just beyond, into the hills at the horizon. She and Alex had hiked those hills in winter, when the quiet snowfall had painted all of the ground cover a slate-tinted white. Among the poplars and birches, Laurie had luxuriated in the sensation of balance as they walked, as if by having Alex's company, the labor of exertion simply collapsed into the movement of necessity, of the unmistakably present.

Right now, Laurie thought, Alex was on the road, perhaps with Mac or Johnny, grabbing coffee or idling the motor of their ambulance in the ER parking lot, waiting for their next call. She hadn't been by in a couple of weeks.

Laurie lay her head back down.

It was hard being still. The phrase *occupational hazard* floated overhead.

✦

"I hear you're thinking about leaving," Alex began bluntly. "Is that true?" Side by side on their knees, she and Laurie were turning over the loam in the ragged, dark plot behind the parish house. Alex had spent the morning cultivating a deep furrow against the fence, composting the bed of asparagus she'd put in the month before. Now they'd worked their way forward, toward the outside edge of the plot. A wheelbarrow full of tomato plants and marigolds waited nearby.

"Where'd you get that idea?"

"I get the skinny from AA." Alex wasn't an alcoholic and didn't attend meetings. But her ex, a frequently off-the-wagon but stalwart member named Cynthia, apparently didn't honor the confidences of the gatherings.

"I'm still here," Laurie answered, brushing off the inquiry. She dug into the muddy dirt with her little spade, relocated a worm, tore out a few weeds. "The regional office called me. I haven't told them anything yet. But when they call it usually means it's time for me to move on."

"But you've been asked to stay, haven't you?"

Actually, the pastoral search committee at St. Andrew's had just approached her. They'd been in the hunt for a replacement since the last fellow, an amiable fifty-four-year-old, had dropped dead in the middle of a sermon the previous April. Within six weeks of his demise, Laurie had arrived on temporary assignment. She spent the first several months of her tenure soothing the congregation, including two women who'd been rivals for the pastor's affections. Eventually she'd earned her own place in the people's hearts, owing much to her conscientious attention to the church's finances. The search committee had offered her a permanent post.

"Yeah, I have that option," Laurie replied lamely. She chopped indifferently in the dirt, ruffling small riverbeds, chucking handfuls to one side. She found the motion of her own hands, the aroma of the earth, and the peculiar order they were creating strangely intoxicating.

"I'm in love with you," said Alex suddenly. "I want you to stay."

Laurie paused with the spade and turned. "Don't complicate this. It isn't about you and me."

"But we have been working toward something."

"Of course," Laurie muttered, digging into the dark soil again. "But this is church business. I have to consider my career. It's not about our relationship."

"If you think so," said Alex under her breath.

"The thing is, I got an offer in Anchorage," Laurie continued. "I can leave the parish life for good, become an assistant director at a retreat center. It would be a big change for me. I'd have the chance to learn something new, to take my life in a new direction."

"A new direction? You've had a new relationship every eighteen months or so for the last twelve years. That seems like a lot of new directions. What about us? Or am I the only one who thinks our relationship has turned serious lately?"

Serious? Maybe that's what it was. Maybe that's why she was hesitating. She looked at Alex slowly, taking in her shining, earnest eyes; her muscular upper arms; the wisps of hair just behind her ears. Could she wake up next to her for the next few years, for the rest of her life? "I, I don't know..." Laurie stammered. "I need a few weeks to make a decision, honestly."

Alex was different from other women she'd dated. She displayed a fierce indifference to what other people thought, but without any arrogance. She was funny. She was kind. She knew how to leave Laurie alone. And she knew how to get her attention: a book of poetry left on the seat of her car, a pound of coffee just when she was running low.

"I don't want you to be coy," Alex said. "You know what I'm talking about..."

"You want me to look in my crystal ball and tell you the future? I can't do that."

Alex tossed another spadeful of dirt toward the back of the garden.

"You mean you won't."

Laurie's response was curt, and then she regretted it. "Look, I'm only in charge of my own future. Don't make me responsible for yours." She gathered a few seedlings from the wheelbarrow and handed them to Alex. Carefully, Alex scooped out a pocket of soft earth and patted the plants into place, one by one.

Alex got to her feet and peeled off her gloves. "Listen, I'm not asking you to marry me. At least not yet. But I find it more difficult each day to bear this sense of how I want to be with you. It's weird, I know. You're like this joyful burden in my head. I get up in the morning and put you on, or slip you in my pocket, the thought of you, the sound of your laugh, your fragrance, your fire. I'm not obsessing about you. But all day long, somehow, I've come to count on seeing you, or hearing your voice. And you've been doing that too. And you know it." Alex brushed at the knees of her jeans, collected the empty seed packets, and tossed them into the wheelbarrow. "So if you're going to leave here—leave me and us and this thing we've been building—you've already waited too long to tell me."

"I'm sorry," Laurie answered quietly. "Going is what I know how to do."

"Then do what you know how to do," Alex said. "If that's what you want. Maybe I've been reading you all wrong this last year. We've been careful about what we've shared about our pasts, and I respect that. I hope—and you've said—that what is between us isn't 'the same old thing' for you. You've seemed happy."

"I am happy."

"Laurie, if you want to learn, really learn something, you have to unmake the world as you know it."

"I don't know what I want."

"You'll figure it out." Alex pulled her bandanna from her back pocket and mopped at her forehead. "You'll have quite a crop of tomatoes by August," she said.

"I'm sure someone will eat them," Laurie sighed.

It was only June.

$\spadesuit$

In the distance, as darkness fell, Laurie heard the rumble of thunder and saw the intermittent flashes of lightning. A slow-moving storm. It wasn't cold yet, but in a rainy breeze, Laurie knew the temperature would drop through the night. No one would find her until morning. By then, disheveled and infected, she anticipated her bones would hang on to the chill like a forgotten T-shirt on a November clothesline.

She felt like an idiot. "Hey!" she called out into the wind. "Anybody? Hey!" Her voice was scrappy and rough; it didn't carry far. Her sound waves escaped like an injured bird out of its trap but too damaged to fly. Useless.

Her neighbors, the Madisons, were out of town. It would have taken a yodel of gargantuan proportions to get their attention anyway, since they both wore hearing aids. She rolled on her shoulder and turned her gaze to the peak of the roof, just a few feet above her. Where was Alex?

$\spadesuit$

It had been a slow start, to tell the truth.

Interrupted in the composition of her Sunday sermon, Laurie was irritated by the doorbell. Her coffee had grown cold, and the radiator was being finicky, only stingily

31

spewing heat for a few minutes each hour. She hugged the navy cardigan closer and opened the front door.

"Reverend Cady," Alex had begun. She doffed her cap and twisted it self-consciously in her hands.

In the ambient mid-morning light, Laurie thought she looked troubled. An ailing parent? An impending divorce? Laurie put aside her irritation and assumed her most pastoral expression. "Yes?"

"I'm here to take care of the yard," Alex announced. "And the garden." Her friendly smile immediately dispelled any notion of psychological disturbance. She was wearing faded sage jeans. A pair of leather gloves peeked around her hips from a tight back pocket, a denim jacket, a Yankees cap. Lean, cute. Just over her visitor's shoulder, Laurie spotted a not-too-old Ford Ranger parked at the end of the driveway.

Laurie stood in the hallway with the door halfway ajar, and she slid her wire-framed glasses up to her forehead. The part-time sexton, George, hadn't mentioned the yard work.

"I need the key, you know, for the shed," Alex continued, gesturing obliquely toward the backyard.

"Right." Where was the key? "What did you say your name was?"

An hour later, Laurie was brewing fresh coffee and staring through the window over the sink, watching Alex drive the tractor around the back lot. Her sermon was still undone, but she felt distracted by the gardener. She fixated on the pattern cut into the soft spring grass; the waves of short and long; the rhythmic, steady thrum of the mower. She watched, entranced, as Alex tilted her head as she made the turns first at one end of the yard, then at the other. After several passes, near the pear tree at the far end of the yard, she turned off the mower.

Laurie stepped back into the shadow of the kitchen,

not wanting to be caught staring. Then she felt stupid. Maybe coffee. Maybe the woman would like some coffee.

Alex was walking toward the house.

Laurie opened the door and called out, "Coffee? I just made a fresh pot..."

Alex had stopped twenty feet away and was staring at a spot over the door. "Huh? Oh, sorry, Reverend Cady."

Laurie repeated her offer.

Alex waved her off with a polite "No, thanks."

Laurie pushed through the screen door and wandered out into the yard. Her coffee sloshed a bit when she walked. "What are you looking at?"

Alex took off her ball cap and pointed to the roof. That's when Laurie noticed her hair, a short, gentle rope of curls pulled back in a ponytail, hanging loosely in a spray colored of hay and flint. "You've got a shingle come up—right there."

"That's something I'll have to tell George, I suppose."

Alex nodded. "You need a new roof. Probably next year. But I can fix that for now..."

"Really?"

"You'll be all right for a few days. George doesn't like heights."

"And you do?"

"I'm not crazy about them. But I can come by tomorrow, if that's all right."

Laurie shrugged. "You sure you don't want some coffee?"

They'd gone on like that for a few months: drinking coffee and exchanging pleasantries. Sometimes Laurie would invite Alex in for a sandwich. Alex planted peonies and ground cover. But one Saturday in September, Alex didn't show up. She didn't call. She hadn't said—in the weeks before—that she'd be out of town or wouldn't be coming.

From the window over her desk, Laurie kept checking the driveway, looking for the little Ford. At 11, concerned, but dismissive of her own agitation, Laurie drove up to County General to make her hospital rounds.

In the clergy office she picked up her visits clipboard. It identified only one patient: Mary Reston, a comatose twenty-three-year-old in the long-term care annex. Mary'd been there since her high school prom night. Laurie headed for the dim, near-empty ward without enthusiasm.

As always, Mary's mother, Sylvia, was knitting, and providing the answers to an old *Match Game* rerun.

"Good morning, Sylvia," Laurie offered, as she took up her position next to the silent, unmoving girl. "How's Miss Mary today?"

"A regular chatterbox," mumbled Sylvia. Her knitting needles kept time with the clicking respirator.

Laurie caressed the young woman's forehead briefly, then lowered her head and prayed silently for ten minutes. "See you next week," she whispered into Mary's unhearing ear. *I hope you die soon,* she said to herself. And end this... "And I'll see you at services tomorrow..." she said to Sylvia. Then she gathered up her briefcase and turned for the door.

"By the way, you know your friend's on the second floor," said Sylvia, her needles pausing.

Laurie already had her hand on the knob. "Excuse me?"

"Your friend came in. Alex Bailey. She's a friend of yours, isn't she?"

"Yes, I know Alex. She works on the ambulance. I suppose she's here pretty often—"

"She definitely wasn't working. She came in this morning, right behind me."

Laurie frowned, trying to make sense of what she was hearing. "Is she all right?"

Sylvia shrugged. "Apparently not."

Alex awoke some hours later. "Hey, got that sermon ready?" Her voice was thin, wasted.

Laurie sat forward. She rested her hands awkwardly on the edge of the bed, between them. "You should have called me. The nurse told me you drove yourself in."

"Have you been here long?"

Laurie felt a space open at the back of her throat, the slightest twist in her gut. It was bad form for a preacher to lie. She'd spent the entire afternoon in the visitor's chair. Had a church member seen her, her quiet posture would have been credited as an expression of rapt piety, but she hadn't prayed at all. She'd found herself staring at Alex's small mouth, wondering what she tasted like. After an hour, she'd even let the paper mask fall away from her face, convinced she was immune to the viral pneumonia that had brought Alex, coughing, pale, and feverish, into the emergency room. "Just a few minutes," Laurie said gently. "You look like hell."

"Nice talk for a preacher," smiled Alex. "Just for that," she added, "you'll have to cut the lawn yourself."

"Hmmm," murmured Laurie.

Alex turned on her shoulder and coughed. She pulled Laurie's hand over her own, cautious of the IV drip. The antiseptic had plumed a yellow stain under the translucent bandage on her hand.

"I wondered where you were this morning," Laurie said.

A wry smile. "Now you know."

"My Saturday seemed kind of out of whack."

"No joke. Mine too."

"Right." Alex's hand was warm. "Do you need anything?"

"I'm going back to sleep."

"All right. I guess I'd better get home."

Alex had closed her eyes. "I feel lousy," she whispered. "Stay a little longer." Her grip loosened, but her fingertips stayed, reading the Braille of Laurie's heart line.

"I will," answered Laurie.

It was dark when she drove home.

Sometime in the weeks after Alex recovered, Laurie kissed her. Not in the backyard, but on a date. A real date. They'd gone to dinner, then off to the university to look at the stars. On the roof of the Science Center, a group of astronomy grad students had set up a dozen telescopes and invited the public to gaze at the moon, the binary systems, Mars and Jupiter.

Scott, an eager-looking fellow in his late twenties, proctored the big scope. In her amiable way, Alex had fallen into an extended conversation with him about his studies. Laurie lingered at the eyepiece of the telescope for several minutes, trying to focus on a planet. Finally, a family with three impatient children gathered behind her, and she relinquished her position.

"I've fished that spot," Alex was saying to Scott as Laurie came up behind her. There, Laurie noticed the worn seam on the shoulder of Alex's jacket; obviously, she'd tried to sew it up herself. The thought of Alex's effort warmed her, even if her workmanship was shoddy. Laurie had come to appreciate her independence, the way she wouldn't waste a thing. "A notoriously slippery shoreline. Dropped my rod and reel and filled up my boots there too, opening day of trout season!"

Laurie marveled at Alex's ease with near strangers. Although Alex seemed shy, Laurie had come to recognize her as simply open and nonaggressive. There was no guile in her, no pretense.

Scott chuckled. "I'm a glutton for punishment, I guess. I'm going back Saturday."

"You won't catch anything but bass now," Alex warned him.

"You could suggest a more productive place?" He raised an eyebrow as he asked. He couldn't take his eyes off Alex. There was a tinge of playfulness in his voice, a kind of *Are you interested?* and Laurie suddenly felt invisible.

"And reveal my secrets?"

Laurie cleared her throat and touched Alex's upper arm. "Hey, sorry to interrupt."

"Oh, you're done. Did you see any UFOs?"

"Not a one." Laurie thrust out her wrist and tapped her watch lightly. "I'm thinking we still have an appointment with a bottle of wine…"

Alex eyed her with slight surprise. It hadn't been on their agenda; in fact, there hadn't been any discussion of events to follow the rooftop expedition. "Oh, right," she agreed. Quickly she thanked Scott and shook his hand.

"Let me know if you want to come along next Saturday," he offered. "I could call you."

Alex grinned. "Sorry, can't make it." She reached for Laurie's hand and held it up for him to see. Laurie felt a rush of embarrassment and delight. What if someone saw them? She was out to the hiring committee of course, but not to the entire congregation. Alex's grip was firm, but not demanding. "I think my Saturdays are taken."

Later, in the parish house kitchen, Alex said she was sorry. "Low impulse control," she admitted, setting her glass of wine on the counter beside her. "I shouldn't have grabbed you like that."

"Don't apologize. You surprised me, that's all."

"Well, I'm not sure about you, to be fair. Not sure about the speed of all this. I'm pretty certain we've been on a date all night."

Laurie nodded slowly. "Yeah, I think that's what I called it when I asked you..."

"So was I wandering down the road too fast?"

The light over the stove cast a buttery glow between them.

Laurie stepped forward. "I'm not in the habit of answering a question with a question, but do you think I should kiss you?"

"Is that what you want?"

"Yeah," Laurie nodded. "That's what I want."

Alex smiled and tucked her hands behind her back. "Bring it on, girlfriend," she said.

So Laurie kissed her. First in the kitchen, and then in the living room, on the floor, in front of the evening news, Letterman, and the late movie, until breathless and unbuttoned, they fell asleep.

◆

It was cold on the roof.

Laurie was lying on her back now, her hand outstretched and aching. Overhead, the clouds were low and crowded, dismally close and rumbling with rain. She wished for a blanket. The cinders in the shingles had begun to imprint themselves on her bare shoulders; she felt dirty and thirsty and utterly miserable.

She rolled toward the nailed-down hand and fantasized about jerking it off the nail. A spider of red infection was already crawling out around the puncture mark. When had she last had a tetanus shot? She couldn't remember.

What a ridiculous sight she might be, she imagined, when someone at last discovers her, stapled to the pitch, her skin raw with irritation from the sandpaper surface. If she were dead, would her rescuer construe her odd predicament as evidence of foul play? She could see the headline in the local rag, the *Askance County Citizen-Dispatch*: "Local Minister Succumbs to Tool and Dies."

Overhead, the gray clouds began to roil and swirl like a gray, velvety concoction, pockmarked here and there with a few stringlets of stars.

The pain in her hand worsened, and Laurie pointed her chin toward the chimney. She felt the shingle-grit adhering to her face and instinctively pulled at her nailed-down hand to brush it off. Bad idea. Again the wave of pain invaded her arm. There was no ignoring it.

Think about sex, she told herself. Think about the best sex you've ever had. The way it starts when you and Alex are arguing local politics, both of you backed into corners and still scoring points, a competitive tongue in your cheek, the good-natured laugh. If there's company, you notice how she lays off the beer, savoring the conversation as an intoxicant, thinking; she wants to be sharp, not just come once and collapse into sleep. She wants you to see how she drops subtle hints for the guests to get lost. She clears away a few of the empty bottles. She dumps an ashtray. Coming back from the kitchen, she stops at the doorjamb and rejoins the chatter, her arms crossed over the denim shirt, where strangely enough, another button has come undone...

Or if you're alone, there's that moment when her grasp encircles your wrist in the middle of *Law & Order* and she says You feel like fucking? and you always do.

Think how it's never been quite like this before, with any other lover. The way Alex looks at you, not with adoration, but with the confidence that whatever mystery you are brewing, she will find it out.

The rain burst open on the roof with the music of a

dropped vial of tiny beads. For a moment, Laurie opened her mouth and drank it in.

♠

Valerie Jean Morgenhaber had almost had her committed. To settling down, that is. VJ adored Laurie. But back in Cincinatti, VJ's incessant cheerfulness and devotion simply got tiresome. And Laurie had put off breaking up with the girl, worried that she would devastate her. Talk about your anticlimax. VJ's reaction had been minimal; a month later she moved in with a plumber named Dennis.

That had been a long time ago. Years, in fact.

The interim had offered up a short list of discreet affairs, until Laurie's work had sent her packing, and she hadn't felt inclined to drag any of the romantic weight with her. No one had really interested her, she told herself. It was the boredom that terrified her, the suffocation of sameness, that peculiar neediness that eventually all her lovers had come to reveal, and that she abhorred. More than once a lover had offered to come along, to follow her to the next ministerial post— until Laurie reminded her she wasn't invited.

Alex hadn't offered. Hadn't begged. Hadn't shown the slightest interest in following Laurie anywhere.

♠

Once the rain started, Laurie let her misery wash over her. The shower came down in a steady wash of white noise, soaking her jeans, slipping under her back, strangely muting the fire in her hand.

She missed Alex. After that day in the garden, they'd agreed to separate; a month had gone by. Even though she'd decided against Anchorage, she continued to put off the committee. For the past few weeks, the loneliness had been unbearable. She missed Alex: her patience, her steadiness, her honesty. She'd missed the sex too.

Without her, Laurie had spent some of the last month surfing personals online, looking at badly retouched pictures, listening to pleas for a partner who "doesn't play games," and reading more than enough skanky bisexual come-ons. She hadn't encountered a single ad that interested her.

In love with Alex? she asked herself. Is that what I am? What would Alex's ad have said? Enthusiastic, hard-working woman who digs laughter, great sex, and small adventures seeks a friendly partner with a bright gaze, open mind, and tender heart. Unnecessary to compare confessions...

That was the thing, the disinterest Alex generally held for the past, both Laurie's and her own.

◆

"Look," Alex told her that morning in bed, just after they had first made love. "It's not that I don't have baggage. But I don't want anyone to carry it for me. It has nothing to do with you and me..."

In the dim, diffuse light of the sunrise, Laurie's curiosity had wrestled with the refreshing nonchalance of Alex's attitude. "If there was something I needed to know about you, about your past—"

"You'd already know it," Alex answered gently, and then pulled Laurie closer. "You're safe with me."

"I believe you," Laurie heard herself whisper.

◆

I'm slipping, thought Laurie suddenly. The rain had made the surface of the roof slicker, and gravity was working its magic on her tired body. Soaked to the skin now, she'd begun to slide toward the rain gutter, just a few centimeters, but enough for the nail-pinned hand to shudder with an excruciating agony. Carefully, Laurie bent her knees and tried to push her boots against the roofline. A little purchase with the right, an inch of upward lift, a moment of numb relief. Then the left gave way, and the pain tore through her hand again, and lightning struck the tree next door.

The utility guy in the cherry picker would have missed her completely if she hadn't yelled. Not that, being forty feet off the ground, you'd expect to be accosted by somebody nailed to a roof. They were still separated by the power company wires, some of which dangled, spitting weak sparks, over the shattered upper limbs of the elm. The cherry picker floated cautiously near a transformer.

"Mother of God, you scared me!" he shouted back, his hands cupped to his face, which actually looked a little pale. The rain had stopped, and a milky moon sent out enough light for Laurie to make out his company jacket. He waved at the truck down below to stop shaking his basket. "Jimmy! Cut the motor!" He turned back to the preacher. "You all right?"

"What time is it?"

"Four in the morning. What the hell are you doing on the roof?"

"I'm stuck."

"Come again?"

Laurie shook her head. "Just get me an ambulance, would ya?"

"Hey, Jimmy!" the utility guy called down to his driver. "Call 911!"

A few seconds later the thread of a faint siren lifted up over the houses and sewed its way through the neighborhoods, mending the night. The utility truck backed up and lowered the picker to the ground, and Laurie could hear the shouts of the men directing the ambulance at the end of the driveway. The flash of rescue lights fluttered silently against the phone poles. A few doors slammed. *The crew's coming through the house,* thought Laurie. *Their boots are probably muddy.* Then the scent of almost-ripe tomatoes followed Alex and Mac up the ladder.

"Jesus, Laurie," Alex said, scrambling gingerly forward to kneel beside her. Mac took up his position on her opposite side. "How long have you been up here? Anything broken, or is just the hand?"

"Just the hand," Laurie said.

"Roll her toward me, Mac. Let's get her up just a few inches."

Mac's hands on her waist were firm, and his lift almost effortless. Both EMTs opened their kits, and Mac began to swab at her shoulders and neck. Alex extracted a pair of pliers. She rocked forward on her knees and examined Laurie's hand. "Son of a bitch," she murmured. "That's gotta hurt."

The moonlight was fading again, and Alex settled back on her heels for a second. Quickly she unzipped her light jacket and slipped out of it.

"Not much, anymore..." The jacket's thin flannel lining was warm across Laurie's bare skin.

"You're freezing," Alex went on. She tore open some alcohol gauze pads and tossed the wrappers over her shoulder.

"I'm going to live." The alcohol burned like dry ice on her hand. "I'm glad to see you."

Alex smiled a slight smile. Then she covered Laurie's hand firmly with her own, letting two fingers lace into the space between Laurie's. She aimed the pliers at the offending spike. "I'm gonna get this out now. You ready?"

Laurie nodded.

"Turn your head, darlin'," Alex whispered gently, and pulled.

♠

Laurie and Alex were back up on the roof the next weekend. Laurie had borrowed a new nail gun, but Alex wouldn't let her handle it, and Laurie was happy to leave it to her. The hand was still healing but didn't hurt much anymore. It was bandaged and tender, but usable.

There were just a few shingles left.

"We're almost done," Alex was saying. "This roof should last the next resident another ten years."

"You think so?" Laurie asked.

"It should. If it doesn't, I can always—"

"You think you'll always be here?"

Alex paused and looked at Laurie. "I reckon..."

Laurie held her gaze a moment, loving her just as she was, just then, and knew.

"The garden looks good," she said, tilting her head slightly toward the brilliant tomatoes. "I want asparagus for dinner..."

Alex smiled, amused. "There won't be asparagus until next spring."

"I know," Laurie answered. "I'll mark my calendar."

the butch of my dreams

lesléa newman

If I've told myself once, I've told myself a thousand times: Unless you're in a coma, Mimi Jankowitz, never, never, *never* leave the house without putting makeup on your face. And do I listen to myself? No.

So there I was at the post office, waiting to mail a package and buy a roll of stamps without so much as a hint of liner on my eyelids or a touch of blush on my cheeks, in sweatpants no less, when who should get in line behind me? Only the handsomest butch to roam the planet since the Ice Age, if not before. She was tall and built to last, with broad shoulders and a thick waist underneath her snug leather jacket. Her legs were so solid, I was instantly jealous of the lucky pair of blue jeans that were hugging them so tightly. She had short, slicked-back dark hair, blue eyes that literally (yes, *literally*) sparkled, and a mouth that looked like it would slide into an easy grin at the drop of a bra strap. Hell, she might as well have had a sticker on her forehead with the words MIMI'S WET DREAM printed on it. I couldn't believe my luck. Why did this have to happen on today of all days, when I looked like something the cat wouldn't even dream of dragging in?

Oh, well. Perhaps I'd bump into her again some other time when I was looking more like my usual glamorous self. She had to be new to the area. This is a small New England college town, and I would have definitely noticed her before. I tried not to make it too obvious that I was noticing her now, but I couldn't help turning around several times to catch a glimpse of her. Once I pretended I was looking at the clock on the wall behind her, another time I turned my head when the door opened as if I were checking to see who had just come in. I even accidentally-on-purpose dropped my keys to see if she would pick them up, but a man on his way to the stamp machines beat her to it. As all this was happening, the line we were waiting on inched its way forward and I reluctantly moved with it. Then when there was no one ahead of me, I heard my name called.

"Mimi."

I started walking toward the counter but then saw that Annie the postal clerk was still busy with a customer. Were my ears playing tricks on me?

"Mimi." I heard my name a second time and realized the sound hadn't come from in front of me; it had come from behind me. Which could only mean one thing. I turned around slowly, licking my lips to moisten them in a pathetic attempt to pretend I was wearing lip gloss, and faced the tall, dark, handsome stranger.

"Mimi." The butch said my name a third time, as a statement, not a question. How did she know who I was? I studied her face openly now and she watched me. When it was clear I didn't have a clue, she said her own name.

"Kim. Kim Kesselman."

"Oh, my God. You look so…"

"Grown up?" she asked, and sure enough, there was that easy grin.

"That's one way to put it."

"Good enough to eat" would be another. I couldn't believe I hadn't recognized the woman I'd been fantasizing about for ten years. When had she returned to town? And when had she lost her baby fat, replaced the horn-rimmed glasses with contact lenses, and finally learned how to tame her hair? She'd been adorable before, but now she was downright dashing. She'd grown into her butchness as I'd always known she would. It was in her stance, in her smile, in the way her hands were jammed into her pockets and her feet were planted firmly on the floor. The woman took up space. She also took my breath away.

"I see you're still trying to sell the great American novel." Kim nodded in the direction of the large padded envelope I clutched to my chest.

"Yeah, well, at least they can't say I didn't try." I shrugged. "I'm nothing if not persistent." *Or foolish,* I silently added. I'd been working on a version of this novel ever since I'd known Kim, whom I'd met in a college creative writing class a decade ago. "What about you? Still nursing literary aspirations?"

"No way." Kim laughed and patted her stomach. "I like to eat too much."

I laughed too, and then Annie called my name, so I sauntered over to the counter, making sure I put a little extra swing in my walk. Hell, just because my face looked like crap didn't mean my ass couldn't look great.

"Hey, Mimi. How's tricks?" Annie was friendly as always. That's the kind of town this is. I'm on a first-name basis with the postal clerk, the supermarket cashier, the butcher, the baker, the candlestick maker. Some people find it suffocating to be so known—in fact, a good friend of mine recently moved to New York City because, as she so delicately put it, she felt everyone she passed on the street knew what color underwear she had on. I'm from the Big Apple, which I left precisely for the opposite reason: There you can walk out your front door wearing nothing but your underwear and nobody would even notice. I've always been a small-town girl at heart. I liked that Annie the postal clerk remembered I had a cold last week and hoped it was better. I liked knowing that her grandson lost his first tooth yesterday and got a shiny silver dollar from the tooth fairy. Under normal circumstances I'd be perfectly happy to stand here and shoot the breeze with Annie all morning. But today's circumstances were anything but normal. All I wanted to do was mail my package, grab my stamps, then leap onto Kim's back so she could carry me off into the sunset where we'd fuck like bunnies and live happily ever after.

Ah…a girl can dream, can't she? I got my stamps and lingered by the door until Kim had mailed her letters. Then she said four little words that were music to my ears: "Need a ride home?"

You betcha! "Sure," I said, quietly slipping my car keys into my pocket. Hell, they could tow my Toyota to Toledo for all I cared.

Kim took my elbow—some femme had sure trained her well—and steered me to her car. She opened the door for me, slammed it shut, then flashed me another grin through the windshield as she walked around to the driver's side and slid behind the wheel.

I gave her directions to my place, and as she drove we talked about this and that—the various jobs she'd held for the past ten years, the places she'd lived, how her sisters were doing. I filled her in on what I'd been up to as well. Neither of us mentioned our respective love lives, though of course I was dying to ask her if she was single and more than eager to tell her I was once again between girlfriends and could really use a little afternoon delight. To get the ball rolling, I decided to beat around the bush, so to speak, and bring up her lurid past.

"What was that jock's name—you know, the one you went out with when we were juniors? She played basketball, softball, soccer, you know the one. She was like Miss Athlete of the Century. Ever hear from her?"

"Oh, God, you mean Loretta?" Kim glanced at me for a second and rolled her eyes. "Some athlete. She was athletic, all right. Except for in the bedroom."

"I told you she wasn't your type. I always said you needed a femme, not a jock, remember?" Of course, back then I was too shy to say what I really meant: Kim didn't need just any femme; she needed me to bring out her inner butch and then some.

"Hey, how about what's-her-name?" Kim was quick to change the subject. "The curvy blond who broke your heart? What was her name?"

"I forget," I mumbled, as if I could ever erase the name *Lydia* from my brain cells. Lydia, who not only openly cheated on me but also wound up draining over half my bank account. Talk about dyke drama. I'll never forget that humiliating night when I cried in Kim's arms about the unfairness of it all. And then we split a few beers and I tried to talk Kim into having sex with me. Since I was being cheated on, I told her, there was no reason I couldn't also cheat. And furthermore, since Kim wasn't getting any action in the boudoir, she had every right to a little nooky with me.

God, I hoped Kim had forgotten that awful night. She acted honorably (much to my dismay), for she was as loyal—and as cute—as a Saint Bernard. She wouldn't touch me, even though the sexual attraction between us was so thick you'd need a chain saw to cut through it. She swore if we were ever single at the same time she'd jump my bones in a minute, but somehow our timing was always off. If I was single, she was seeing someone. And when I was on the loose, she was always attached. And even though all I got from her was a chaste kiss on the forehead the night of my failed seduction, things were different between us from that point on. And then we graduated and she moved away. Kim had grown up in this town and always said she wanted to live in a big city. So she went off to San Francisco, and except for in my dreams, I never saw her again.

"Is this your building?" Kim asked, cutting into my thoughts.

"No, the next one."

She pulled into my driveway and turned off the ignition. A loud silence filled the car. A silence I knew I'd have to break, since it's always the femme's job to make the first move. But it's also the femme's job to make the butch think she's making the first move. So I merely asked, "What brings you back to town, anyway?"

"My mother died."

"Oh, I'm sorry."

She shrugged, and I knew not to press further. Kim's mother was a card-carrying Christian who had told her daughter on numerous occasions that she was going straight to hell and it was her own damn fault. I knew there wasn't much love lost between them.

"So I'm cleaning out the old homestead," Kim said almost to herself. "And then if I never set foot in this town again, it'll be too soon."

"Did you come by yourself?" I asked.

"Yep," she said, which gave me the answer to the question I was really asking: *Are you single?* She had to be, since no self-respecting femme would let her butch come clear across the country to perform such a painful task by herself.

"How about you?" Kim turned in her seat to face me and leaned her arm against the steering wheel. "You flying solo these days?"

"Yeah," I nodded, and then asked the next logical question. "So do you want to come in?"

"Of course I want to come in," Kim said.

Oh, my God! My mind raced around the apartment. I thought I'd picked my dirty clothes off the floor and at least piled last night's supper dishes in the sink, but I wasn't totally sure. And what about the bed? Had I made it? And more importantly, when was the last time I'd changed the sheets?

I tried to remain calm, or at least look calm, as Kim got out of the car, came around to my side, and opened the door for me. I took her arm and smiled as we walked up the steps. At the door I let go of her sleeve to fumble in my coat pocket for my keys.

"Wait," Kim said just as I unlocked the front door. "Maybe this isn't such a good idea."

"You're right," I nodded. "It's not a good idea at all. It's a great idea. A fabulous idea. The best idea I've heard all day. All week. All year." *Down, girl!*

"Oh, Mimi." Kim smiled and shook her head slightly. "I don't know. I want to come in—what fool wouldn't?—but I don't know if I should."

"Oh, c'mon, big boy." I crooked my finger and winked. "Let's have a little fun."

"Mimi," Kim sighed my name again. "I could never just have a little fun with you. You know that. We share too much history. And besides..."

"Besides what?" I tilted my head to the side in what I hoped was an attractive manner.

"Besides..." Kim paused and knit her eyebrows together,

51

like she was trying hard to find the exact words to say what she needed to say. As I watched her forehead crease in concentration, I remembered how precise her writing had been in that class we'd taken so long ago.

"Ah," she said, as though a lightbulb had just appeared over her head. "Remember that story Mrs. Morrissey told us in Introduction to Creative Writing?"

"Which story?" I asked. "She told us a lot of stories."

"Oh, right." Kim looked down and blushed, and I was glad to see she was as nervous as I was.

"Let's sit," I dropped down on the top step of my apartment building's stoop and Kim sat down beside me. "So," I prodded her, "Mrs. Morrissey…"

"It was toward the end of the semester, and that weird guy with the sparkly Elton John glasses, what's-his-name, Danny something…"

"Danny Schmidt. Oh, my God, he was always writing those poems about cabbages, remember?"

"Yeah, what was that about?" Kim asked. "Anyway, he kept pestering Mrs. Morrissey to tell us how to get our work published. So finally, even though she said it was extremely difficult to get your work into print—"

"Tell me about it."

"She agreed to give a lecture on publishing. She told us about all the different kinds of rejection letters you can get from editors: the unsigned form letter, the signed form letter, the signed form letter with a personal note at the bottom, the personalized letter, the no-thanks-but-try-us-again letter—"

"I have an entire collection upstairs," I informed Kim, motioning over my back toward the building. "Want to come up and see?"

Kim threw me a look and continued. "Mrs. Morrissey said even if your writing is good, it doesn't mean it will ever get published. And she told us about this writer who sent a story to a magazine and waited for months until he finally got a reply. It was a personal, handwritten letter. The editor said his story was amazing, fantastic, the best story he had ever read. But there was no way he could publish it."

"Why not?"

"Because the story was so extraordinary, it made every other story the editor ever read sound like shit."

I smiled. "I'm sure Mrs. Morrissey didn't say 'shit.'"

"All right. It made every other story sound like poop."

"That's better."

"The point is," Kim raised one finger, "if the editor published the writer's story, it would raise the magazine's standards to an impossibly high level no other writer could ever hope to meet. Eventually the magazine would have to cease publication, as would every other magazine in existence. Literature would no longer exist. So even though it was with great regret, the editor had to do the world a favor and return the story to the writer."

"Oh, yeah." I looked up into Kim's dazzling baby blues. "I vaguely remember that story. But what does it have to do with us?"

"Don't you get it?" Kim asked, gently tucking a strand of flyaway hair behind my ear. "If I made love with you, Mimi, it would be so amazing and fantastic, I'd never be able to make love with anyone else again."

"Maybe you wouldn't have to," I said softly.

"But we live in such different worlds," Kim reminded me. "After a while, we'd have to make some decisions. And I doubt you'd move to San Francisco—"

"You know I hate city life."

"And I would never move back here. So sooner or later we'd be right back where we started."

"Except we'd be older and wiser," I pointed out.

"Or sadder and more broken-hearted."

"Maybe." I had to concede her point. "But don't you think it'd be worth it?"

Kim sighed, and a look of pain passed over her eyes. Someone had hurt her badly, very badly, and I could see she wasn't ready, at least right now, to take a risk like that again.

Oh, well, what's a girl to do? I reached for Kim's hand and squeezed it tight. "That's the nicest rejection I've ever gotten," I told her. "And believe me, I've gotten plenty."

"It's not exactly a rejection," Kim said.

"But you're not coming in."

"No," Kim said. "I'm not. But I'm glad we bumped into each other. Now I know you're still alive, still here, and still more beautiful than ever."

"You're going to break a girl's heart, you know that?" I held onto her hand for dear life.

"Mimi, it's better this way," Kim patted my knee. "This way I get to keep you forever."

"What do you mean?"

"I mean…" she paused and covered her face with one hand. "I can't believe I'm telling you this. I…I dream about you," she mumbled. "I…you know. I fantasize about you."

"Me too," I whispered. "I dream about you too."

"But it's more than that." Kim's eyes swept over my face. "You're my harbor, my haven, the place I retreat to when I feel all alone in the world. Every sailor needs a port in a storm, Mimi. And I need you. I need you right here." She lifted our clasped hands and placed them over her heart.

"Wow," I said. I didn't know how to feel because I was feeling so much. Flattered, turned-on, sad, disappointed. "But Kim," I said, hope springing eternal. "Couldn't we just—"

"No, we couldn't just." Kim cut me off at the pass. "We're lesbians, Mimi, remember? We can't *just* anything. We'd have to process and analyze and go to therapy and—"

"Yeah, yeah, I know." This time I cut her off. "But Kim," I had to keep trying, "wouldn't you like one afternoon of unbridled passion to remember me by?"

"Yes, but...Mimi, don't. Please don't."

"How about a kiss then?" I'm nothing if not persistent—or foolish—remember?

"Okay," Kim said. "What harm could a little kiss do?" She stood, and still holding her hand, I stood with her, shut my eyes, and waited. A few seconds passed. Then Kim, gentleman that she was, raised my hand to her lips and planted a tender kiss across my fingertips. Surprised, I opened my eyes and looked at that stunning face one last time. Then I withdrew my hand, kissed the spot Kim had kissed, and placed it over my heart as the butch of my dreams descended the steps, got into her car, and drove away.

lesbian father

lisa e. davis

Driving the lonely stretch of highway in western Massachusetts from our house to town, I'd often thought they seemed to manage fine without me—my partner Marilyn and our three-year-old son Ethan. We'd hired Sancha, a college student, to cook, clean, do mountains of laundry, and play every afternoon with Ethan, who still slept at night in the big bed between me and Marilyn. That stymied any adult sexual urges that might've survived Ethan's introduction into our life.

We both cuddled him instead. I bathed him when I got home from work, the way I'd done since he was an infant, and we shared long conversations about floating rubber duckies and dinosaurs upside down and right side up. "Look, Lala," he called me. I loved having a moniker; I'd never liked my name—Leila—definitely a cat's name, or a hooker's. When bath time was over, I gathered Ethan in his big towel and sniffed the fragrance of baby soap and shampoo.

Things weren't going so smoothly with Marilyn. I

knew how tired she was, so I put up with her nagging. But she really got under my skin when she complained about how I looked after Ethan. His bathwater was too hot or too cold. His socks didn't match, or didn't match his T-shirt. He was eating too many sweets. And on Friday, she'd screamed at me down the long, icy driveway with Ethan in his car seat, off to nursery school: "You forgot his hat. You're going to give my baby pneumonia." Fine, I forgot his hat. "Thank you." She was frazzling my nerves, but the part about "my baby" was what really pissed me off. I didn't dispute that she was the mommy, but Lala and Ethan loved each other too. No one was going to separate us; we were pals.

Marilyn hadn't always been so possessive. Once upon a time she'd been anxious to share.

Before we decided to have Ethan, Marilyn, and I had been together seven years. Our relationship seemed steady and enduring. She wanted to have children. "We'll prove that family means love," she said, "not what we grew up with." A certified social worker with a psychotherapy practice, Marilyn didn't fear the future, or the past and its scars.

But I wasn't so sure. Sitting on our sofa, in our little house on one of those woodsy New England roads, we'd watched the seasoned birch logs blaze in the fireplace, our fingers intertwined. "You know, we have so much together, and children don't guarantee happiness," I said cautiously.

My mother had convinced me of that long ago. "You talk just like your father, Leila," she'd complained. "You even walk like him." I could neither verify nor deny, since he'd run away to Canada to avoid the draft in the 1970s, never to return. But I suspected Mom's complaints were her way of saying I was too butch for her taste, of blaming him for saddling her with a lesbian for a daughter.

Marilyn had problems of her own that I didn't like to remind her of. "Children are a big responsibility," I said, cradling her head against my shoulder to soften the blow. "And ever since I've known you, you've been raving about your mother, how she married too young, had her life eaten up by children and a worthless husband."

Marilyn's thick chestnut hair curled over her shoulders, eyes steely-blue like a blustery autumn sky above Provincetown harbor. "I'm not a victim like my mother," she replied, a tear starting down one cheek. "I have choices, and I won't let her bitterness hold me back."

And that was that. We invested thousands in donor sperm at 500 dollars a pop, mostly Marilyn's money. My job at the bookstore only paid enough to cover a few bills and essentials. We started out inseminating at home, but after the third delivery all the way from California of an enormous refrigerated cylinder with a tiny vial of sperm buried deep inside, curiosity got the better of the FedEx person, who asked, "What are you doing with that, anyway?" We moved on to the gynecologist's office. She had a steadier hand or more practice, and after another thousand dollars or so, we hit pay dirt.

The pregnancy was good. Marilyn glowed with health, all rosy pink like a great peony opening, and I trembled just to touch her. She confessed she no longer felt beautiful, but I pooh-poohed that. "I've never wanted you more," I whispered before I plunged between her legs. The miracle of her fecundity pulsated all around me, and I felt life stir, dark and bloody.

The amniocentesis showed we were having a son, which conformed to statistics weighing in on the side of lesbians giving birth to male children. Some sort of legacy from Amazon warriors, we figured. I liked the idea of being lesbian father to a boy, with penis and balls (not just a rubberized facsimile), who would grow up to have narrow hips and big shoulders—all the things I'd always wanted. We would hike, play games, talk sports. Any doubts I buried deep alongside my other fears of parenthood.

In the last months, as mother and son waxed massive, I became like one of those worker bees at the center of the hive, the ones you see on nature programs, that exist only to serve the Queen Bee—Marilyn—who would bear young. No frills, no sex; I brought food and kept her warm and comfortable.

But none of that bothered me. Both of them needed me, and I felt part of something miraculous. Being part of something is better than being left out.

Then in the fall, snow threatening, he came, with powerful screams and an insatiable hunger. "Isn't he beautiful?" I said to Marilyn as she fed him. His tiny hand closed around my finger, and I forgot everything in a wave of gratitude for his robust health. I thought the three of us were getting to know each other, getting on really well.

That was interrupted when the door to Marilyn's room opened wide, filling up with some people I hadn't seen in years and others never. "I had to call my mother," Marilyn admitted, the one she'd sworn never to speak to again every time she talked to her on the phone. Mom gathered Marilyn and the newborn to her bosom. "He looks just like your brother when he was a baby," she declared proudly. Then there were aunts and uncles, a distant cousin, and Marilyn's grandmother weeping over the baby, who'd weighed in at a whopping eight and a half pounds and measured twenty-one inches. "He'll be tall like his great-grandfather," the old woman sputtered, as though our son had given her life new meaning. And I guess he had.

After everyone had had a chance to admire him, a nurse whisked the baby away. Marilyn took up the slack by introducing me around to the relatives who weren't in the know. "This is Leila, my partner," she said. "We'll be coparenting."

Silence resounded like a thunderclap, and all eyes in the room turned my way, stationed as I was at the foot of Marilyn's hospital bed like a sentry. In those eyes I saw some befuddlement, some hostility. Marilyn's mother nodded pleasantly, and the cousin from New Hampshire shook my hand. "Welcome to the family, Leila," he said lamely. An uncle cleared his throat. "Well, what are you going to call him?"

"We haven't decided," I stammered, though we had pretty much settled on Zachariah after Marilyn's maternal grandfather, the tall one. People would call him Zack for short, which evoked both daring and cheerfulness, we thought.

Now it was Marilyn's turn to look befuddled, but she didn't give me away. After another half hour of buzzing around gnatlike, the relatives went off to dinner.

"I'm sorry about the name business," I explained to Marilyn.

"That's okay," she smiled at me. "I figured you had something up your sleeve."

"I guess I didn't realize," I said, "you were so into family."

"Oh, you know I'm not." She laughed. "They're harmless, and they'll go away soon. Then it'll just be the three of us." She paused sweetly. "Why don't you go home and get some sleep?"

"Maybe later," I replied out of a mounting vigilante fear I tried to suppress. If they came back while I was gone, they might kidnap the baby, even Marilyn. My blood froze. If anything happened to her, they'd have legal rights to the baby. The precariousness of my situation bore down hard. If I didn't have the money to adopt right now, I'd better start saving and get the process rolling.

"About the baby's name," I added, "you know my father's never been more than a shadow to me—"

"I'm sorry," she said; maybe, I imagined, the way she talked to her therapy clients—too bad for you, better luck next time.

"Anyway," I continued, "I wondered if maybe we could give the baby *his* name, Ethan, as a connection, you know, to my side."

"Zachariah Ethan... That's beautiful, darling"

"Ethan Zachariah," I suggested coyly.

"Of course." Marilyn took my hand. "That's even more beautiful."

That was before.

∮

Things started to go wrong once we brought Ethan home. He was happiest when he was eating, and Marilyn got up to feed him at all hours. A cry, a whimper, and she was on her feet. If he fell asleep in bed between us— Marilyn's teat in his mouth—we got a little more rest. I was up at 6:30 A.M., and Marilyn had moved her therapy practice home to a space in the basement that had a separate entrance. Though some of her clients didn't want to make the drive out of town, most of her evenings were busy with tired, depressed, anxiety-ridden people headed home from work.

We were almost paid up at the sperm bank and gynecologist, but exhaustion had taken its toll. One night while Ethan was dozing, we sat together over Chinese takeout I'd brought from town. "I know you're tired, darling," I began. "Maybe we could take a little vacation, just over to the beach, like we used to."

"Not with the baby," she replied. "He's too little."

"He'll be fine," I reassured her. "And we could relax, get closer."

"Oh, Leila," she patted my hand, "in a few months. I don't think I could do it right now."

Then on a weekend she knew I had to work, she took the baby on a three-hour drive to visit Grandma and Great-grandma, driving all that way alone. I don't think I ever forgave her for that.

Time passed with no vacations and little respite from a relentless routine. But Ethan thrived, and grew strong and willful. He was often indulged when someone should've said no, I thought. "He's spoiled rotten," I said. "And the older he gets, the worse it's going to be."

Then he'd hide behind Marilyn and peer out at me, his lip stuck out, face all screwed up for a good cry. He was such a ham, I had to laugh while he ran off screaming into the bedroom chasing the cat or something. Ethan was quite a guy.

Once he started nursery school, he and I drove in together every morning. "He's having some trouble adjusting," one of the staff told me when I came to pick him up.

Uh-oh, I thought. "What did he do?"

"He's just a little aggressive with some of the other children," she confided. I could imagine.

"Do you like school, Ethan?" I asked him on the way home.

"No," he hollered, "no, Lala," and struggled with the straps on his car seat.

"Why not, precious?" I tried again.

"I want to go home."

"That's where we're going." A rubber ball from the

backseat bounced off the windshield and into my lap. "Watch it, Ethan," I warned. He squealed with delight.

A week or two later a call came for me at the bookstore. "Leila," Ethan's teacher said, "I'm afraid we've had a little incident here."

My pulse fluttered. "Ethan, is he all right?"

"He's fine." Her voice was stern. "But I'm afraid you'd better come over."

I did. Our Ethan had wrestled another boy for a wooden train engine, then smacked him over the head with it. The other child had a big bump.

I walked Ethan to the car. "Do you know you hurt Frederick with the toy?"

"He wouldn't give it to me." His lip stuck out a mile.

"He doesn't have to give it to you. You could wait until he's through playing with it."

"I didn't want to."

"You can't do everything you want to." He thought that over and threw his rubber ball at the windshield. That time it bounded harder and caught me in the eye. It was a snowy day, and I swerved. "Ethan!"

I pulled to the side of the road and opened the back door. He glared at me defiantly. I took his tiny right hand and slapped the palm. "No, Ethan. That's dangerous." I paused, thinking this was long overdue. "You can't have the ball in the backseat." I snatched it off the floorboard, turned toward the woods, and lobbed it a good twenty yards into the underbrush.

Ethan screamed as though I were murdering him. "No, Lala, no!" he cried pitifully.

I got back under the wheel and eased onto the highway. When we got home, Marilyn was waiting. The nursery school had called her too. As soon as he was released from the car seat, Ethan manufactured more tears on the way into Marilyn's arms. "Lala hurt me," he wailed, "and took my ball."

"Oh, Leila," she moaned as she swooped Ethan up to his room. She spent the rest of the time before the first client was due, comforting him. "I thought we agreed never to hit him?" she confronted me.

"Are you kidding, Marilyn?" I was fed up. "I slapped his hand, after he'd brained another kid with a toy and almost put my eye out with his damn rubber ball."

"You should've brought him right home. I'm his mother."

"What do you think I was doing?" I retorted. "And if you're his mother, what am I? Don't I have any say here?" The long postponed adoption flashed across my mind, with its impossible price tag that read LESBIAN FATHER. That was me.

"Well, I don't want you hitting him again," Marilyn insisted.

"Suit yourself," I said, and started for the door.

"Where are you going?" she said. "I've got clients."

"Cancel them."

Halfway back to town I had a couple of beers at the local gay bar, talked to the bartender and a couple of cute girls. It was more fun than I'd had in months. When I got home, Marilyn and Ethan were both sleeping peacefully, curled up in the big bed. I squeezed in and put an arm around Ethan. He was getting to be such a big guy, taller than most of the other kids. I didn't want him to grow up a bully.

The next morning I was up before anybody and off to the bookstore. Saturday was our busiest day, with all the college students on the loose with money to spend. In the middle of the afternoon I returned a longing stare from Catherine, who worked at the bookstore too, a tall blond who'd asked me out for a drink before. I had always put her off because, after all, I was as good as married with children. She'd seen the photos of Marilyn and Ethan behind the counter. But if she didn't mind, I didn't. "Hey, it's Saturday," I said. "Do you want to have that drink tonight?"

Catherine didn't hesitate. We ended up at a local coffeehouse instead of a bar, where it wouldn't have been smart to be seen together. I sat across from her and talked bookstore for a while. She seemed so young, like Marilyn when I'd met her, before she became tired and angry. I wondered what it'd be like to sleep with Catherine, just a quick roll in the hay with no kid in between.

"I'm adopted, you know," Catherine was saying. "I've never tried to find my real mother." She took a sip of coffee. "You know how it is...'if they didn't want you the first time, why should they want you now?' sort of fears."

"It must make you feel really insecure," I replied, my mind drifting to Ethan, the adoption. I would try to be the best parent I could, but would he always wonder about a father? When would he ask, and what would I say?

"Leila?" Catherine's voice startled me. "I was telling you," she said, no wrinkles around the eyes but a terrible yearning, "for years I didn't know what to do with myself."

"I understand," I stammered.

"Now I'm going back to college. I can start this summer, just one course." She paused. "What kind of degree do you think I should shoot for?"

As she laid bare her dreams, I thought maybe Catherine wasn't the type for a roll in the hay. Neither was I, of course. Neither of us was very hungry, so we split a sandwich. At about 8:30 P.M., I told her I'd better be getting home.

"Sure," she said, not pressing me to stay longer. "I'll

see you Monday." She didn't even look disappointed. She'd just wanted a friendly visit, someone to listen. Suddenly I wanted badly to get home.

Once I got out on the highway, I was glad we hadn't been drinking, because it was snowing heavily, New England zero visibility. I crept along the road.

Marilyn came out on the porch in a sweater when she heard my car plowing up the driveway. "Leila, thank God you're all right!" she said, and hugged me as soon as I got close enough. "Where were you?"

The distress on her face was painfully real. "Why didn't you call?" She shivered in a thin sweater.

"You know I always forget about the cell phone," I joked, and pulled it out of my coat pocket. "I just stopped off to have coffee with Catherine, the woman I work with. I think she's going through a really hard time."

Marilyn looked fragile. "I never heard you talk about a Catherine."

"There's nothing much to tell. She's just somebody who works at the bookstore. She's going back to college, that kind of stuff."

Marilyn seemed relieved.

It took me a while to get all my winter gear off—boots, hat, coat, scarf. I sat on the sofa in front of the fireplace. "I'm going to make a fire," I said.

"Ethan tried to stay up to say good night. And he didn't like me giving him his bath." Marilyn laughed. "He said I didn't know the animals' names or how to play with them. He wanted you."

We hadn't had much time for sitting by the fire the last few months, maybe years, and the logs were dry and crisp. With a little coaxing the fire blazed up. Marilyn was waiting for me on the sofa. "We've got to talk," I said.

"I know. I've been awful and stupid." She was crying.

I took her hand. "I want the adoption proceeding to get under way. It's too risky for Ethan, and for me."

"Of course," she agreed. "I'll help you get the money together. We should've done it long ago. If I hadn't been such a fool."

"Oh, you're not so bad."

"I've been stupid and jealous..."

"Jealous of what?"

"You and Ethan. He loves you so much, and you always know what to say, and how to make him laugh. He saves all his games for when you come home."

"You can't be serious?" I laughed at her. "He's been your baby from the beginning. I've tried so hard not to be left out."

"I'm so sorry," she whispered into my shoulder. "I guess I never really learned to share." The fire crackled.

"It's a hard one, one Ethan'll have to learn too." I paused. "Don't you think he could start sleeping in his own room soon?"

"He's up there now," Marilyn said, and snuggled closer.

if they only knew

karin kallmaker

→

"Told ya."

After I thank the waiter for the rubber chicken, vegetable medley, and rice pilaf with yellow sauce, I give Ellen a withering look. "Don't be ungracious."

"Told her what?" Laurie, to Ellen's right, offers the basket of sourdough rolls.

"The menu."

"This isn't the first charity dinner we've been to together." I accept the basket from Ellen and pass it on to Nora, on my left.

After a murmured thank-you, Nora asks, "How long have you two been together?"

This is always the best part of the evening for me. "Twenty-five years."

"Really? That's amazing! Congratulations."

Those who heard my answer have the look of people doing math in their heads.

Nora's companion breaks first. "Either you look ten years younger than you are, or you guys got together—"

"Sixteen." Ellen lets crumbs from her roll sift onto her vegetables. After the first five years I stopped trying to get her to stop mauling her bread. Closing cupboard doors was much more important. "Beth seduced me."

"I did not."

"You had that blue shirt, and after I told you it made your eyes look bluer—"

"You also mentioned something about it making my figure Marie Antoinettesque..."

"I don't recall that part."

"You never do."

Addressing myself to Nora and her girlfriend, I continue with the true accounting of Ellen's actions. "After that she wore that shirt three times a week. I was completely smitten."

"Smitten?" Ellen makes a threatening gesture with her fork. "You had the hots for me. 'Smitten' sounds like we're yodeling our affections across the Alps."

"How did you stay together?" Laurie, with a vacant seat next to her, seems interested beyond charity dinner politeness.

I shrug. "She's my best friend."

"Friendship is important, sure." Across the table the newlyweds have come up for air. The brunette takes another long swallow from her wine. "But I think lesbians really overemphasize the whole 'being friends' thing. I mean—I know so many couples who are together because they're friends. They're not having sex anymore, but they still consider that a relationship."

I can feel Ellen bristling. "Day in and day out, year in and year out, it's friendship that endures," I say. "Passion goes and comes back, hormones and bodies change, but friendship is always there."

The brunette puts her arm possessively around her

blond paramour. I can't see their name cards. "I think it's great and all, you guys being together so long, but is that really the only model for a successful relationship?"

"Of course not. I'm Beth, by the way." I add a nod because it would be impossible to reach across the table of eight.

"Suze, and this is Ilene." Ilene, apparently, does not speak.

"What brings you to the awards tonight?" It's enough of a diversion, and Suze expounds on her commitment to the lesbian community while I sneak a glance at Ellen.

She's looking at me, and her eyes are twinkling.

We already sent the money, she says to me in the car. We don't have to actually show up. I point out the great parking space. She agrees, but she's still not making any move to open her door.

She turns in the seat, abruptly. Another button has come undone on her blouse.

"It's been ages since we made out in the car."

"What about last week?"

"That was the van."

She moves closer. She's wearing the black bra with the lace. In the streetlight her skin shimmers. Her breasts are golden and round, and I am washed over with remembering her arms around me last night. "Pull open that blouse some more and we'll get arrested."

"Was that a request?" Her fingers move sinuously to the next button. "All I want is a kiss."

"Right." I'm on to her wiles. After all these years I know exactly what she wants.

"You know it'll be chicken, vegetables, pilaf, and sauce. A mediocre dessert, endless speeches, and you'll fall asleep. Let's make out and have burgers on the way home instead."

"Make out?" I curve my palm over the top of one breast. The shudder that runs through her seems to make the air around us vibrate. "Baby, you need more than that."

"Last night it was you." She's breathing hard.

I swallow hard, remembering.

"You're right," she whispers. She lifts my hand to her lips and touches the tip of my index finger with her tongue. "I want a lot more."

"So we'll go to the dinner?"

She makes an exasperated noise. "What is it with you and your industrially prepared chicken fetish? I'm never going to figure that one out." She rebuttons and gathers her purse.

"It'll give me strength."

"You're going to need it," she warns. She opens her door and turns to me. In the glare of the overhead light her hands go to her breasts, simultaneously teasing them and offering them to me. "I intend to make you sweat."

From time to time I think it's important to make her stomach flip-flop the way she does mine. I have to clear my throat first, but I finally manage, "If you're not careful, I'll fuck you between dinner and dessert."

I fight down the butterflies—which Ellen's eyes can so easily rouse in me—by finishing my dinner. I almost don't have to look to know she's left half the chicken, all of the carrots, and none of the pilaf.

Suze and Ilene are honeymooning again. I really don't mind, though it's a little distracting. On the other hand, I think, if they want to do a scene on the table, I probably won't drift off during the speeches.

Ellen's hand snakes over my thigh. I shift my weight so she can slide her fingers a little farther along the seam of my trousers.

Her hand feels so sure of what it's going to do. The

movie theater is nearly deserted, but my lord, surely she isn't going to actually...

Her fingertips stretch out the waistband of my sweat-pants, then slip downward. My legs reflexively open for her. I can't stop my hips from tipping upward in welcome.

I snap back to the conversation, aware Nora has begun a serious discussion with Ellen.

"Life just gets busy, doesn't it? I've never thought sex was the be-all and end-all. I get tired of the blanket assumption that if we don't have fuck buddies and pierced nipples, we're sexually unfulfilled." Nora sends a sidelong look at the newlyweds. "Especially if you're over forty."

"I will admit," Ellen says, "that our sex life isn't what it was when we first got together."

Through her hand between my legs and I can feel her silent laughter.

"Whose is?" Nora squeezes her girlfriend's hand.

Squeezing back, she says, "As long as we both have what we need." She gives Nora a kiss on the cheek.

"Yes," I say solemnly, to make Ellen laugh more. "Our sex life is not what it was."

Everything feels good. The slightest touch to my shoulder makes my body ripple with response. I feel waves of pressure between my legs. My eyes feel glued to her gym uniform. It's the way she walks and stands and everything about her. I want to touch her and she's letting me, and I think I'm going to pass out.

Later, on top of the pink-and-white bedspread my mom tries to make me like, she lets me again. It all feels so good. Her hair smells great and my head is swimming with wanting to touch under her clothes, but I'm not sure I can stand it. I don't know what this feeling is, like something's going to blow up inside me. How can she be so calm? I want to make her feel the crazy-dancing way I do, but I don't know how.

I feel so alone, all of a sudden, and she is a stranger.

"I don't know what to do," she whispers.

She makes everything okay, right then, and she always does.

Twenty-five years she's made me feel like the strongest woman on the planet. I squeeze the hand between my thighs. She knows what to do now and so do I. It just takes practice.

I'm trembling just enough for her to know. She takes her hand away, and after a moment to drink a little wine, she rubs my shoulder in what looks like an innocent gesture.

"Can you keep up with me, baby?" She's thrusting herself down so hard on my fingers that I have to re-center my body or she'll knock me backward.

"As long as you need it." I'd have never dared to fuck her like this all those years ago.

She's panting. Up on her elbows, trying to stay with the moment. "You need...to work out that shoulder. Build up those muscles...oh..."

She starts the long groan and slips all the way on to her back. I hear my name in the keening of her worship and I feel like a god.

"Lesbian bed death." Laurie has had enough wine to feel confessional. "That's why I'm single again. I don't know what happens."

It may not be PC, but I just can't help the pang of sympathy I feel for anyone who is alone. "If you know it's forever, then patience is a little easier. You can see how everything has a cycle."

Suze leans away from Ilene to allow the waiter to collect her plate. "I think the ridiculous insistence on exclusivity is the death knell, frankly."

Ellen shrugs. "I think fidelity is a profound way to demonstrate trust. And trust is everything. No trust, no sex. No trust, no laughter. If you don't trust someone to hold up their end of the relationship, how can you trust enough to be vulnerable even more intimately?"

Ilene finally speaks. "I could never close myself off from the beauty of women. I notice them and want them, and that's who I am. Suze trusts where my commitment is."

I've really tried to understand, but I always fall short. I can't imagine a life different from the one I lead. My head knows it's not for everyone, but secretly in my heart I'm sorry for everyone who doesn't have their own Ellen. "I don't consider myself closed off. There are a number of attractive women here tonight. I'm going home with this one, though, just like always."

Suze and Ilene aren't bothering to hide their pitying glances before they turn to their wine and each other.

Ellen crosses her eyes at me.

The waiter puts down the dessert. Carrot cake.

I look back into Ellen's eyes, a thrill shooting down my spine.

I excuse myself. I don't look back.

My heart is pounding. I didn't think, in the car, when I made my threat, that we would ever...I mean, I'm not quite sure. Will she?

I can't always read her mind.

In the quiet rest room I wait, fighting guilt. What if a handicapped person needs the stall? But it seems like the rail will be handy and there's more room—a tap on the door.

I open it slowly. She's unbuttoning her blouse.

For the length of two heartbeats I feel sixteen again and I don't know what to do. But practice has helped.

I yank her inside and push her up on the rail. Her back is to the wall and she's kissing me hard. I fumble with the button on her heavy silk slacks, the zipper, then I've got it open and there's enough room to touch her.

She hisses and I know the sound she wants to make. I hear it echoing over the years, layers of it saying she is mine and she wants me.

I'm inside her and I feel her gathering. I put my hips behind my hand and feel the breath being knocked out of her body. Her nails are digging into my back and it all feels so good, like the first time did, except I know what to do now.

Another kiss. She tightens. A flick of one fingertip. Her legs jerk. Back to the same place, pressing hard.

"You know you want to," I whisper. "Right here. I'll give you more at home. But right now you need this."

She turns to liquid, and I have to keep her trapped against the wall or we'll both fall. I have a brief but primal fear that her arms are going to snap my neck and, at the same time, that her pelvis is going to break my wrist. I hold her because she trusts me to.

When her feet are under her again she brings her hands to my breasts. I shiver. I am a vast ache of wanting.

She watches me respond to her touch. "That takes that smirk off your face."

"Maybe, but we both know who got done and where."

"I was just helping you keep your promise."

I look down. "This will be a dry-cleaning bill to remember."

"It's your own fault. I wouldn't have done that if you hadn't made me."

"Honey! You're not the one who's going to have to go back in there looking like you're incontinent."

"Blame it on a faucet." She breezes out the door, looking perfectly coiffed. I have a brief but deeply arousing fantasy of wiping the smirk off her face—up against the sink, watching her face in the mirror while I have her again.

She catches my gaze in the mirror and her hips move. She reads my mind sometimes. Then, with a delightful giggle, she splashes water onto my slacks. "Damned faucet."

I chase her out of the bathroom, then decorum demands we behave. Thank goodness our table is near the back.

She slides into her seat and picks up her fork. Leaning toward Laurie, she asks, "Is this any good?"

Laurie looks noncommittal. "It depends on what you like."

I dab at the front of my pants with the napkin, just in case anyone noticed, and mutter, "Damned faucet."

Ellen makes a choking noise, then tries a second bite of the carrot cake before pushing it away. "For the calories, I'd rather have a Snickers."

Reaching into my jacket pocket, I say, "Sorry, sweetie, I picked wrong."

The lights dim as she eagerly takes the small bag of M&Ms. "You are so good to me." Leaning closer, she murmurs, "Sex and chocolate. You are such a stud."

I realize her blouse is misbuttoned. Before I warn her I glance around to make sure no one is looking. From the surprised look on her face, I can tell that Laurie has noticed as well.

Her gaze travels back and forth between us, then her grin flares. I feel the hot red flush break over my forehead. "Honey, your blouse."

Ellen makes a gulping noise and quickly rights it.

I snuggle up behind her, positioning my chair so I can spoon against her back.

Speeches. At least an hour of them, I think. I want to take her home right now, but I don't have the strength to move.

She shifts slightly, then turns a little, and the best part of her shoulder is under my cheek. I close my eyes and tuck my hand under my cheek so I can smell her on my fingertips.

I know she'll wake me if I snore.

prague posts

leslie k. ward

Jen switches on the lights. The spots fade up, sending triangular-shaped beams down onto the Kopecky paintings, hanging every few feet along washed terra-cotta walls. I drop my backpack at the far end of the counter and flip open our CD folders, looking for some appropriate wake-up music. Nothing too abrasive, but not too sleepy either, or I'll stumble around in this daze all morning. I toss in Ani by default, my groggy head still not equipped for an actual decision.

In a coffee shop, in a city, that is every coffee shop, in every city, on a day that is every day.

Yep.

Jen is putting the espresso machine back together after soaking the filters and group handles overnight. She scrubs the coffee baskets with special sponges, the ones she cut the corners off of so we (I) wouldn't mix them up with the regular sponges. Special sponges and kid gloves—she shines her coffee machine every morning like I bet she shined her first two-wheeler. I can picture it, little Jen all knees and elbows, hunched over the mag wheels of her brand-new Huffy, wiping each rim clean with her dad's V-neck beefy tee. I'm sure she stood back, hands on her hips, head cocked to one side, eyes all squinty like she does right now, giving her hard work the once over.

Jen thinks about coffee the way some people think about fine wine, the way my father thinks about cigars. For some, espresso is a habit, for me it's a craft, but for Jen, packing and pouring is an art, one of the highest caliber. I feel almost guilty pouring myself a Pepsi Light, but I get over it as soon as I hear the the fizzy whoosh of the bottle top. Jen and I share a need for caffeine, but I find coffee too bitter, even with buckets of sugar and whipped cream. Jen say she understands but teases me relentlessly. This morning she tells me I have the oh-so-distinguished palette of a twelve-year-old. I'm too busy picking out my favorite color straw to respond.

I finish the grocery list, open the register, and decide Jen will have to deal with the postal ladies. They smoke like chimneys, those girls, griping and gossiping and filling three ashtrays every morning. We used to have only two morning regulars, but I guess word got out about our lattes, because now we host a postal extravaganza every weekday at 10 A.M.

Most days I enjoy the animated start, watching the café spring to life as soon as we open the doors. Today, however, I'm savoring our lazy morning calm, reluctant to include any extra participants. I open a few cabinets in a halfhearted attempt to locate two shopping bags. I stare blankly into each open door, forgetting to look for the bags, finding them anyway. Several minutes tick by and the caffeine creeps through my system, crisping the edges of my morning haze. Mobile and motivated, I kiss Jen goodbye and set off for Havelák, the open-air farmers' market at the end of the block.

Havelák is already bustling with energy as growers rush to set out their best stock, artists lay out their favorite prints, and the marionette dealers struggle to untangle spaghetti nests of puppet strings. I meander through the carts, thumping melons and squeezing tomatoes. Digging into messy pockets, I pull out a handful of lint-covered hellers. "Kellen hellers," Jen calls them. I think these aluminum coins are ridiculous. They're practically worthless, fractions of a single crown, costing more to produce than the value stamped on the front, but since I don't want to end up with a jar full, I wipe off the lint and count out exact change for a kilo of carrots. I also pick up some fresh strawberries, even though we don't need them, and brainstorm a daily special. When I've gathered the last of the produce, it's off to the bakery for the day's bread and pastries.

Jiri recognizes me as soon as I come in. He gives me a kindhearted smile as I make my way to the counter. He knows exactly what I want but lets me order anyway so he can correct my Czech. *"Tri krat, plundra makova,"* I say, giving it my best shot.

"Plundrou makovou," he chuckles.

"Plundrou makovou," I repeat, imitating his wide fish-mouth endings.

"Lepsi." Better. *Plundrou makovou, plundrou makovou, plundrou makovou.*

We hammer out the rest of my order, and I promise to practice the rough patches for tomorrow. Jiri stamps my receipt, hands it to me with my change, and bids me *ahoj*. The other customers don't seem to mind my impromptu Czech lesson, although I've gotten the death stare from grumpy *babickas* on plenty of other occasions.

When I return to the café, Jen has just finished putting a batch of coffee into the roaster, and a comfy, toasty smell meets me at the door. I watch the beans toss around in the machine, slowly turning from pale-green to dark, shiny brown. Jen scribbles the details in her roasting journal: time, date, bean origin, roast level. She jots notes in the margins. Sometimes I think if I showed this journal to our customers they would be loyal for life. If they understood Jen, if they knew how much she cared about every bean, I'm sure more people would linger over their espressos, proudly sip their macchiatos, gush over every creamy latte.

I put away the groceries and record the receipts. Jen pours out the beans to let them air. They sound like pebbles in a rain stick cascading from the glass roaster, pitter-pattering into the shallow cardboard box. I bring over the poppy seed pastries I bought for our breakfast, along with a few fresh strawberries and the best double-shot I can muster.

"*Plundrou makovou pour vous,*" I entreat, tangling languages.

Jen laughs, puts the coffee and pastries on the counter, and wraps me in her fuzzy sweater arms. She showers me in gentle good-morning kisses and gets all goofy like I love, planting exaggerated smooches on my forehead and nuzzling my neck until I'm bubbling with giggles.

"Thanks for breakfast, sweetie," she says, the words muffled below my cheek so I feel them more than hear them.

"*Není zac,*" I reply. No problem. Not this morning. I can't even think of one. Of course, I'm not going to try.

Jen and I moved to Prague and opened this café nine months ago, all in the name of Grand Adventure. We definitely got what we bargained for in the adventure department. Aside from the standard excitement of moving to a foreign country, learning a new language, and starting a small business, Jen and I have seen everything from murders to floods here. I'd like to say we've come through unscathed, but my conscience knows better. We are changed, although we won't ever know how much, or if it's for the better.

♠

"CALM DOWN! CALM DOWN! CALM DOWN!" I growl through clenched teeth, hitting my thighs over and over with balled-up fists. I know they'll be purple-black by tomorrow, covered in huge welts that scrape against my jeans when I sit down. It's not the first time. I can already feel them stinging-hot, like my eyes, squeezed tight to hold in the tears. I can't face another gulping, gasping break-down, so I fight to regain control, straining at the seams, reigning in the flood.

The soft thud of fist into flesh jerks me out of the mael-strom of emotion and back into my body, but only for a moment, until the jolt of pain subsides. Then it washes back over me, and I'm flailing again, drowning inside myself.

Jen opens the door and steps out of the bathroom, freshly showered, wrapping a towel around her waist. I don't even notice her. She starts to say something, some-thing light, something apologetic, something tender, but then she sees. In a heartbeat she is all around me, hugging my arms tight against my body, pressing my head into her damp chest. *Shhhh, shhhhh*, she breathes, rocking me back and forth, back and forth. I convulse and sob, exhausted from holding it in. She smells like warm and soft and shampoo and new towels and I'm so grateful to have her here, to save me from myself. We sway this way until my crying becomes a hiccup, then she cradles my cheeks in both hands and kisses the tears from my eyelids.

"You really scared me," she whispers.

"I scare me too," I confess.

She helps me stand and leads me to the bedroom, to the big, fluffy bed that is really two beds pushed together. I'm still sniffling, so she brings me a roll of toilet paper, but not before she puts the cat in my lap to keep me company. And then we are kissing and then I am crying and the wave that washes over me this time isn't full of hopelessness but I'm swept away all the same, swimming into something wet and wonderful. Backs arching, bodies twisting, we slip and tumble over each other, slick with sweat, saliva, tears, and sex.

And when we are spent, flung on the bed like seaweed, I hear the soft poof of the cat landing on the down comforter. High-stepping over our entwined legs, she curls up in the warm crook of my armpit and purrs me to sleep.

♠

"I can't believe we're going to eat this." I wrinkle my nose at what looks like deep-fried sneaker sole lying limp on the greasy paper plate.

"You wanted adventure," she replies, pulling the plastic knife back and forth over the rubbery flap.

"Is this really supposed to be cheese?"

"Only one way to find out," she huffs, trying in vain to tear off a chewable hunk.

"I mean, I wasn't expecting gourmet, but this? Banzai wouldn't even touch it." That cat eats everything.

I quit complaining for a second and take another look around the dingy bus station diner. Everything is painted a squalid teal. It reminds me of the inside of an old swimming pool. Slices of indistinguishable cakes line the streaky Plexiglas dessert case on the counter. They look half their original size, shriveled and dried up under crusty, crumbling frostings. A big jar of Nescafé sits on the shelf behind them, next to dusty cans of pilsner and cola bottles with faded labels. It's a sorry sight, even without the sallow-faced, overworked waitress. I look back at Jen. She's chewing for all she's worth, bless her heart.

"You're right," she admits with a mouthful of half-chewed rubber cheese. "Thif if terrible."

"No kidding," I say, feigning surprise. "I'm going to brave the bathroom. Good luck with that manhole cover."

When I return, I hand the key and its bulky wooden handle to Jen, who has since thrown away her culinary experiment.

We came into this diner during a leg-stretching break from the bus ride to Bratislava. Our business visas still haven't come through, so we have to leave and reenter the country every three months to re-activate our tourist visas. It's a nice excuse for a vacation, I guess. This time, however, we couldn't close the café for more than a day, so we're taking the five-hour bus ride to Bratislava for a brief lunch date with Jen's cousin. Two hours in Slovakia and we have to get right back on the bus for the five-hour ride home. Some vacation.

Jen is still in the bathroom and I'm getting antsy, so I gather our things. When she returns I suggest we go outside and wait by the bus. She nods enthusiastically.

Once we're out the door, she puts her arm around me, although it's a little awkward since we're both wearing backpacks. We stumble down the steps, trying to stay linked, hobbling along like drunken camels. When we reach the bottom, she leans over and kisses me with her cheese-greasy mouth. Her lips slide oily over mine, her tongue tastes salty in my mouth. Blood rushes to my cheeks, among other places, as I suck the salt from her tongue and nibble the corners of her greasy bottom lip.

I don't know if she's falling or pushing, but my back

ends up against the railing, my body pressing against hers, and I'm barely even thinking about my sunglasses getting crushed in the front pocket of my backpack. I'm also barely even thinking about the dozens of waiting strangers hopefully too busy staring at bus schedules and checking their watches to notice us. I'm normally shy in public, hand-holding and goodbye kisses notwithstanding. But the absurdity of making out in a bus station parking lot grows on me, and soon we're a (quiet) frenzy of undulating passion. Jen's polyester jacket swooshes and crackles as our hands wriggle under bulky backpacks, searching for skin. My thigh is pressed firmly between Jen's legs and she's just about to reach her hand into the front of my unbuttoned shirt when out of the corner of my eye I see the bus. It's leaving. Without us.

We scramble to untangle and race after it, yelling and waving our arms in the air, shirts flapping open to the world, backpacks thumping behind us. When we reach the platform, the bus is already pulling out of the station. Panting, Jen falls down onto the pavement and pulls me down with her. That's when she starts to laugh. Pretty soon we are both in tears, holding our sides, hawing and guffawing.

"We could always get some more cheese," I suggest, in between ragged breaths.

Jen falls flat to the ground, arms sprawled out on the pavement, howling with laughter.

♠

It's a crisp day in early autumn. One of the first days I can remember the leaves starting to trickle down from the trees. Jen and I are walking through Olsanska cemetery, looking for the grave of Franz Kafka. We entered through the overgrown gates at the far end of the cemetery, the section closest to our apartment. There's a map, but it's completely indecipherable and lacks the all-important "You Are Here" red dot. We decide Kafka would be proud, and resolve to take our chances, happy to be spending time together away from work.

Huge oak trees shelter the grave sites, which are no longer attended to by relatives and friends. Ivy creeps over the headstones and winds up the tree trunks. Some of the granite slabs have tumbled over. Here and there an angel is missing a head, a cherub is missing a pudgy arm, St. Peter stands guard at a door fallen from its marble hinges. A few birds are chirping, and a cool, autumn breeze rustles the leaves on the trees, sending one or two spiraling off like wayward helicopters. It's peaceful here, full of the stillness that permeates the deepest recesses of the forest. It truly feels like a final resting place, like the souls buried here have found their home in nature. Thick green ivy covers them like a blanket, pulling the stone into her folds, protecting her reclaimed children from the waking world.

We walk the winding paths, saying nothing. Jen links her hand with mine, our fingers intertwining. The first of the fallen leaves crunch on the ground, and I deliberately shuffle my feet to send them billowing up in small swells.

Passing under another overgrown gate, we enter a newer section of the cemetery. A paved path replaces the trampled leaves. The graves here are neat, tidy, tended. Flowers adorn the tops of some; lit candles in smoky red jars cast a faint glow over others. People are milling about, quietly paying their respects to the dearly departed.

I think: *One day this will be us.* One day one of us will be here, looking down on a little patch of earth while the other looks down onto the world. Maybe it'll be me who brushes away the leaves or maybe Jen who lights a candle, but hopefully we'll both be thinking fondly of each other, looking forward to the time when we meet again.

◆

I can't believe this will all be over soon. The 200–year flood hit Prague last month, and even though the café was spared, most of our business receded right along with the floodwaters. The metro stopped running because of damage, and it's a pain in the arse to get downtown nowadays. All the tourists went home early, and with the sensationalized coverage from CNN, it's no wonder everyone's rerouting. I think most of them are still waiting downstream for the floating beer kegs from flooded Czech breweries to wash ashore. Wherever they are, it isn't here drinking espresso, here where it counts.

Our finances are lean from starting up, and after only nine months running we can't afford to hold out until things turn around. So that's it, party's over. Jen doesn't like to talk about it. I catch her sometimes at other people's cafés, her head buzzing like it did in the beginning and she's saying things like *if only* and *I bet if we could just...* I hate to do it, but I have to interrupt her with *We can't* and *I won't* and remind her of the parts of the story she's forgetting; the ugly, unfair parts that deflate the happy ending she's imagining, because I know this one isn't real and she deserves a real one. Then I watch her face fall, and sit with her through a painful, awkward silence. If we get into an argument, which we often do, I let her get mad at me instead of the world because I know I can walk away and for a minute it all goes with me.

Of course, it isn't always like this. Sometimes it's like it was last night when we were out having pizza and I asked her what love was even though I know she hates those questions. For me, questions come with answers; for Jen, they come with a million more questions, questions about questions. It's what makes me a hypocrite and her a philosopher.

But last night, while the kitchen staff wrapped up our leftovers, she started answering, and while I can't tell you what she said because I promised I wouldn't hold her to it, I can tell you it was enough that she said it.

More than enough.

dance lessons

andi mathis

I wasn't the only lesbian at Billy's wedding.

My cousin knew lots of gay girls from lots of places; he'd always moved comfortably among all kinds of queers—he was a publicist for a fashion magazine—and often had contact with them.

Jody and Stefanie were a lovely couple, and as they took to the dance floor, I watched the way they moved, and the way I knew I did not. If Kathleen had not left me a month earlier, I would have stumbled out there with her in my arms, trying to make the steps look effortless. The way Jody and Stefanie did.

I'd recently been introduced to them at a Kathleen-less Sunday brunch at Billy's apartment. We'd been sitting around playing Trivial Pursuit, vying for pie slices over questions about Oscars and hockey, when I first became jealous of them.

"What country has the largest sheep population?" Billy was asking the questions; I was pouring the mimosas. His fiancée, Renee, had declined to join in the fun, opting instead for a jog around the park. Jody tamely elbowed Stef, who had been subtly caressing the hairs at the nape of Jody's neck. Her fake Aussie accent was dead-on. "You can take this one, mate," she grinned.

"Australia?" answered Stef with mock innocence.

"You are correct!" said Billy with his best Regis Philbin impression.

We were all feeling a little loose, so I suppose some impromptu celebration wasn't uncalled for. The gals immediately leapt to their feet and performed a little *uh-huh, it's my birthday* bump-and-grind duet, and then simply sat down again. The entire interlude had lasted twelve or fourteen seconds, but it was the unscripted ease with which they had acted in concert that amazed me.

Kathleen and I never did that.

Despite our best efforts, we hadn't discovered ourselves in possession of inside jokes; we traded no meaningful glances; we didn't finish each other's sentences. And I doubted we ever would.

Which was strange, I thought, because I was so in love with her. I had come to savor the sound of her name in my mouth, the way she'd tuck a hank of her thick brunette behind an ear, the reckless speed at which she drove, the cut of a jacket on her broad shoulders. I loved her in a thousand ways, but I hadn't told her enough.

After my last indiscretion, she'd made it quite clear that she didn't want me to talk to her. We were over, finished, done.

The night of the Trivial Pursuit game, I felt Kathleen's absence, and I was miserable.

And now at the wedding reception it was even worse. As a witness to the joyful pairing of Billy and Renee, my awareness of my singular status was acute.

The presence of Jody and Stefanie—their heads bent

over their champagne glasses as they disclosed secret amusements to each other—didn't help either.

The DJ cued up some smooth George Benson, and it was lively enough to encourage folks to show off their rhythm and coordination. Jody had one hand on Stef's hip, and they held each other with unflappable nonchalance, swinging in a way that didn't seem practiced at all. They evidently had internalized the beat, and still talked back and forth as they danced, as if they were strolling side by side on a Sunday afternoon. The music was almost superfluous. Even if there had been no music, I imagined they moved like this, communicating in small gestures and even syncopation, no matter where they were.

They were laughing. Jody pulled Stef closer and whispered something in her ear.

The movement tugged at my heart.

I had loved dancing with Kathleen, despite my two left feet. Maybe it was the effort that thrilled me, to think that somehow we were trying to read each other. I loved her expression when she danced, somehow mildly surprised and on the edge of saying something, her economical motions always intimating that there was more to come, her paced sway slightly self-conscious.

I tried to dance with her, I really did.

I was embarrassed at my awkwardness, and I would stammer with some sheepishness, but Kathleen paid no attention. With her arms around me, she'd fix me with a stare of confidence that insisted, *Come on. It's just dancing.*

Watching Jody and Stef, I was sure it wasn't that simple. It wasn't that their dancing was all that complicated. It was their disregard for inhibition.

I wanted what they had: the abandon of all doubt; the joyful leap of faith; the comfortable silence that said it was possible to celebrate each other; the balance that springs from the movement of two, perfectly matched.

George Benson gave way to some disco-glitter melody, and my companions came back to the table. Jody dropped into her chair, looking a little winded. Stef went to the bar to fetch three bottles of Molson Export. Jody watched her go.

"No dancing for you?" she asked me politely.

"I'm not very light on my feet." We didn't know each other well. Neither Jody nor Stef knew anything of Kathleen; they'd never seen me with anyone but Billy. "You and Stef seem pretty well-suited. You're so graceful out there," I remarked, indicating the throng of jitterbuggers behind her.

"We like to dance."

Something in the music caught her ear, and she shifted enough in her chair to indicate that she wanted to watch the dancing. After a few minutes, I spotted Stefanie making her way through the crowd.

"Ladies? Some liquid refreshment?" Stefanie set down the beers with a flourish. "Thanks," I said.

She pivoted to Jody and lifted her hand to the flush of Jody's cheek. "You're warm." The gesture was so impulsive, so natural, I almost felt as if I should turn my head.

"You wore me out, partner," Jody responded, and lifted her beer. "Nothing a little of this won't fix."

I diddled with my cake fork, uncomfortable with the offhandedness of their intimacy. Even though Kathleen wouldn't have tolerated such caring gestures in public, she wasn't immune to my attention. I'm not the maternal type, but I do have impulses. Once in a while Kathleen would ask me to drive my elbow into her back to loosen a knot she'd acquired from her desk work; I often cooked things I hoped she would like. We'd been good to each other, in ways that had tried to mark us as a couple. But in general, my sweetest whispers of affection were often things she didn't hear, imparted as she drifted off to sleep, deaf to my attention.

For some time I wondered if it made her uncomfortable for me to tell her I loved her, but that's probably not important anymore. I'm not sure—in the few times I know she heard me—whether she believed me or not.

And I'm not sure I believed her. She once confided to me that she thought it possible to be in love every day of your life for as long as you might live. At first I thought she was being facetious, over-romanticizing. It was the flush and freshness of our relationship, I told myself. She couldn't really believe all the charm and excitement would last, could she?

Maybe I should have realized the trust implicit in such a confidence. I think now, in some way, I must have seen the gravity in it, and felt the weight and responsibility such a secret wish might hold for me. It scared me. As much as I wanted to live up to that dream, a lifetime of failure had taught me to ensure that this relationship would fail too. I scoffed at her wish, and betrayed her trust.

A merengue beat roused my tablemates to the dance floor once more, and I waved them on. They started off falsely, giggling and staring at their feet for an instant, until I could see Stef mouth, "Ready? And three..."

A critic might have remarked on their flawless execution, and as the women danced, I noticed that others occasionally stopped and watched them. The merengue's a slave dance, and I imagined the close ranks of women chained together. What magic connected one woman to another? Of what was the invisible chain between Stef and Jody made?

God, I wanted that bondage for myself.

Making love with Kathleen, I had sensed how possible and near that enslavement was. Her appetite and fierceness were always met by my own, and at least in bed, I held deep convictions about intimacy, trust, and fidelity. When I didn't want to make love we rested, and I felt released in her patience, and yet held in her heart. I was, truthfully, terrified of her rejection, but she didn't waver, even when I held her at arm's length. She accepted each kiss as a gift, and I did as I had learned to do. I took all of her joy for granted.

Billy came by my table to see how I was doing. I gave him a big hug and teased him about his tuxedo, and sent him on to greet other guests. He adored Kathleen and had told me she was the only woman he'd consider leaving Renee for. I knew that was true. He'd been hard on me since Kathleen left, placing the blame on me. I guess that's fair. Last week, a witness to my grief, he finally stopped bitching at me.

"That was great!" Stef exclaimed to Jody as they returned to the table. They ignored me. I played with a half-full cup of coffee and feigned distraction.

"Well, we've cut a rug or two over the last few months," replied Jody.

"You've got that right." Stef wiped her hand across her brow, and as she did so, her sleeve rode up, exposing her watch. Jody reached for her wrist. Again, the freedom of their physical familiarity twisted a knot in my gut.

"What time is it?" Jody couldn't quite read the watch.

"Jesus, it's nearly 6."

"What time is your flight?"

"Eight-forty. My parents will have kittens if I don't make it tonight. I guess I'd better get moving. Where is my coat?" She quickly made a beeline for the coat check.

Jody started gathering up the little party favors and

Stef's handbag. She fumbled under the table and came up with a pair of shoes. That seemed odd to me. I shrugged to Stef as Stef slipped out of the flats she'd been wearing. Jody took them from her and examined them closely. "You're going to need a new pair soon," Jody said. "This left exterior is taking a real beating." She ran a finger gently over the edge of the shoe.

"Oh, crap. Must be too much cha-cha," smiled Stef.

"Or tango," Jody suggested. I was sure I detected the lilt of lasciviousness in her voice.

Bundled into their coats, Stef and Jody exchanged quick kisses then acknowledged me.

"Good to see you again," Stef said perfunctorily but pleasantly. I shook hands with her. "I'm sure I'll see you at Billy's."

"I guess we'll have to wait until after the honeymoon," I replied with a wry grin. "Goodbye."

Like Jody, I followed her across the room with my eyes and waved briefly before she disappeared past the bar.

The crowd was starting to thin, but I guessed the party might last another hour or so. I wanted to go home, but I'd promised Billy's brothers a ride, so I was committed to the bitter end. At least I wouldn't have to endure any more public displays of affection.

Jody cleared her throat. "So," she began, "are you sure you don't dance?"

I held up my hands palms out in front of me. "Honestly, I'm a bull in a china shop."

"I don't believe you."

"It's the truth."

Jody nodded in reply. We sat in silence for a few minutes, listening to the music and the dull clank of china plates being removed from the tables.

"You guys seem so relaxed out there," I started. "You look great together."

"Thanks. Stef's a wonderful dancer. She works hard at it."

I hadn't meant to insert a pause, but I didn't want my voice to betray my envy. "I love the way she holds you."

Jody's expression was puzzled. "What do you mean?"

"You know, like she really cares for you."

Jody shook her head. "Yeah, she's got a thing for me. I thought twice about asking her to come to the wedding, but I guess it was all right. We had a talk last night, and I think I set her straight. I'm not looking for a relationship right now, at least not anything long-term or committed, if you know what I mean."

I guess it was my turn to be confused. "I thought you two were a couple."

"Really? Whatever gave you that idea?"

"Trivial Pursuit? The way you dance together—"

"Oh, that. Forget about it. Stef and I are just friends. Heck, I've only known her for about a year. She was one of my students. Took one of my classes. Came in for extra help. We got acquainted, had coffee. You know how it goes."

I felt embarrassed. "Geez, I guess I misunderstood," I mumbled. A flicker of panic shot through my stomach. I'd projected so much on their harmony, on their accord. My jealousy had been wasted. I felt cheated, misled. How could I have invested so much mental energy in something that wasn't real? "The way you dance...you looked so connected..."

"No harm done," Jody said dismissively. She waited a bit, as if disconcerted by my false impression. She brushed a few crumbs from the light linen tablecloth, shaking off the thought. "So, what's your story?"

"Me? I'm single," I answered. "Since last month."

"Sorry. Were you with her for a long time?"

I should have lied then to Jody, but I told the truth. "No," I confessed. "We were only dating for six months." Not even. I should have said, *I think Kathleen was the love of my life.* I should have said, *She made everything right.* I should have said, *When I was with her, I began to believe that forever was possible.*

"Well," continued Jody, "maybe it's best to get out early. You know, if it's not working... Are you dating?"

"No," I answered quickly. "I don't think I'm ready."

Jody reached across the table and patted my hand gently. "You'll feel better soon." Her hand was cold.

For a moment we sat quietly.

"I think I'm gonna get going," Jody said abruptly. She sighed. "I'm not as young as I used to be. I'm totally danced out."

I quickly took a visual survey of the room. More guests had been leaving through the last twenty minutes. "Yeah. In any event, your choices of dance partners are quickly diminishing." I spotted my Aunt Eleanor, who, I knew, would dance with anyone except a lesbian.

"Thanks for the company," I said. "I'm sure we'll run into each other again."

Jody stood up. "Look," she said matter-of-factly. She reached inside her jacket and extracted a business card. "Let me know when you're ready to get out in the world again." She slid the card across the table. "Here's my number. Give me a call. Maybe we can get together or something. Or you can just drop by."

I got to my feet and shook her hand briefly. "Thanks. Maybe I will. Drive safely."

She ambled slowly across the hall, and I watched her, until she was consumed by the huddle near the door.

Suddenly, I didn't want the assured rhythm of the peerless dance partner, the counted-out steps of the predictable waltz, the unassailable balance of some Fred-and-Ginger routine. I might never be a good dancer, but I could hold my own. Perfection wasn't real anyway.

I knew I wouldn't call Jody.

I wanted Kathleen. *Come on,* she'd said. *It's just dancing.*

I picked up the card and read it: *Arthur Murray Studios. Jody Beck, Instructor.*

I tore it in half, tossed it on the table, and got myself a drink.

glad all over

anne seale

———————————→

The Crosstown Pod Mall was home to a video store, a martial arts studio, a wig shop, and Big Daddy's Ballroom, the sponsor of our annual gay pride parade.

Every third Saturday in June the parade started at the Gay Alliance Building and ended twelve blocks later in the Pod Mall parking lot, where Big Daddy was ready with a portable stage, industrial-size speakers, and a fleet of beer trucks. Big Daddy never missed a chance to make a buck.

This year, as always, Sherry, Doris, and I marched with the League of Lesbian Activists. Our current target was the local bishop because of his decision to cancel a gay mass that had been held for years at an inner-city church. My dearly departed Gladys had been Catholic, and that mass had meant a lot to her. I nodded my cardboard miter at the parade watchers with enthusiasm, chanting, "Say hey! Say hey! Where are we supposed to pray?"

When we were a couple of blocks from the Pod Mall, the pavement began to shake from the pulse of Big Daddy's giant woofers. I handed my corner of the banner to Sherry.

"That's it for me," I told her. "I'm going back to my car."

"Don't you dare!" Sherry said. "It's getting harder and harder to pry you from your cushy recliner. We got you out on the town for once, and you're going to stay out!"

Sherry, Doris, Glad, and I used to hang around together, raising hell at bars and parties almost every weekend. We called ourselves the Fearsome Foursome. But now that Glad was gone, I'd gotten in the habit of staying home, turning down all invitations except an occasional dinner with friends. The last place I wanted to go was Big Daddy's.

"The music is way too loud," I told Sherry. "I'm trying to make my eardrums last as long as the rest of me."

"They're not going to wear out in the next hour." She turned to Doris. "Honey, tell her she can't go home yet. It's not even 5 o'clock!"

"It is early, Julia," Doris said.

"My feet are sore," I told them.

"Well, so are mine," Sherry said, limping a little for effect.

"There are too many people."

Sherry stamped one of her "sore" feet and said, "If you don't get out and see people once in a while, how are you ever going to meet anybody?"

"I don't want to meet anybody. Nobody can replace my Gladdie."

She heaved a sigh. "Look, we'll stay for just an hour or two, okay? Then we'll walk you back to your car, won't we, Doris?" Neither sentence was really a question.

Since our contingent was near the end of the parade, the parking lot was mobbed by the time we arrived. Onstage, six men in sequined evening gowns gyrated to the beat of the bass-heavy music. Several more danced on top of the beer trucks. Their stomping rocked the vehicles, sloshing beer out of the pitchers on the counters.

"I'll get drinks," Doris shouted over the music. "You two find a place to sit."

We looked around. Folding chairs lined the perimeter of the parking lot, but they were all filled. Sherry approached some young men seated nearby. "Excuse me," she said loudly, "my friend here has a condition and needs to sit down. Would you mind giving up your seats?"

Two of the young men regarded me with pity and got up. Sherry gave them a beaming smile.

"I don't have any such thing," I said.

"Shhhh," Sherry said, pulling me down next to her. She turned to the fellow seated on her other side. "Actually, we need three," she told him.

He tried to ignore her, but she said it again, yelling directly into his ear. He gave her a withering look, then rose and strode off. Sherry immediately covered his chair with her upper torso and stayed that way until Doris got back with three paper cups of beer.

We sat for a half hour or so, sipping and people-watching. Some old friends spotted us and came over. They leaned into us, trying to carry on a conversation despite the steady boom-boom-boom. I turned my head to hear a comment, and out of the corner of my eye I saw Gladys. She was wearing the red shirt with the big white gardenias I'd bought her in a shop on Maui when we were there celebrating our twenty-fifth anniversary.

"Ohmigod!" I cried, jumping up.

Sherry grabbed my arm. "Julia, what's wrong?"

"I don't know. I'll be right back." I pulled loose and pushed into the crowd. I was too short to see over heads, so I wedged between bodies, watching for the brilliant red of the shirt. At one point I caught a glimpse of it, but a party of revelers pushed in front of me and I lost it again. Stepping up my pace, I ruthlessly shoved people aside.

Suddenly there was an opening in the crowd. I ran into it, tripped over something, and went flying. I came to rest against the back of the red shirt, my nose buried in one of the white flowers. It smelled like Gladys. I almost fainted.

The wearer of the shirt turned and helped me right myself. It was Glad all right, but a young Glad, the Gladys I'd met twenty-nine years ago on my first visit to a woman's bar. I stared at the sweet Glad face under the short Glad haircut.

"Are you okay?" she asked.

"Oh, yes, thank you," I told her. "I tripped."

"What?" she yelled over the music.

"I tripped over something," I yelled back.

She looked at the ground behind me. "It was the electric cord. They should have taped it better. Are you really okay?"

"Yes. Excuse me for staring, but you look just like...a friend of mine."

"What?"

"I said you look like someone," I yelled back.

"No kidding," she said, and returned to what she'd been doing, which was surveying a table of rainbow-motif merchandise. I watched as she inspected a 2X purple tank top.

"I don't think that's pure cotton," I said, standing on tiptoe to be nearer her ear. "There's polyester in it. Forty percent, at least."

She checked the tag, then looked at me. "You're right. How did you know I only wear cotton?"

"This shirt is cotton." I touched the sleeve and ran my finger all the way down to her wrist. The fine black hairs tickled familiarly.

Wrinkling her brow, she jerked her arm away.

"I'm sorry," I said. "It's just...you look so much like her."

"Who?"

"Her name was Gladys."

"What?"

With all the "say-heying" and yelling, my voice was giving out. "Do you have a minute?" I asked.

She hesitated, then nodded.

I grabbed her hand and led her out of the parking lot and around the corner, where the noise was somewhat muted. Reluctantly dropping her hand, I faced her. "My name is Julia."

"Bailey," she said.

I touched her sleeve again. I couldn't keep my hands off her. "I like your shirt."

"Yeah? I got it at a rummage sale last month. This is the first time I've worn it."

"The Gay Alliance rummage sale?"

She nodded

I felt like an idiot. Why hadn't it occurred to me? After three years of grieving, I'd finally felt strong enough to get rid of Glad's clothing and had donated it to this year's sale.

"I'm sorry if I alarmed you, Bailey," I said, "but you're the spitting image of my lover, Gladys."

She glanced around nervously.

"...who died," I added.

"Oh. Sorry." She stared at the sidewalk. To her young mind, death was an embarrassing subject.

Okay, I said to myself, *you've got her. What are you going to do with her? Take her home and hang her on the wall next to the picture of Glad?*

Picture of Glad! Of course! I riffled through my purse for my billfold. Finding it, I removed a photo of Gladys in her leathers, one foot on the peg of her Harley.

Bailey took the photo from me and examined it closely. "Wow!" she said.

"Amazing, isn't it?"

"Sure is. Is that a Shovelhead?"

"Excuse me?"

"The bike! '75 or '76, I'll bet. Not many of those around anymore."

"This one is. I've got it." It was the one thing of Glad's I hadn't been able to get rid of. It sat in my garage, greeting me every day as I came and went.

"You've still got it? Do you ride?"

"No. But look at the woman in the photo. She's older, of course, but don't you think you look like her?"

She studied the photo. "A little bit, maybe. She uh...died, you say?"

"Yes, a few years ago."

"So would you be willing to sell the bike?"

"The Harley? No, I couldn't."

"Oh. Well, nice to meet you, uh...Julia." She extended her hand for a shake.

I grabbed at it like I was drowning. "Wait! Let me think it over. In the meantime, why don't you come have a look at it?"

"Well, okay. When?"

"How about tomorrow evening? Say, 6 o'clock?"

I wrote my address on the back of an old receipt with an eyeliner from the depths of my purse.

She gave the Harley a last loving look before handing back the photo.

♠

The next day at 5:55, I slid a pan of fried chicken out of the oven and put it on the table next to big bowls of mashed potatoes and buttered corn. Then I removed my apron and ran to the front window. Within a few minutes, a battered pickup glided up the street. She was right on time, just like Gladys on our first date and every date after that.

When the doorbell rang, I waited a minute or two, then opened the door. "Why, Bailey," I said as if I'd forgotten she was coming. "Please, come in."

She entered and sniffed. "Smells good in here." She looked around the room. "Nice place." Her glance finally fell on me. "Wow. What is that thing?"

"It's a kimono. Glad gave it to me. Look, there's a dragon embroidered on the back." I turned in a slow circle, tugging at the short black satin. When I came round again, the front gaped, showing a great deal of my still-great legs. Bailey's ears turned red.

"Are you hungry?" I asked.

"Hungry?" she said, pulling her eyes from my lower third.

"I just took some chicken out of the oven. That's what smells so good. I'd be glad to share with you."

"Yeah, sure, I could eat," she said, following me to the kitchen.

"Have a seat." I indicated Glad's place, already set with the good china. "Will you have some wine?"

"Sure." She stole glances at my legs as I moved about the kitchen.

I poured wine for both of us and heaped our plates with food. Bailey waited until I took a bite, then dug in.

"You're a good cook," she said between mouthfuls.

"Thank you. This was Glad's favorite meal."

She gave me the same wary look as yesterday when I'd touched her arm.

"Have another glass of wine," I said.

I soon excused myself and went to the bedroom to freshen my makeup. The Harley looked good, its shiny blackness a dramatic contrast to the white wall behind it. This morning I'd filled the tires and gently polished the body with a soft cloth and a little Turtle Wax. Except for the step up from the garage, it hadn't been too difficult getting it into the house.

When I returned to the kitchen, Bailey had cleaned her plate.

"Seconds?" I asked.

"No, thanks. So where's the bike?"

"Follow me." I led the way down the hall.

At the bedroom door, I stepped aside to let Bailey enter. She paused, taking in the scene. "You keep it in your bedroom?"

"Why not?"

"Whatever." She crossed and knelt before it, examining the tires.

I followed, standing just behind her, fighting the urge to lean over and run my tongue along the rim of her ear.

"Can I mount?" she said.

"Oh, yes, mount away," I told her.

She gripped the handlebars and threw a leg over, easing into the seat. "What a steed!" she said. "Have you decided whether or not you want to sell?"

"I'm sorry. I can't." There'd been no decision to be made.

"Too bad. It's a great bike." She dismounted

How could I keep her from leaving? "Do you have a tattoo?" I asked.

"Uh...yeah."

"Where?"

"On my arm."

"Can I see it?"

"I don't care." She pushed up the left sleeve of her T-shirt to reveal an amazing tattoo, a gold lightning bolt wrapped in a coiled black snake, its forked tongue caught in mid flick.

"How beautiful!" I told her.

"Thanks. I designed it myself. Did she have one?" She nodded at Glad's photo on the wall above the bed.

"Yes. It was on her shoulder. A heart with my name on it." My eyes began to fill. *Get a grip, Julia. Tears are not seductive.* I blinked and forced a smile. "I have one too."

"A tattoo? Where?"

I shrugged out of my kimono and let it fall to the floor. Bailey's jaw dropped. "Find it," I told her.

Her indecision showed on her face. *Am I out of here?* she was thinking. *Or should I go for it?*

I stood totally still. It was up to her now.

After a moment Bailey's expression changed. Her eyes grew dark and her lips formed a sly grin.

Oh, good!

She picked up the kimono. "Put this on."

"Really?" I said, disappointed. Had I read her wrong?

"I undress my women."

I nearly swooned with relief. Taking the kimono from her, I put it on again, tying the sash into a big gift bow. Bailey looked at me for a long while, and after pulling the kimono to my waist, lifted me and sat me sidesaddle on the seat of the Harley. The leather felt smooth and cool on my bare bottom.

She crouched before me and inserted her hand between my knees, forcing them apart. Holding my eyes with hers, she said, "I've been wanting to do this since I walked in."

"Do what?" My voice was shaking.

"This." She ran her right hand up the inside of my thigh and grabbed my crotch. I gasped.

Very slowly she began rotating the hand, which contained most of my pubic region, as if she were turning a water faucet on and off. It worked—my fluids soon began dripping. "That feels good," I told her.

"Just good?" she asked. One of her fingers escaped the gripping fist and dipped in and out of me every time it passed. I swelled into her hand, growing wetter by the second. My nipples hardened, straining against the black satin. I wanted her to remove the kimono now so she could squeeze and suck my breasts as Gladys used to do. "Oh, my, I'm so warm!" I said, hoping she would get the idea, but she didn't.

The leather seat was getting wet, and I started slipping all over. Bailey scrambled to her feet and leaned over me, putting her left hand in the small of my back. Holding me tightly against her chest, she continued to work me. I groaned into the front of her T-shirt and ground my forehead against her breasts. "Oh, Gla…" Oops. "Oh, Bailey!"

More fingers—I couldn't tell how many—joined the first. They slid into me deeply with each revolution of her hand, then slid out again. Each withdrawal felt like abandonment. I pushed my pelvis into her, trying to prolong the stroke.

Bailey started making weird whistling sounds alternating with strangled croaks. I leaned my head back and peered into her face. Her teeth were clenched, her eyes tightly shut. Her cheeks and forehead were scarlet. Sweat dripped from her jowls. My word, I thought, what if this young woman has a bad heart or something? What was I thinking? Maybe I'd better cut this whole thing short.

"Take me!" I cried dramatically. "I can't stand it. Take me now."

The hand froze. "Are you telling me how to make love?" she asked.

"No." I said quickly. "It was just a suggestion."

"I'm not her, you know." Sweat flew as she jerked her head in the direction of Glad's photo. "I'm Bailey. B-A-I-L-E-Y! I do things my way." Obviously, she didn't share my worry that she was in danger of collapsing.

"I'm sorry, Bailey," I said. "You're right." Her facial redness had faded a little, and I felt better about the whole thing. Her hand was still on me, the fingers frozen at my threshold. I wiggled my butt, hoping to get them moving again.

"Okay then," she said. In one motion, without removing the vital hand, she lifted and flipped me so that I was lying on my stomach on the sodden seat, my head hanging down on the far side. I saw the reflection of my startled face in a circle of chrome. My kimono was gone, I don't know how or where.

"There it is," Bailey said. For a moment I thought she'd read my mind, then I realized she'd found my tattoo.

With a couple of thrusts, she brought me back to where I was before the hiatus, then threw herself on top of me. Her belt buckle dug rhythmically into my back. I figured her hand was moving between my bare clit and her clothed one. It was a thrilling concept.

I was the one making weird noises now.

We rocked with abandon, and the Harley rocked with us. I hoped it wouldn't fall over, crushing my head against the wall like a raw egg. I didn't worry about it long, though, because the fingers hit my quick, and I came with a vengeance.

When we were able to move, Bailey turned down the bed and lifted me in.

"Thank you, dear," I said. "That was wonderful."

"Yeah," she said, straightening her clothes. "I've never done that on a bike before. You'd better towel it down pretty soon."

"Are you leaving?"

"Yeah."

"When can you come back?"

"I can't. I'm moving to Iowa next week. Going to be pretty busy."

I sat up. "Iowa! What for?" I was born and raised in Iowa and couldn't wait to leave. It was hard to imagine anyone *moving* to Iowa.

"Got me a girlfriend in Des Moines. I met her on the Internet, in a chat room."

"A what?"

"You don't know what a chat room is?"

"No."

She said she couldn't believe I wasn't online. Sitting on the side of my bed, she regaled me with the wonders of gay sites, lesbian bulletin boards, and butch-femme chat rooms. Then, after writing down her e-mail address in case I ever decided to sell the Harley, she took off.

After I recovered and dried off the Harley, I called Sherry and Doris and invited them over. I intended to pick their brains about how to buy a computer. Doris used computers at work and knew all about that kind of thing.

I was sure, now, that another Glad was out there somewhere, looking for me, and I was going to find her. I just hoped she wasn't in Iowa.

the measure of grace
achy obejas

———————————→

Judith scampers up the stairs, excited, teasing. "You
didn't recognize my voice? How could you not recognize
my voice?"

I should have, of course, after spending last night listening to her talk for hours and hours. We sat in a
Japanese restaurant where they served Hawaiian drinks
with little paper umbrellas, and she told me how her new
lover had cheated on her, how she couldn't get the visual
part out of her mind, how fingers might hook into bodies
and mouths fall on each other.

"You really didn't recognize my voice?" she asks,
standing at the door while I rub my eyes. She'd rung the
doorbell and called up on the intercom. I'd stumbled out
of bed, literally crawling on all fours in my surprise,
climbed up the wall to the button that released the lock on
the door downstairs, and called through the small micro-
phone. "It's me," she answered.

"Who's me?" I asked, perhaps too indignantly, perhaps
inconceiving.

Even if her voice hadn't filled the night before, there were three years of it prior to that. We were together that long, lived together for two and a half of those. I should have recognized that timbre, but for now I consider it a good sign that I didn't.

"You woke me up," I tell Judith. "I wouldn't have recognized my own mother." I wrap my bathrobe around me. Suddenly I feel transparent. "Everything's okay," she says, smiling, not apologizing for coming over unannounced, for not having considered that I might not be alone—although I am. "I took your advice, I apologized," she tells me, not thanking me for that good advice.

"Congratulations," I say, feeling her on my heels to the kitchen. It's as if she's breathing on my ankles. I turn on the hot water in the kitchen sink and wash the coffeepot. The cats scratch up my legs to tell me they're hungry, but they don't make a sound.

◆

Before we broke up, Judith said she wanted a girlfriend with means (unlike me), preferably a Jewish girl (like herself). Last night she expanded on her theory. "I'm convinced now," she said, "that I'll never date outside my own class again."

I wasn't angry when she said this, just embarrassed. I could see my friends might be easily horrified, but I wasn't: Love isn't about politics. Love, I've discovered, is not so ethereal, religious, or correct. Ultimately, it's about what fits, what makes life easier. Since my bank account made life more difficult between Judith and me, we couldn't stay together. I know that now.

"I knew what I wanted all along," she told me last night, "but you didn't have a very clear idea of what you wanted."

"Sure I did," I said. "I wanted you."

Then she blushed the deepest, darkest pink. I felt no shame at all.

⟡

"I apologized profusely," Judith says, reaching into my cupboards with all the familiarity of a spouse or a room-mate. I'm uncomfortable with it because we are neither; we'll never be either again.

She pulls out a pair of cups with Mickey, Goofy, and Minnie decorations, immaculate leftovers from our vaca-tion to Disneyland, the land of future-past. I don't want to feel nostalgic, so I jerk open the cupboard after she's closed it and set down a cup with gaudy Christmas graphics, always out of season. Judith notices nothing.

"I realized you were right, honey," she says to me, but I feel as though she might just as easily be talking to her-self. "If there's something real between Danielle and me, we'll survive all this."

I want to tell her that's not what I said, but I haven't had my coffee yet. I want to remind her that I said she had a right to be jealous and upset but not a right to be vicious or sarcastic. I want to shake her by the shoulders, throw her up against the wall, and ask her why she always twists everything I say. I feed the cats instead.

⟡

Last night I got an earful about Danielle, this WASP she's mad about, this very rich, very cool WASP who has her wrapped around her little finger. Except for the WASP part, Danielle's everything Judith has ever wanted. I tor-ture myself by imagining them together, their bodies spooning one into the other. Judith knows this, but last night she didn't even blink as she told me story after story about the two of them, even as she acknowledged her own nightmares. "I can always tell with Danielle," she said, "when she's with somebody else."

I wanted to tell her it was useless boasting to me about her nonexistent intuition.

"Just like with you," she continued, taking her turn twirling the paper umbrellas in our drinks. "You remember how I always knew?"

I shrugged, choosing not to confirm this lie again. The amazing truth is, she never, ever, knew. I remember one time I came home with the smell of another woman still on my breath, my only attempt at camouflage a cigarette inhaled in the hallway, and Judith smiled and hugged me at the front door, never—and I mean never—suspecting. She was so sure about me: that I might even consider infidelity never entered her mind.

Eventually, after I'd tumbled with a few strangers, I realized I'd become so enamored of her image of me that I couldn't bear to tell her the truth. So I told her half-truths: confirmed, for example, that whatever crush she'd suspected I had on somebody was on target. Last night I wanted to kick myself for ever letting her believe she had any telepathic powers at all. I'm reaping what I sowed, I told myself, biting my lower lip, hoping for a big, black sore as recompense.

"The problem is this nonmonogamy," she said, staring out the window of the Japanese restaurant. "I just don't understand it. I just don't get how one person's shadow or ghost doesn't intrude on the other."

She looked up at me, as if I might understand. "I don't like the woman," I said, sighing, hating the mere thought of giving Danielle any credit at all, "but you have to give her points for honesty on this one, Judith. She told you she wanted to be with other women. She even told you who, and to a certain extent, when."

She nodded. "Oh, I know, I know, but I thought, after we were together, she wouldn't need anybody else," she admitted. "I called her up and left her a really nasty message. You know, I have this very visual imagination. I can just see her with this other woman, and that's what hurts."

I took a deep breath. When I'd been with somebody else, Judith had worried about whether I'd gone down on the woman, pleading with me to tell her I hadn't, that I'd reserved what she considered to be the most intimate of acts just for us. I'd refused to discuss it, insisting whatever happens between two people is their sole province and nobody else's. Besides, I'd reserved nothing. "Christ, stop obsessing," I said, "just because you have such a problem with oral sex."

"Oral sex?" she asked with genuine surprise. "Oh, yeah, that," she said, catching herself, and me. I felt as embarrassed and doomed as a mouse who's lost her tail, and possibly even her life, over that old stale-cheese trick.

"Isn't that what you meant?" I asked, not looking at her for the first time during dinner, focusing instead on the chopsticks carefully balanced on a little tray of inky soy sauce.

"Well, yeah," she said, but her smile and her sudden flush told another story.

Hard as I tried to blacken my mind's screen, in that instant I pictured Judith and Danielle as garishly as if they were performing in a porn film composed mostly of close-ups. I swallowed hard and took another deep breath. I knew nothing could be worse than crying in front of her, and I was on the verge. I gathered my senses, leaned back in my chair, and smirked.

114

"I guess you can teach an old dog new tricks," I said.

It was her turn to shrug, but it was, in its own way, another boast. She couldn't wipe that grin off her face.

You're supposed to love me, I thought, no matter what. I wanted her to be more careful with my heart, that's all. I wished she could hear herself, the damning reckless-ness of her stories. I had no question about her need to tell them, but since I couldn't stop from listening of my own free will, I hoped she'd love me enough to spare me their pain. I wanted her to take it all back.

♠

"We talked for four hours," Judith says, pouring the cof-fee into her cup, then into mine. She ignores the Christmas cup, insisting on Disneyland instead. "Sugar?" she asks, as if she needs to ask. How long were we together? How many fucking cups of coffee did she pour for me over how many mornings and afternoons and evenings and all those nights I stayed up all night?

I practice another smirk, but she won't acknowledge it. She hands me the cup, sugar melting at the bottom of it, unstirred.

"It was the best conversation we've ever had," she says. "I feel like we're cleansed, like we bonded. We are just so good together."

I take a gigantic gulp, letting the coffee burn the inside of my mouth, wondering what "good" means and how she can know that from six weekends with Danielle. The cats, disgusted, turn from their half-full bowls and walk away.

"I told her you helped me think things through," she says sheepishly, then she leans toward me and kisses me on the cheek. Her lips are full and warm. "She says we have a very interesting relationship." I swallow the hot coffee,

breathe air. "I hate the word *interesting*," I say, totally irritated. "It's a non-word, it means nothing. Can't Danielle
commit to anything?"

Judith's surprised. "She was trying to be supportive."

"Supportive, my ass," I say. "I was supportive; she's
a bitch. Why couldn't she just say we have a good relationship?"

But I know the answer to that: We don't.

♠

Judith sighed. "She's what I want," she said at the
Japanese restaurant, taking the paper umbrella from her
drink and trying to fold it.

"Those aren't meant to fold," I told her, nodding at the
umbrella, once stiff and now sort of drooping from the
drink and the sweat on Judith's fingers. She ignored me,
pushing carefully on each little toothpick spoke, caressing
each one down until it developed a willingness to fold.

"It really doesn't matter what she does," she went on.
"I don't want to change her, I just want to find a way to
accept her. I love her, I really do." I gritted my teeth and
said nothing. In my head I had a tally sheet in which I held
against Danielle every sin Judith's forgiven her.

"Over time," Judith said, covering my hand with hers,
"I think you'll grow to care about her too."

I yanked my hand away.

"Not a chance," I said.

And I meant it.

♠

The cats are hiding under the couch, a sign I take to
mean that they're on my side. Judith is kneeling on the

floor, trying to coax them out, but they won't be entreated so easily.

"Why are they mad at me?" she asks in all innocence.

"Because you deserted them," I say, but I really mean, *Because you deserted me.*

"That's ridiculous," she says. "I visit, I bring them toys. Are you filling them up with your stories? Are you trying to get them not to love me?"

I think: *No, I'm trying to get me not to love you. It's harder but more important.*

"I have to go," Judith says, standing at my doorway again. She touches my cheek. "You really were so wonderful. You really helped me through last night."

I want to know why I can't help myself, why I can't find comfort, why I feel like a dark, hairy beast trying to swim among swans.

"I have to go," she says. "I'm meeting Danielle for lunch."

"Please," I finally say, "just leave. I can't take much more."

Judith is startled, as if she just remembered we were lovers once. "God, I'm sorry," she says, hurling her arms around my neck. "It's just that you're my best friend, my best friend ever, and I want to tell you everything."

But I don't want to know everything. I've told her this a million times. I only want to know the important things: that she misses me, that she loves me, that I remain the most important person in her universe.

♠

The cats and I watch Judith leave the building and cross the street to her car. She practically skips across the way, not looking in either direction. When she's right dab in the middle of the street, a car lunges from the corner, its grillwork ready to swallow her. But the driver's alert, and the brakes scream loud as a siren, bringing the metal hulk to a dead stop inches from her. Judith jumps, then holds her heart with her hands and laughs from nervousness. I can see her chest heaving. The driver, who rolls down his window to curse at her, is just as relieved.

I close my eyes for an instant, trying to keep down all the images of what might have happened. I want to rush down there in my robe and slippers and slap some sense into her. I want to tell her she's a fool; a careless, insensitive bitch.

I jerk open my window, the spring screen, and the storms. The cats scamper. "You fucking asshole," I scream down at her. "Don't you know how precious you are?"

Judith looks all around, bewildered. There's no question about it: She doesn't recognize my voice.

no puffin

jane eaton hamilton

The Cannon Beach Hotel is a surprise to both Annie
Newman, a gynecology resident, and Sally Larson, a geriatrician, because it is modern and sprawling. They would
have preferred, they both agree, something small and
quaint and old, but they're booked for two nonrefundable
nights. The reservation agent, when Annie called, made
this quite clear: There was a two-night minimum. Was that
all right? Annie agreed, and gave her Visa for the first
night, and Sally's for the second.

They are late, they explain to the sullen teen, Marilyn,
behind the registration counter—a late departure from
Canada. A last-minute delivery at the hospital.
Unavoidable, and there was then all that border traffic.
The pregnant girl—Annie estimates she's only sixteen or
seventeen, but eight months along—stares malignantly
from half-cast eyes. She hands over a form for them to fill
out, slides along behind her desk on a chair with casters,
and slides back with a map in her hands. She pulls out a
drawer full of slots and chooses their key from hundreds.

She scowls and shakes the map. In red pen, she Xs in their room location as well as the route to it through the maze of bland contemporary buildings. She hands them this as well as two Visa receipts.

Marilyn's mouth downturns. She says, "I hope you enjoy your stay with us, doctors."

In the car Sally says, "Surly little fertility goddess."

"I see three girls like her in a week," says Annie.

"Ugh," says Sally. "I don't know how you can stand gynecology. Women's parts are so..."

Annie laughs.

"I don't know. Smooshy? Boggy?"

"Someday you'll be pregnant and take that back."

"I've never even looked at myself down there, and believe me, I'm certainly not having kids. No, thanks."

"You're not?" Annie herself waffles—yes, no, the urge warring with her desire for an uncomplicated future.

"Actually, I'm infertile."

"I'm sorry."

"God, don't be." Sally waves away her concern. "I made my peace with it long before med school. Now anything that smacks of maternity turns my stomach. My maternity rotation was a killer. Give me old gals and their dried-up bits any day."

Cannon Beach, Oregon. Annie has been here before. She visited with her parents and siblings when she was a little girl, then she came with a single friend, Karen, during what she thinks of as her young, wild years—Cannon Beach was a disappointing destination that time. More recently, she came with her husband, Derek, en route home after a driving trip to L.A. Annie ought to have known of a good place to stay, therefore, but the little B&B she stayed in has vanished; the others were already booked because it's Easter.

When Annie wrenches the car door open against the wind and slips behind the wheel, Sally consults the map. "Go straight," she says.

Annie parks under a large round sign. It's the black outline of a bird, faintly reminiscent. Whatever kind it is—a toucan? Something energetically tropical?—it is outlawed here. There's a red circle around the edge, a red line through the bird itself. She clicks the trunk open for Sally, who takes out their bags and climbs up a stairwell while Annie opens the back car door and roots around for apples and oranges that have spilled from a sack.

Sally comes back to announce they were given the key to an occupied room.

Annie makes a disgusted noise.

As they drive back to registration, Sally tells Annie that she walked in on someone. She mentions a couple flailing about on the bed, whips.

"Really?" Annie is astonished.

Sally grins and expands her lanky frame outside the car. "A messy room is all I found. With a baby asleep in a crib and the TV on. I'll just get our right key."

When Sally walks back toward her, Annie feels a familiar thud inside. She knows what it is, finally she knows what it is, but she longs for the days when the feeling was innocently unidentifiable. Annie has fallen in love. She feels a bit of a fraud for luring Sally away; they both, after all, have husbands and fidelity vows back home, but she tells herself it is just that she loves Sally's company. Besides, sex? Annie is appalled by her strong interest. Ugh, she thinks generically, a woman. Then she sees Sally and melts.

"There's a restaurant next to the bar," Sally says, holding her hair against the wind. "It closes at 10."

Their key fits the lock of a vacant room, and they carry

their bags inside, flipping on the overhead light. Annie has chosen a deluxe room with both a view and a whirlpool, but the room is nevertheless cramped and unattractive. The walls are painted a stark white; there is only one piece of art on the wall, a landscape of Haystack Rock above the bed. And what does this locally famous rock look like? Brown, conical, bleak.

Sally says, "One bed?" She raises an eyebrow, a question.

"If we wanted a spa, we had to share a bed. I won't bite."

Sally smiles. "Is that a promise or a threat?"

Other than that one looming bed, the only place to sit is in one of two vinyl straight-backed chairs. But at least the spa in the nondescript bathroom is commodious, and there's a closet with extra pillows and blankets. There is, Annie reminds herself, a view that will become evident in the morning. Of the rock featured in the painting, where puffins nest. Suddenly the outlawed bird sign swims into her mind and identifies itself as a puffin. "No puffin," she says and laughs.

Sally looks at her quizzically.

"I'm just happy to be here, finally." Annie wedges herself around the chairs and a large round table and pulls the cord that opens their drapes. She slides the door wide. It's too dark to see the water, but they can hear it, the eager, horrible surf. Annie steps out onto the little concrete balcony, with Sally following.

"The famous rock is somewhere out there," Annie says and gestures south. The wind catches them in gusts, but the night is clear; the moon is clipped to the sky like a broach.

Sally lifts her toss of black hair from the nape of her neck. "I work too much. I haven't had a weekend off since Christmas."

"Me too," says Annie, and adds, "I'm glad we have an excuse to get to know each other better."

It is cold in the wind, and late, and dark, so they head down for dinner. They consult their map and set out across long stretches of tarmac. Sally holds open the first of a set of heavy doors: Country music surges out toward them. The bar and the dining room aren't separated except by a middle aisle; the dining room is very nearly empty. But apparently the restaurant is already shut down, early by ten minutes; a waiter insists they sit in the bar if they want to eat.

They carry their coats across the aisle. Annie begins to relax. She is here with Sally. They discuss smoke wafting from the far side of the room: Yes, they are hungry; yes, they can accept the air quality in order to eat. "What would you like?" Annie says. "What interests you?" Sally wants to know. They open their large, laminated menus like bird wings.

Annie orders a Caesar salad and smoked salmon fettuccine. Sally decides on prime rib.

"Cholesterol surprise," Annie says.

"My favorite," Sally says. "Next to being here at all." She takes Annie's hand in a way Annie can't interpret, though it gives her a small shiver. "And with you."

Annie reminds herself that Sally says this kind of thing all the time, to everyone, that it signifies nothing. Or possibly it does? Sally too has a crush? Annie's heart flutters. She doesn't dare let herself hope.

The waiter arrives with a basket of different breads. One is wafer-thin, with sea salt and rosemary. As well, there is cornbread and crusty French bread. The little tub of butter is whipped and unsalted. Annie and Sally dig in thankfully but are less than happy when a table full of guests—including the cranky pregnant desk clerk,

Marilyn—arrives to sit right next to them. There is laughing and, alarmingly, smoking, plentiful smoking, smoking by six of the eight tablemates, in fact, and even by Marilyn. She isn't old enough to be in this bar, or to order liquor, or even to buy cigarettes. Where is the baby's father? The girl's parents?

"Oh, for pity's sake, her again?" says Sally. "Miss Having-a-Child-at-Twelve."

Annie laughs. "Some of the girls I see really are twelve. They're seven months along and no one knows they're pregnant. Sometimes even they don't know they're pregnant."

"Those are the ones who have their babies in the bathroom between Home Ec and History and stuff them into trash bins."

Annie flashes Marilyn a look. "Sometimes it works out." Annie crosses her fingers for this one.

"I had a hysterectomy," says Sally.

Annie has to lean forward to hear her.

"Post-self-induced abortion, actually. I was just a kid."

Annie doesn't know what to say. She turns her chair away from Marilyn. She's getting a headache. Pain flares at her temples. "Can we move?" she asks the waiter when he appears with her Caesar salad and Sally's green salad.

"Can we sit away from the smoke?" says Sally.

But the waiter refuses to reseat them. The dining room is closed, he says, and says again.

"But if we sit here," Annie says, "or there, which is probably no more than ten steps away, what is the difference? I fail to see a difference."

"Aren't other people eating there?" Sally asks.

The waiter says, "They arrived before closing time."

"So did we!" cries Annie.

"It's fine," says Sally, putting a hand on Annie's arm.

"I'd rather go back to our room anyhow and have a proper drink or two in a congenial atmosphere."

They order their dinner to go. They have to wait, slouched against the lobby walls, for almost fifteen minutes, but finally they're on their way.

The food spread out on the wobbly table in its Styrofoam dishes smells delicious; from the cooler she brought along Sally produces strawberry margaritas she has premixed as well as an elegant arrangement of red tulips, which bend from their vase as soon as Sally unwraps their cellophane.

"I have candles," Annie says, and fetches them.

They turn down the lights so the decor fades. It's too windy to open the window, but they leave the drapes open. Sally tries to cut her steak with the provided plastic knife, says "A stethoscope would be easier," and takes out her Swiss army knife. They eat, drink, complain about their residencies, their upcoming orals. They talk about where they have signed on to practice. Annie will join a downtown eastside clinic, while Sally is staying on at the hospital as a geriatrician. As they always do, they wind up discussing their husbands: George, who is a luthier; Derek, Annie's husband, who teaches history. Annie is happy, relatively, with Derek: They are old pals, content, but Sally is not doing well with George. Lately she suspects him of having an affair.

"What would..." Annie considers how to shape her question. "Would you leave him?"

Sally pushes her chair back, swinging her long legs up to the windowsill. She shakes her head. "There's something in me that insists I stay. My Mormon past?"

Annie says, "You should get to be happy, though. Life's too short."

"George isn't evil," Sally says. She pours a second margarita. "Besides, better the jerk you know... Anyhow, I can have my fun if I want to. I've just never really wanted to."

Annie stares out to the darkness. "You have an arrangement?"

"On the sly, I mean."

"I think about leaving Derek, but I just can't imagine it."

"Aren't you guys the perfect couple?"

"Well…" Annie says. Is this her chance to say she's fallen in love with someone else, that the feelings are stronger than she ever had for Derek, that she fears she might be a lesbian?

"Come on, give. I've had my suspicions." She twirls a lock of hair around a finger. "I'm really drunk."

"You've had suspicions?" How horrible, thinks Annie. "It's just… Okay. I am interested in someone." Annie looks at her lap. "But for complicated reasons, nothing will ever happen."

Sally sits forward. "You're interested in someone? Who?"

Annie shakes her head.

"Tell me."

"Uh-uh," says Annie. She grins, but she isn't feeling happy. She feels scared and lost and like she wants to flee. She stands up to stretch.

"You swear nothing's happened?"

"Believe me, I'd know if it had."

"Anyone I know?"

Annie closes her eyes and steels herself, shrugs.

Sally stands. "Well, if you're not going to tell me, let's at least go play chicken with the waves."

They don't have a flashlight, so even picking their way down the rickety staircase is precarious, but once on the sand they fly toward the roar of the surf. The wind pushes them along. The ocean is elemental, furious, huge, foaming at the mouth, rabid. They try to stop short of the waves, but since they can't see, Annie gets soaked. Sally follows the ebb of a wave, closer, closer, then jogs backwards when the next wave surges. Annie, drunk, scoops mittfuls of ocean and tosses them at Sally, who screams and runs. Annie chases Sally down the beach in the dark, but Sally, all legs, easily outdistances her.

They are thoroughly frozen when they get back to the room. They toss off clothing, Sally going unself-consciously down to her underwear before putting her hair into a clip. "Whirlpool?"

Annie rinses the margarita glasses while Sally fills the tub. Annie relights the candles and douses the overhead. Sally moans with pleasure in the curve of the tub as the water level rises. Annie uncorks a bottle of wine.

Sally pours the wine and hands Annie her glass.

"I'm drunk enough already," says Annie as she submerges. She forgets to sip and before she knows it Sally is refilling her glass, then once again after that. Annie tries not to stare at Sally's small breasts, at the arrows of her clavicles, at the ropes of tendons in her long neck, at the wet tendrils of her hair. She could run her tongue along those clavicles like a slick marker. She tries to medicalize Sally, to see her as a selection of bones and sinew and skin. She runs down diseases in her mind, the more disfiguring the better—nasal cancer, eye amputation, breast cancer.

"Tell me who it is you like," says Sally. The jets are so noisy she has almost to shout to be heard.

Annie can't admit to her infatuation. Even though her inhibitions are lowered, she still considers consequence. Sally could be disgusted, appalled, revolted. After all, lesbianism, out of the blue? Except on reflection it isn't out of the blue, because Annie remembers crushes on girls as far back as elementary school. But Sally could think she's been tricked here, exploited.

"Come on, who's the new love interest?" Sally says, and with her toe prods Annie's calf.

"Hey," says Annie. "Don't."

For a minute Sally regards her assessingly, the way she must look at a patient during a competency exam. Then she says, "It's me, isn't it?"

"That's not even funny. Of course not." Annie is mad suddenly. She pulls herself to the side of the tub. "I'm so drunk. I'm dizzy."

"Whoa," says Sally as Annie teeters.

Annie tries to rise. "I can't stand up."

Sally gets out, water cascading from her skin in sheets, and wraps Annie in a towel, rubbing it across her arms. She leads Annie into the bedroom, pulls down the covers, tucks her into bed. Annie's head is swooning. She shouldn't have had the wine so fast. Deny, she thinks. Deny, deny, deny, or ruin everything.

After a few minutes, Annie catches the pungent smell of a joint. She sees Sally silhouetted in the window, makes out delicate puffs of cloudy smoke.

In another minute Sally climbs into bed, pulling Annie close for a hug.

The room is dark, but Annie can make out Sally's features, her lips. They scan each other's eyes. Annie whispers, "Okay, it's you."

"You're shaking," Sally says. Then: "I have eight years of postgraduate training. I figured as much."

"You knew? And you still came to Cannon Beach?"

Annie feels Sally shrug. She's flabbergasted when Sally kisses her.

At first her shock makes Annie stiffen, but in a minute she relaxes. A few minutes later, when Sally's hand is against Annie's breast, Annie bites her lip hard enough to taste blood.

♠

In the morning, when she wakes, Annie can't remember where she is and what happened, but when she does, her eyes snap open. There is Sally across the bed, lying on her back, arms akimbo, softly snoring, not a blanket or a sheet in sight. It's true, then. Annie's head throbs from tequila and wine and she thinks with guilt and regret about Derek, but then she drifts along on sensations and emotions, and no doubt on a sea of endorphins. She swats thoughts of her marriage away like mosquitoes. She is very nearly humming when she rolls to rest her head on Sally's shoulder. Sally comes to consciousness in a flail of arms. Annie laughs and pulls her close.

"Oh, my God, Jesus, don't." Sally jumps from bed, arms raised in defense.

For a second, Annie assumes she's forgotten a patient, left an urgent chart on her desk. Sally scrambles for her clothes while Annie, despite herself, admires the stark shape of her spine, its knobs and buttons. She stretches luxuriously.

"Come back to bed, sweetie," Annie says at last, bemused, raising on one elbow.

Sally's hair is wild as a puffin's nest. "Forget everything!"

She is not looking anywhere near Annie. Annie raises on one elbow and pats the mattress. "Everything? Surely, not quite everything."

"Have you taken leave of your senses?"

Has Annie? It wasn't a dream; they really made love, sex like Annie has never experienced before. Far into the night, she told Sally she loved her. She remembers that, doesn't she?

Sally is dressed in record time, spends barely two minutes in the bathroom before putting on her coat. "I'm going to breakfast," she says shortly.

Annie finds Sally at a corner table drinking coffee with her chin in her hand, staring out toward Haystack Rock. The sky is the color of unpolished pewter and coddles the top of the rock like a smudgy halo. Rain sheets the beach, cold, forbidding.

"Hey," Annie says as she sits.

Sally doesn't speak.

"Can't we talk, at least?"

Sally stares at Annie coldly.

"Don't do this," Annie says, leaning close. "Don't pretend."

A waitress interrupts to request Annie's order. "Would you like your orders together, ladies?"

Annie says yes at the same time Sally says no.

"At the same time," Annie says firmly.

Sally raises her palms. "What am I doing that you so object to? I'm trying to eat my breakfast in peace."

A six-foot white rabbit with a basket of bright eggs hops across the dining room, one floppy ear bent double. Annie says, "You owe it to me to talk about this."

"About what?" says Sally. "I was drunk, I was stoned, I wasn't responsible."

"Oh, that's crap," says Annie sitting back. She drains her orange juice in one long gulp. "That's such horse pucky. I wasn't alone, and I wasn't the aggressor either. You seduced me."

"Shh," hisses Sally, thinning her eyes, scanning the room for who might have overheard, pressing her lips into pale slashes as the rabbit hops up to roll handfuls of garish eggs onto their butter plates.

"Please, can't we just forget it?" Sally puckers her mouth

as if tasting something sour. "I never meant anything like that to happen. I never wanted it to." She looks furtively around. "I'm not...that way. I never wanted to be. I refuse it!"

"Sally, really, that's stupid."

"Maybe we should go back to Vancouver."

"We just got here!"

Their eggs arrive. Sally's are poached, Annie's are sunny-side up.

"Look who's here," Sally says bitterly. Across the room, the pregnant teen, Marilyn, is rubbing her belly, hand swinging like a metronome.

"She probably has to work."

"Don't defend her," says Sally. "She's a slutty little bitch who can't keep her knickers up."

Were you? thinks Annie. When you were self-inducing your abortion, is that what you thought about yourself? Pretty hard-line, she thinks. Pretty ungenerous. "Stop being so touchy."

"Pun intended, I assume?"

"Sally, calm down."

"I am not gay." Sally stabs her eggs so they bleed onto her plate. She hisses it again: "I am not gay!"

"Fine, okay. You are not gay. You just seduce women. There's a difference." Annie wipes her mouth. "There's a big honking difference."

♠

Haystack Rock projects absurdly out of the water, a hulking monolith. Annie pulls out binoculars to spot puffins, but her heart isn't in it. She doesn't know where Sally has gone, but she stormed out of breakfast and wasn't in their room. Annie is hurt, bewildered, confused—yet still alarmingly aroused. The bad weather feels like punishment. She's read up—the literature in the drawer beside the bed. The puffins gather here in March and nest until July. It's as far north as they go; when their young are flight-worthy, they return south. Black dots careen through the viewfinder; occasionally a flash of orange appears, and this, Annie knows, must be a puffin's beak. Black and squat, puffins are mostly unremarkable birds—it is only this orange bill, and their white faces, that mark them as interesting.

The whitecaps have smoothed out, leaving a glassy sea. It seems to Annie as if she can see forever—eventually sea meets sky in a vague gray line. In the shallows sperm—shaped bull kelp slop around slick algae. Sandpipers pick through the mud on tall, stilty legs, occasionally scared into flight by young children or dogs. There are a good number of tourists despite the weather. Some of the children have blue or red plastic buckets and shovels, garishly bright, but the rest of the beach hues are subdued and wintry. Annie picks through the tidal flats at the foot of Haystack Rock. Won't Sally come to her senses? Then she thinks: What would coming to Sally's senses entail? Sally won't leave George. Annie couldn't leave Derek, could she? She loves Derek.

The Pacific Henrica is the best, brightest starfish on the coast, a luminescent red, but Annie spots only one, seeing many of the more common ochre star. Little red cucumbers are tucked up under a rock. Anemones are profuse and various, and she tickles their soft middles, making their purple or fluorescent green hairy sides close up like sandpaper around her finger. Annie's hands come out of the water red and frigid. The rain comes at her face like tiny scalpels.

"Annie?"

Annie turns. Rain has flattened Sally's hair and drips from her nose and chin.

"I'm sorry. About back there?"

"Okay," says Annie, pushing hair from her face.

"And uh, about last night. It was just that when I woke up...I mean, I've thought about doing that before, but I... I mean it was a mistake. It was weird."

"Good weird, though."

"It's wrong." Sally scuffs her toe on a rock. She looks down the beach as if someone will step forward to second this.

As maybe they would, if they knew, thinks Annie. "It isn't wrong."

"You'll forget it, though, right? You won't tell anybody."

Annie shrugs.

"You have to promise me. You won't ever say a word, not even to Derek."

"I'm not ashamed of it. I keep telling myself that maybe I should be, but I'm just not."

"But we're married."

"Sure," says Annie, "that's not so great."

"We're women."

"That's okay."

"Says you."

Annie nods. "Says me. Yup."

❧

That night Annie and Sally drive into Cannon Beach for dinner. Place after place is brightly, encouragingly lit. The town is hardly more than two-horse: just a straight row of clapboard buildings dolled up in cheerful paint to attract attention, store after store of dresses and toys. They choose a little place that advertises Marionberry pie, a favorite of Annie's.

Sally had wanted to drive home, but Annie convinced her to stay. Annie promised to go back to just friends, and not to mention or allude to what transpired between them. What Annie always worried about is already happening; their friendship is changing. There will always, from now on, be this secret between them, and sooner or later Sally will decide it's easier not to see Annie because of the things it stirs up. They order and sit in stilted silence, until one of them thinks of something to say. Finally, they discuss the rotten provincial government back in B.C., the cutbacks to hospital services, the chance of a doctor staying afloat in a private practice, the way they both entered a specialty partly in order to earn more money. They both have loans the size of large mortgages to pay off.

Annie is not thinking about her career, though she's continuing her side of the conversation. She's thinking: I had my tongue there, on Sally's cheek, on Sally's earlobe. What she's thinking is that she may not be wired straight and that this explains why she has always lacked passion with Derek.

"Annie," Sally says after their dishes are cleared. She reaches across the table and takes Annie's hand in hers— but surreptitiously, Annie notices, checking first to see whether the waitress can see or other diners notice.

Annie pulls away. "Why did you do that?"

Sally shakes her head.

"Well, don't, okay? It's hardly fair after telling me to back off."

Annie can't believe Sally's insensitivity, making Annie swear then going right ahead and breaking the promise herself not hours after she made it. "I'm tired," she says suddenly.

"Let's get back. Let's not have dessert," says Sally. "If we get some sleep now, we can get an early start tomorrow morning."

"I don't mean now. I mean in general. I'm terribly tired," Annie says.

♠

During the night, with Sally in pajamas twisted tight to the far edge of the bed, rolled up like a cocoon in a separate blanket, Annie dreams of moving. Of having to be out of her house, her condo, of not having found a place to go. She runs up and down a west end street rapping on doors, begging for accommodations. Later, when she appears to have moved, she's in a house so big she can't begin to occupy it. There are always more rooms, and then still more. Bedrooms and kitchens and offices and bathrooms: rooms after rooms after rooms begging her to fill them, to decorate, to make of their bare walls and floors and appliances a home.

When she awakens, Sally is again sprawled on her back. Annie can't help herself. It's like a drug; she stares hard at her to memorize the planes of her face, the shape of her miraculous fingers. Disgusted with herself, Annie slips from bed, dresses, and lets herself out of the room. It's early: The day is hardly broken; just like Annie, it hasn't decided yet what it wants to be. She pads down to the parking lot and around the northern edge of their stucco building. There are the stairs—wooden, with a handrailing. Annie's feet sink in the sand; her progress toward the water is clumsy. Still, out there things churn reassuringly. She breathes the salt air deeply. It's really cold. She has to be determined, she thinks; she has to be motivated. This is what she needs: to be alone in the gray, cold dawn; to have it buffet her, to have it scour her clean. For she sees clearly now, after her dream. What she is going to need is a fresh beginning. Something entirely new, where she doesn't bring the old, safe her along, where the walls are bare and there's no old furniture. She has to leave Derek.

She decides to walk to Haystack Rock, which is when she notices a figure, indistinctly, off a little distance to the south, back up against the break fence where the beach is dry. Under what is probably Annie's hotel room window, in fact. Annie gradually sees it is Marilyn, the much maligned Marilyn from the lobby, hunched over her knees, brown hair tossing.

Annie hears a slight keening sound, eerily caught and whipped by the wind coming up off the water. When she's close enough, Annie touches Marilyn's shoulder to see if she can help.

Marilyn lifts her head. Her face is wild with fear, her eyes round, her nose red with weeping.

Annie says, "Can I help? Can I do anything?"

Marilyn's eyes are glassy. All traces of sullenness have vanished. "The baby's coming out. I can feel it."

Annie kneels and holds Marilyn's closest knee. "Did your water break?" She thinks whether she and Sally have brought any supplies—no, they haven't. Then Annie realizes her doctor's bag is in the car trunk.

"Something's coming!" Marilyn cries.

Annie will have to examine her. She eases Marilyn back and has her raise her hips so she can tug off her pants. Her panties are a fluorescent orange, smudged with blood and mucus at the crotch. She eases them over Marilyn's hips. She says, "Have you had any contractions? Any pains?"

But the girl only shrieks.

The wrinkly blue sole of a foot appears. That's what Annie sees when her hair whips away from her face—toes. As soon as she's registered them, the foot recedes back into the birth canal. Annie bends, explores, and analyzes. Marilyn's water must have broken at some earlier time.

136

Yes, a foot—and is that the cord? Yes, the cord, dangling from the cervix. Her heartbeat quickens. Has it prolapsed? She feels for the foot again, and, holding it beside the cord, pushes them gently back inside the womb. If the cord has cut off the blood supply, the baby will be dying.

Marilyn screams.

Annie tries to remove her hand so she can go for help, but the baby's leg slips back out. She scans the beach for assistance. It's fully daylight now, but they are quite alone. She tells Marilyn she's delivering a footling breech and needs to get to the hospital. "Just concentrate on relaxing. It's important the baby stays inside. Everything will be fine, but I'm going to have to call for help. Loudly, so someone will hear us."

Annie calculates the distance to where Sally lies sleeping. Under their window, maybe fifteen feet distant, is a lower-floor patio. She calls, "Hello! Hello! Help!"

Over and over she calls. Marilyn is holding steady, breathing in ragged gasps, tears flowing silently down her face. Annie doesn't think she's in transition; it wasn't pushing that forced the foot out. "Help! Help!"

At last, after perhaps four minutes, the lower-balcony door slides open. A man appears, tying on a robe. Annie yells for an ambulance.

The moments pass. Annie is anxious for the man to reappear. Marilyn is pasty-faced, ashen. When the fellow reappears to say the ambulance is on the way, Annie shouts for him to awaken Sally. "Room 211 above you!" she cries. "She's a doctor! Tell her to get my medical bag from the car."

Annie has to see the youngster through another contraction before Sally appears, loping across the sand, Annie's blue doctor's bag thumping in her hand, shirt half undone, shirt flapping. Sally takes Marilyn's vitals. She calls out measurements that are, thankfully, not hopelessly abnormal. And then the ambulance is heard, the wail of its siren.

There is rapid consultation. Annie cannot be moved, it's agreed. The ambulance crew, a man and a woman, with Sally's assistance must lift both Marilyn and Annie in tandem onto the stretcher, because it is crucial that Annie's hand not be displaced. Marilyn lies flat, heaving, her face streaming with sweat and sand and salt. Annie kneels between her legs, her forearm cramped. The ambulance crew lifts them; Annie teeters and almost falls. Sally steadies her. She thinks of herself, briefly, as a sort of modern-day Cleopatra, being carried toward her future. How has it come to this ironic twist, that she, on the cusp of lesbianism, should be lifted across an Oregon beach on a litter, her hand trapped inside the body of a woman? With her lover/not lover trotting along beside them, judging both their morals harshly? A crowd has gathered.

♠

It is nearly noon before she and Sally settle in for lunch in the hotel dining room. They had meant to be already on the road by this time, but they are minor celebrities—other diners whisper and point or stop by their table. Over and over, Annie repeats that Marilyn is the proud mom of a baby girl, five pounds, three ounces, both fine. Is it true the baby was born on the beach? No, this is not true. In the hospital, like most babies. Well, then, is it true the baby nearly died? Here Annie hesitates. "Marilyn could have run into trouble, but luckily, everything worked out perfectly."

Sally says she's proud Annie thought to check the desolate figure on the beach, proud she was able to divert disaster. For disaster was exceedingly close, both of them admit.

They go over and over it. In fact, they can't stop. Just when they do fall silent, one or the other will start up again. Annie will say, "But I never even noticed how cold it was!" Or Sally will say, "You are a hero, Annie, an absolute hero." Or, "No good will come of that girl's life."

Sally stands and gives her a neck massage. On the side facing away from the dining room, the people, she tenderly, incautiously scrapes her finger up Annie's cheek, her message irrefutable.

Sally says, "Did you imagine she'd name the baby after you? She probably thinks you'll be good for some cash."

Annie is disgusted, a little, by Sally. She sips a tall, sweating glass of champagne and orange juice, getting a bit drunk. And she realizes she is a little like a footling breech herself, half out. She knows that because of Sally she'll want to go back in, but only so she can be reborn the right way. She picks up her wineglass. "But let's not talk about work."

"Let's not," says Sally. She takes her seat and presses her knee against Annie's. "There's something else we should discuss."

"Is there?" asks Annie and moves her leg away.

But Sally cannot quite bring herself to say.

"Is there?" Annie repeats.

Sally touches her hand. "There is."

la llorona

amy hassinger

————————➤

In a small pocket of the city, where imported palm trees lined the sidewalks, where tiny backyards of plum and lemon trees and occasional swatches of green lawn were framed by steep wooden staircases, where old Victorians stood in various stages of disrepair against the clear sky, painted brightly in pinks, blues, and purples, there was heard every morning, at the rising of the sun, a wail. This wail keened out over a small courtyard, waking the inhabitants of the apartments that surrounded it. It began like the whistle of a teakettle, a thin ribbon of sound that grew broader, heightening until it became a wide, wavering vibrato, a careening sheet of noise, a bright flag flapping in a gale. Immediately, the Colombian construction worker in the shotgun two-bedroom on the third floor rolled over and stretched himself out of bed; his wife groaned and sat up next to him, listening for their son. The newlywed computer programmers, whose bedroom windows overlooked the courtyard, snuggled tightly for just a few minutes more, before they rose and jumped in the shower together. The waitress in the first-floor apartment who worked the night shift finished her cigarette and took a last bite of her sandwich before tucking herself in for the morning. The earnest young yoga teacher went to stand by his kitchen window, sipping his green tea, and gazed toward what he thought might be the source of the sound, hoping to catch just a glimpse of the wailing woman. Though he tried, he could not identify the source of the cry. It seemed to come from all around, to bounce off his walls and high Edwardian ceilings, and to hang in the air like the fog shrouding the Twin Peaks above.

Poor lady, thought the Colombian woman as she fixed an egg for her son's breakfast. *She's been abandoned by her lover, left to care for her infant child alone. The woman's overworked,* thought the waitress who worked the night shift, as she fell into bed and closed her eyes, *with feet she can't stand to lift.* "I bet she's a crazy old hag, with a hunchback," said the computer programmer through a mouthful of toothpaste, "who can hardly stand up." His new wife laced her hands around his waist. "With sunken eyes," she said, "and just one or two yellowed teeth." *Oh, how lonely she must be,* thought the earnest young yoga teacher, *how desperate, how empty.*

No single story was approved by the neighborhood as a cause for the wail, but they did latch onto a name. The professor of Chicano studies who lived two floors below the yoga teacher dubbed her La Llorona, the wailing woman. As she told it, "There's a Mexican legend about a wailing woman—La Llorona, *se llama.* She bore children she didn't want, and she drowned them in the river. But she was haunted by her crime and now she wanders the streets at night, weeping for her dead babies. She dresses all in white, like a ghost, and if you look at her face, you will die. This woman wails like her." She dropped her voice to a whisper: "I think she's done something terrible. *Hay mal-dad en su casa.*"

♠

Nina's view of herself was not quite so mythic. She led a balanced life. She ate well: a bowlful of oatmeal cooked with apples and raisins for breakfast, a salad at lunch, and a good balance of protein, complex carbohydrates, and vegetables at dinner. She arrived at 8 o'clock sharp every morning at her office downtown—she worked as a parale-gal at Pearson, Ricker, & Stores, a corporate law firm—and she arranged her lunch in the staff refrigerator and attached the wrist cushion to the base of her computer keyboard. She stood up to stretch her wrists, back, and shoulders every hour and a half, to minimize the chances of developing carpal tunnel syndrome. Every evening after work she set the StairMaster at the Wellness Center for twenty-five minutes on interval training, then took her pulse as she walked to cool down—a consistent 115 at the end of her workout, 75 when resting. She was fit, trim, wore sneakers to work and took public transportation as much as possible, and drank only one glass of wine a week—with her dinner on Friday nights—to cut down on the risk of heart disease and help her sleep.

Every morning Nina rose at 5:45, wrapped herself in a silver silk robe her mother had given her when she was still alive, shuffled into the kitchen to put on the coffee, stretched her back and hamstrings in four Sun Salutes, and stepped into the shower. As the water hit her face, wetting her short blond bob and her upturned nose, she stretched her mouth wide, stuck out her tongue as far as she could, opened her throat, and said what she thought was "A-a-a-a-a-a." This yoga pose was called the Lion's Roar, and its purpose was to stretch and strengthen the tongue, lips, throat, and vocal cords as well as to greet the day. Nina believed this "A-a-a-a-a-a" was nothing more than an extended guttural sigh. She was not aware of the way the sound, once given the opportunity to escape, surged from her like a great freshet breaking a dam.

On the Christmas of her twenty-eighth year, she met Gladys. Nina had planned to meet Tony at the firm's year-end party. Tony—also a paralegal, as well as the self-designated matchmaker of the firm—brought Gladys. Gladys's hand was sweaty when Nina shook it. Nina looked for an inconspicuous place to wipe off the sweat and Gladys handed her a towel she kept in her large black purse—one that reminded Nina of Mary Poppins's bottomless carpetbag.

"Here—indulge yourself," said Gladys. "I know my curse."

"Oh, no," Nina said, shocked at Gladys's straightforwardness. "I must have spilled something on my hand—some water from my glass." She took the towel and wiped, then folded it carefully in threes before handing it back.

"Gladys and I have known each other for ages," gushed Tony. "I can't even remember where we first met, Glad. Was it at Nero's masquerade that year? When I went as a Chiquita banana? Oh, no it wasn't, no it wasn't!" Tony grabbed Gladys's elbow. "It was Judy. She had us both over for that wine-tasting party. I remember, I invited you too, Nina, but you came up with some excuse. Glad, Nina is a yoga goddess. You should get her to show you some of her moves. She was the one I told you about who got that nasty kink out of my back months ago—remember? Oh, God, it felt so good, even though I was sore for days afterward. You should, Glad, you should try it."

"Tony always talks too much when he's trying to get people together." Gladys lifted her bug-eye glasses, set them higher on her nose, and considered Nina, as if she were a fruit with a small spot of mold.

"Gladys! I am *not*! I just thought you might be interested in one of Nina's major talents—just out of courtesy, at least. God. I swear, sometimes..." Tony stomped off to the bar in a huff, leaving the two of them together.

"You're straight, aren't you?" Gladys said. Her eyes were sharp and small—a bleak gray, like a foggy morning. She had a wide nose with a flat bridge, and her heavy glasses kept sliding toward the tip of it. Her black hair coiled like wires from underneath a fisherman's cap, which she wore slightly askew. She chewed on her lips as she watched Nina—they were meaty and over-red, and constantly glistening. A mole protruded from the corner of her mouth, and from time to time she stuck her tongue out to touch it, almost involuntarily, like a frog feeding on flies. Nina was slightly repulsed by her physicality, her sloppy clothing—cotton sweater hanging hip-length over a long, shapeless skirt and ankle boots with splashes of paint on the toes. Yet she also immediately admired her in a childish way, the way a young girl looks up to an older one.

"I knew it," Gladys continued. "Tony always pulls this one on me—he doesn't seem to get it that not everyone in San Francisco goes both ways." She sighed and put her hand on her hip. "I warned him. I said, 'Look, Tony—is that woman over there a dyke? Because if she is, I want you to introduce me. But only if she is.' I knew he knew you. He knows everyone. 'But,' I said, 'you'd tell me if she was straight, or married, right?' But all he would say was 'Oh, Glad, she's perfect for you, you're going to love her, Glad, please let me introduce you, *please*'—in his eternally faggy way." Gladys rolled her eyes and picked a piece of lint off her breast. "Ah, well."

Nina blushed, suppressing a giggle. She felt all of a

sudden like a maiden in a Renoir painting, with porcelain skin and florid cheeks. "I'm sorry," she said.

"That you're straight?" Gladys raised one eyebrow. "Look, I'm famished—are you here alone, anyway? Because I hate mingling, and I really hate eating alone. Excuse me," Gladys tapped a suited shoulder and wove a path through the crowd. She did not wait to hear Nina's reply. Nina followed.

The firm had rented out a hotel ballroom. The place had been empty when Nina arrived. The clicking of her heels on the floor had echoed against the walls as she walked to find her name tag on a table clothed in white linen. But now it was filling up—men in suits and ties moved to and from the bar like eddying water, holding glasses of wine and cocktails above the heads of the crowd. Women stood in tight circles, sipping and talking, glittering under the chandeliers. Splashes of red marked the occasion—red dresses, ties, sweaters, socks. A sprig of mistletoe hung over the entry way, and one man stood directly underneath it, tapping every woman who passed by, pointing above him, shrugging, like there was nothing he could do but follow custom, and kissing the victim full on the lips. Nina felt stifled. She removed her blazer and hung it on the seat behind her. She considered checking it at the coatroom—she did not want it to get stained by spilled wine—but the crowd was thick by now, and she was hungry.

"I'll tell you, I don't know why I came. Look at that idiot over there, under the mistletoe. How much do you think he's had to drink already?"

"Claude? Oh, I don't think he even drinks at all."

"He does that sober? Unbelievable." Gladys took a large glug from her bottle of beer. She tucked a swatch of hair behind her ear and looked up at Nina over the tops of her black frames. She reminded Nina of an animal—some kind of woodchuck or gopher—the way her eyes wrinkled at the corners and scrutinized her shamelessly. "I should tell you right away, if we're going to be friends: I can read minds.

"I don't tell everyone I meet," Gladys continued, shoving forkfuls of salad and pasta into her mouth as she spoke, "because you know how people get. They start asking me for favors, or worse, acting like I'm slightly off and they're just going to humor me about it. Like, it's not something I live with every day of my life, for Christ's sake. It's not easy, you know. It gets distracting. For example, I can hardly hold this conversation because I keep hearing that man's voice over there—see him? The one swaggering over to the bartender—you know what he's thinking?" Gladys dropped her voice to a whisper and leaned in toward Nina. "He's rating every woman he passes on a scale of one to ten."

"No," laughed Nina, turning to see who she was talking about.

"I'm not kidding. I heard it when I passed him. I was a four. Bastard."

"Oh, I can believe it," said Nina, playing along. "That's Paul. He's slept with at least five of the summer interns."

"I'll tell you something else," said Gladys. She sat back in her chair.

"What? Are you going to read my mind?" Nina raised her eyebrows coyly.

Gladys bit her bottom lip. "You're hard to crack. I'm getting some foggy signals. I sense intelligence, stubbornness, even obsession. One thing I can see: You like me." She spat the pit of an olive into the palm of her hand.

Nina had never met someone so forthright, so ready to say the first thing that came to mind. She was enjoying it. It was a nice change of pace from her own prison cell of a mind—the neatly arranged cell, with its bedspread smoothed and its sheets hospital-cornered, and the sink and toilet scrubbed daily. Nina walked through life with a vague sense of claustrophobia, no matter where she was. Her thoughts paced. She obsessively arranged, planned, and parceled. She made lists: to-do lists, lists of videos to rent, of books to read, lists of possible birthday gifts to get her father or her boss, lists of pros and cons for every decision she had to make:

Eat out with Tony after work?

Pros	*Cons*
Social time	*Will miss workout*
Expensive	*Calories!!*
Quesadillas	*What will we talk about?*
T. won't bug me about	
getting out more	

She made lists until every choice loomed like a growling beast in the hall, until she learned to simply remain in her cell, behind the barred door, sitting with her hands folded on the edge of her small bed.

"Okay, Glad, I've forgiven you." Tony sat down next to Gladys. "There's absolutely no one interesting here tonight. I've tried, I really have. Derek is being a complete flirt, as usual, and he's making me so jealous I just feel like biting everyone I see him with—but, of course, I won't, because I'm a gentleman. Unlike some people. Push over, will you?" Tony scooted closer to Gladys, tugging the tablecloth with his elbow. "Nina, did Gladys tell you she's looking for an apartment? And she's been looking for only...*three months*! It's so depressing, isn't it? I mean, if you can't find a place after three months of looking, and they're all so expensive anyway—why do we live here? Don't answer that—it's because of the boys. I know—"

"Actually, I have a room." Nina said, smoothing the wrinkled tablecloth.

"What?" said Gladys.

She blushed. "I have a room."

"Oh, my God, this is fate. I knew it. I knew you two would hit it off."

"Is it available?" asked Gladys.

"I don't know. I guess it could be. I've been using it as storage space. But I guess I could consider renting it out to you."

Tony gasped. "Nina. You're an angel."

"Can I come see it?" Gladys asked.

"Sure," said Nina.

"Now?"

Tony gasped again. "Oh, let me come too, Nina," he said. "I can't stand to stay here with Derek and his waggling, wandering prick."

Gladys flared her nostrils at Tony. "Spare us, sir."

"Sorr-y." He said. Nina giggled.

◈

The room Nina had was small. There was a closet—a sliding door opened onto racks of rarely worn clothing. Old scarves, hats, and gloves lay on a high shelf—relics from her days back East that she hated to throw out. Several overstuffed pillows were piled in the corner next to an antique spinning wheel, empty of wool. A rolltop desk abutted a single window, which looked onto a brick wall. Against the far wall was a narrow bed with a bright orange spread pulled tightly over the mattress. The floor was finished hardwood, the ceiling high.

Tony flopped onto the daybed and laced his fingers around the back of his head. "This is amazing," he said. "Total serendipity. Who would have thought Nina would just happen to have a room sitting empty in the land of astronomical rents? It's like you were just waiting for Gladys, Nina. I told you one of these days I would turn your life around if you just let me." Tony propped his weight on his elbow. "Now, Nina, in all fairness, you should tell Gladys about La Llorona if she's going to consider living in this neighborhood."

Nina raised her eyebrows.

"Come on, you know who I'm talking about. The wailing woman? Don't tell me you haven't heard of her!"

"What?" asked Gladys.

Eyeing Nina doubtfully, Tony said, "Glad, everyone in this neighborhood talks about this woman who wakes up every morning and cries. Early. And I mean she *cries*—not just like a little whimper. This woman has *lungs*."

"Who told you that?" asked Nina.

"My friend Peter. And Jodie. And Clyde from the café. Everyone. It's a local legend. Anyway, I'm just saying you should know, Glad, just in case you have a particular aversion to loud weeping."

Gladys shrugged. "I don't mind a little mystery in my life."

"Oh, I can see it now. You two are going to become old maids together, loving each other in secret, acting all proper and straight in public. Like Virginia Woolf and Vita Sackville-West. Like Sarah Orne Jewett and what's her name. One of those Boston marriages. Can't I join in?" He sat up, grabbed Nina's hand with both of his. "I'll build a little bedroom alcove in your back room, Nina. I'll be so quiet and serene. I'll make breakfast and you two can wander out of your love nest and look out at the city, holding hands. Won't it just be divine? Oh, Nina, honey—you're blushing. It's too sweet!"

149

"Shut up, Tony," said Gladys. But Nina saw her mouth curl into a tiny smile.

Gladys moved in the next day. She had been living at the youth hostel for the past few months; so much of her stuff was in storage. Nina helped her pack, running back and forth from the storage unit to the U-Haul trailer, where Gladys stood. She had a way of just standing that seemed chaotic and maniacal—pencils sticking out of her weedy hair, her hands waving over boxes, steadying them. Nina did the heavy work, cowering at Gladys's commands: "Not there, Nina! Put it here—that's a fragile one." More than once, as she trudged up the several flights of stairs under the weight of yet another box of books, Nina felt her throat clutch with an emotion she could not quite identify: fear? Apprehension? Excitement? Here she was, inviting a near stranger to move in with her. It was without a doubt the most reckless thing she had ever done. She had given it no forethought, made no lists. It had simply happened. She had been compelled.

Sunday night, after Gladys and Nina had spent the day lugging boxes up three flights of stairs, unpacking various articles of clothing, dozens of books, piles of old magazines, scraps of tin and bottles of glue, and a bronze sculpture of a satyr, after they had shoved all of it into every corner of the small room and had closed the door on the mess for the evening, they sat down at the kitchen table and shared a bottle of wine and a pizza. Chaos lurked just beyond the kitchen threshold, yet Nina was amazingly content. With shy admiration she listened to Gladys talk, and did not protest when Gladys refilled her wine glass. Her cheeks glowed.

As Nina rinsed their dinner plates in the sink, she looked out over the small courtyard at the moonless black sky pricked with starlight. The whole neighborhood was quiet. A song boiled in her: She hummed.

"What is that?" asked Gladys, coming up behind her.

"What?" She turned around.

"You were humming." Gladys repeated the melody.

"I guess I was," Nina said. She hummed the strain again. "It's a hymn my mother used to sing to me as a kid. I can't think of the title." She dipped her hands in the soapy water.

"It's nice," said Gladys. Nina felt Gladys's chilled hands against the nape of her neck, then on her shoulders. She prodded Nina's muscles with her thumbs. "You're tight," she said. "All that lifting."

A new warmth thrummed in Nina's thighs.

♠

That week, it rained. The sky hung like a gray pall over the neighborhood. Colors intensified: The pink stucco of the yoga studio across the street grew rosy, the green of the median strip became deep, oceanic under the white-gray sky. Even the lemons on the tree in the courtyard seemed to cast their own yellow light. Rain blackened the streets and lifted the smell of wet tar into the air. Stray fliers, cellophane wrappers, Styrofoam containers, and scattered leaves that had collected in the gutters washed into sewers, down alleyways, out of sight. Most people stayed indoors if they could, their windows shut to the blowing rain. La Llorona fell silent.

The neighborhood hardly noticed her missing cry. If they thought of the wailing woman at all, it was in passing. *The rain must soothe her,* thought the earnest young yoga teacher as he sipped his tea and watched rivulets stream down his kitchen window. *It drowns her out,* decided the newlywed computer programmers. The professor of Chicano studies lifted her head from her desk: *She must have nowhere to go. She is huddled somewhere beneath a bridge, a newspaper her only shelter. Tormented soul.* She mouthed a silent prayer.

On the first day of the storm, Gladys suggested that Nina call in sick. She and Gladys pressed against each other under a single umbrella, pointed it into the driving rain, and ran together to the video store. They rented four movies and spent the day on Nina's couch, huddled under a comforter, eating chips and salsa and watching films: *Breakfast at Tiffany's* and *Casablanca* (Nina's choices), *Heavenly Creatures* and *Women on the Verge of a Nervous Breakdown* (Gladys's choices). The second day of the storm, Nina called in sick again, and they spent the morning making deviled eggs and chocolate brownies, then spent the afternoon eating them. "How many times have you been in love?" asked Gladys, licking batter from the spoon.

"Not really ever," said Nina, startled by the question.

Gladys squinted at her from over her heavy frames. "Not even as a teenager?"

"I had crushes, I guess. I went out on a couple of dates. But I was never really in love."

"Bullshit. You had to have some major heartbreak, Nina," Gladys said, a smudge of chocolate on her front tooth. "You're twenty-eight! How could you have avoided it?"

Nina shrugged. "I've always been kind of shy. It just never happened."

"A secluded heart," Gladys shook her head. "That's what you've got. Sad. Sad. Sad." With each "sad" Gladys touched the tip of the chocolatey spoon to Nina's face.

"What is that? You sound like it's some kind of disease." Nina batted the spoon away. She wiped the sticky batter from her cheeks and forehead.

"It is. Secluded heart–itis. Either that, Nina, or…" Gladys narrowed her eyes, "you're hiding something from me. In which case, there will be hell to pay." She roared the end of her sentence, brandishing the spoon like a prophet's staff.

Nina laughed.

Nina had planned to go to work on the third day, but for the first time in her life she forgot to set her alarm the night before, so when she awoke to the smell of Gladys's pancakes and fresh coffee at 9:30, she figured she'd already missed one meeting, and if she stumbled in this late, any excuse would seem transparent, so she might as well just take one last day off. They spent the day painting glass jars and bottles, and when they were through, they lined them up on the windowsill. Gladys's were ornate, raucous with vegetation: yellow speckled petals, prairie grasses swept with wind. Nina's jars were decorated with stripes of solid color: red, blue, green.

"I always wanted to be creative," sighed Nina. "I guess it's just not in me."

"Bullshit," said Gladys. She spattered blue paint on the table as she waved her paintbrush. "Everyone is creative."

"You sound like my mother."

"A wise woman then, your mother. Where is she now?"

"Dead."

Gladys painted, silent. "How did she die?"

"Breast cancer. It was a couple of years ago."

"What about your dad?"

"High on heroin."

Gladys considered Nina over her frames.

"No, I'm just kidding," Nina said. "He's in Massachusetts still. He's fine. I don't see him much."

"That was not funny. What if he was high? How would I know?"

"I thought you could read people's minds."

"Ha," said Gladys. She pursed her rubbery lips into a cinched circle.

Nina touched her finger to Gladys's mouth. "Hey," Gladys whispered. She leaned into Nina. Her breath tasted of citrus. Nina's mouth felt tiny against Gladys's full lips, almost breakable, as if she were a glass miniature of herself.

"There! I'm your first woman," said Gladys, her palm cupping Nina's chin. "I've deflowered you."

"Well, hardly," said Nina. "My lips, maybe."

"The question is, Will I be your first love? If I had to answer that myself, I'd say yes."

"A bit presumptuous!" laughed Nina.

"Still and all, it'd be yes."

That night, Nina and Gladys slept under the same covers. "What do you believe in, Nina?" whispered Gladys. She laced her right arm under Nina's and traced a fingernail across Nina's nipple. Nina shivered.

"What? You mean God?"

"God. Beauty. Yoga, maybe."

Nina thought. "Can you believe in yoga? Mainly I do it to stretch."

"Well, I can tell you what I believe in," Gladys said. "I believe in chance. Fate, if you like. A mysterious force of some kind. Chance brought me everywhere I've yet been."

"That's something," Nina said, for lack of anything better to say. A tense silence rose between them.

Gladys propped her head up on an elbow. Her voice was brusque. "You're telling me the only reason you do yoga is for physical exercise?"

"Are you angry at me?" Nina asked quietly.

"No!" Gladys shouted. She glared. "I just think you're missing something. There's more to it than that."

"Like what?"

"Like...finding peace, or self-knowledge. I don't know what! More than exercise, though."

"I don't know, Gladys. I just do it because I do it. I guess that sounds pretty boring."

"Hmph," said Gladys.

"Uch," Nina said, suddenly indignant. "Why do you need to know what I believe? How do I know what to believe? Nothing! I believe in nothing."

"That's sad for you," murmured Gladys. Soon she fell asleep. Nina lay awake, listening to her light snore. She was virtually buzzing with anger and humiliation. How could Gladys assume such an intimacy with her this early in their friendship? Just because they were in bed together didn't mean Gladys had the right to know everything about her. Asking her what she believed? It was invasive. And yet she was mortified at the way she answered Gladys's question. To believe in nothing? It wasn't fully true, she knew, and yet she did not know what else to say. She did not know what she believed. Was that the same as believing in nothing? Nina turned over on her side, away from Gladys. She stared at the small patch of sky that she could see through her bedroom window. A thought looped through her mind: *This woman is important. This one thing is important.* Toward morning, Nina slept.

On the fourth day, Nina went in to work.

Tony rushed to her cubicle and leaned over the divider, spilling coffee on her desk. "Nina," he said, whispering so everyone could hear him. "What has gotten into you? Don't even try to tell me you were sick. Did you guys get it on? I'm amazed at you, really. I never thought in a million years you would let another person move in there."

Nina swabbed the coffee from her desk with a handful of Kleenex. "I know. But why should I worry? Should I worry?"

"No, no, not at all. No, I think Gladys is a doll—you guys are going to be a great couple."

Nina did not protest.

"I mean, by now I guess you know something about how she can be, of course. I wouldn't call her a tactful person, Nina. But, you know, she has a good heart. It's just only sometimes she goes a little nuts. What I'm saying is, well, she's got kind of a weird past."

"What do you mean?" said Nina.

Tony pulled at his nose, looked around, and noticed a man in a brown suit standing at the front desk. "Oh, shit—first client. I've got to go take care of him, doll. We'll talk later—lunch, okay?"

But when Nina went to find Tony at lunch, he was gone, no note. Nina sat by the fountain in the lobby alone, unpacked her brown bag, and spread a cloth napkin on her lap. She wondered what Tony had been referring to.

When she got home, the door to Gladys's room was closed. Nina slammed the front door behind her and walked by Gladys's door, yawning loudly. Gladys did not emerge. She dropped her gym bag heavily on the living room carpet and pressed play on the message machine. A low female voice spoke on the tape: "Gladys. Come on. Pick up, honey. I know you're there. Gladys!" There was a thudding sound, as if something had been thrown against a wall. "Goddamn it!" Click.

Gladys's door opened when the message ended, and she emerged. Her eyes were flittish, her hair matted on one side, as if she'd been lying down all day. "I didn't want you to hear that," she said, her voice heavy with resignation.

"Who was it?"

Gladys fell onto the couch and stared at her hands. Her face held an exaggerated expression of pain, tragic and austere. "I suppose I can't keep it from you much longer, Nina. Sit down." Nina sat next to Gladys. "That was my ex, Athena. She found me here. I don't know how, but she did."

"What do you mean 'found you'?"

Gladys looked at Nina wearily. She took a deep breath. "When I was sixteen I ran away from home. I grew up in rural Missouri, where they don't take too kindly to lesbians, if you know what I mean, and I knew what I was— so when I could look eighteen if I wore just a little of my older sister's lipstick, I took off. Snuck out one night and hitchhiked to the nearest Greyhound station in Gilman Falls, where I took the next bus to Nevada. I started working for this carnival there, as the mind reader and fortune-teller. That's where I met Athena. She was the strong man— she used to dye her mustache hairs black and twist the ends with hair gel. Once I saw her bend the barrel of a shotgun like it was a paper clip. I'm telling you, she was the real thing. Anyway, she took care of me—let me sleep in her tent, paid for my food, bought me new clothes. She was the first woman I was ever with. And I loved her for a while, I guess. Needed her, anyway." Gladys sighed heavily.

"We traveled together with that carnival for three years. Until one day, I found out that our next stop was Gilman Falls, Missouri. I didn't know what to do. I knew that my parents would go to the carnival, you know, bring the kids— I had six younger sibs, besides me and my sister—and I worried that my mother would come to get her fortune told. I had seen her do it before. But where could I go? You see, there were these heavies at the carnival, guys who carried clubs around and looked at you with tiny smiles in their eyes, like they were just waiting for you to try something."

"Heavies?" Nina was doubtful.

"Oh, the whole place was a front. For drug running. It was a huge business, really. We transported the stuff all over the country. Every booth had some kind of compartment where the stuff was stashed. They made deals after-hours. I remember walking to Athena's trailer one night and seeing

Grimes, the guy who operated the Ferris wheel, loading some boxes into a pickup truck with local plates. I kept walking, pretending I hadn't noticed anything, but he saw me."

Nina nodded.

"I knew they would go after me if I decided to take off, you know, and I didn't really know how to protect myself. And I suppose at the time I didn't want to leave Athena. Anyway, I decided to keep on, do the job, and just try to keep a low profile. I stayed in my booth the whole time I was on duty, so the only way I'd be screwed is if my mother decided to get her fortune told. Which, of course, she did."

"What did you do?"

"Well, I knew it was her right away when she set her foot in through the curtain. My mother is a large woman—300 pounds large. I felt the whole booth shake and I saw the purple flowered housedress she always wore, and I had no doubt in my mind. So I ran out the back. I jumped through the back curtains, but I couldn't leave right away—I had to peek, I had to just get a glimpse of my mother, for God's sake—and I tried to do it by just pulling back the curtains the tiniest bit— but she saw me. So I tore off. She was shouting, 'Gladys! Come back to your mama! Come back to the righteous path!' But I kept running, all the way to Athena's booth. We didn't even stay to get our pay. We just took off on her Harley, beaming that light toward the West, toward San Francisco, the Promised Land."

"What about the heavies?"

Gladys snorted. "Yeah, well, they followed us, all right. But they didn't count on Athena. She used to race her bike on off-weekends, and she tore up the ground like you've never seen. They tried to keep up, but she lost them on a back road. At least one of them bit the dust, and maybe the rest of them decided that it wasn't worth it. I mean, why run after two dykes who just disgusted everyone anyway?"

"Wow." Nina was entranced.

"So we settled down. I guess we were happy for a few years. Athena got a job as a bouncer and she worked every night until 3 or 4 in the morning. I temped and went to movies at night when she was at work. I started messing around. She was never home, and it was the first time I had been around all these beautiful women who liked other women and didn't even try to hide it. Athena came home early one night and found me with someone. She broke the woman's arm over her knee."

"Oh, my God."

"I was scared to leave for a while, but I finally did. I finally just packed up my stuff and left. I moved around from hostel to hotel to friends' floors, just kept mobile for—God, almost seven months now. Hasn't been much fun. I thought Athena finally had lost track or had given up. Thought it might be safe to find somewhere more permanent. But I guess not. She's found me."

"Well, Jesus, Gladys, I mean, what're we supposed to do?"

The phone rang and Nina jumped up, hugging one of the couch pillows to her chest. She stared at Gladys. "What should I say? If it's Athena? What should I tell her?"

"Let me answer it," Gladys said. She walked over to the phone and picked up the receiver. She lifted it, waited a beat, then placed it back down in the cradle.

"Gladys! What if that was someone else?"

Gladys looked at Nina over the top of her glasses as if to say, *Please, be sensible, we know who it was.* "Now," Gladys said, pacing meditatively around the room. She ran her fingers over items she passed: the lopsided bowl Nina had made in her high school pottery class, her Nancy Drew books with their blue-and-yellow covers, her crimson silk scarf with the long fringe that covered the table, on which sat her collection of tiny glass figurines—a collection she had begun when she was eight and had continued to add to as an adult. "We have a few options, the way I see it. One: We can leave, go on the run, borrow Tony's car or something, and just take off for Mexico."

"*We?*" asked Nina.

Gladys ignored her. "Two: I could run, get on the next bus out of town."

"And leave me to face her? Great idea."

"Or, we could outsmart her. Which, I might add, would not be terribly difficult." Gladys turned abruptly to face Nina, put her hands on her hips, and said, "I say that's what we do."

"How? She's going to show up here furious. She probably won't even ask any questions—she'll just haul off and hit me once I answer the door."

"Exactly. Which is why I'll answer the door."

"Oh, brilliant. And then what, Gladys?" Nina's pulse had quickened now, and she too was beginning to pace, although her steps were not meditative but brisk, almost military. She hugged the pillow tighter.

"Then, I'll introduce her to you, my mentor Madame Genevieve, the renowned fortune-teller and mind reader, who taught me all I know."

"That is ridiculous."

"No, Nina. It's perfect." She grabbed Nina by the shoulders. "Athena is very superstitious. She was always trying to get me to tell her fortune, but I never wanted to—I put her off by saying your loved one couldn't do it, it was too dangerous, whatever. I made up some excuse. But you can be my mystical teacher, who I've come to for help. There's something that's been haunting me about my lover, Athena, and I had to come to you, because you're the only one I know of who can tell me what it is. We decide together that the only way to break the curse that I sense, the foreboding I feel in every bone in my body, is for you to tell Athena's fortune. You know, tell her what she's really feeling—that she no longer loves me. She will absolutely fall for it, no question."

"I'm not really an actress, Gladys."

"We'll figure that out later. But she could be here any minute. We've got to fix things up." Gladys swept the collection of glass figurines off the crimson scarf and draped the scarf over the floor lamp, which cast a reddish gleam. Nina yelped and ran to inspect her figurines. "Put those away somewhere, Nina. Those are not the trappings of a princess of mystery."

Gladys moved from item to item, carrying the TV and the VCR into her room, pulling the table out and draping it with another scarf—this one turquoise, with threads of gold wound through—setting candles up at the corners of the room, clearing the shelves of the Nancy Drew books, and instead placing a grapefruit on one shelf surrounded by inches of space, an orange on another, a blue glass bottle on another. She ordered Nina to remove all the furniture except a wooden stool and several pillows, which she placed around the room against the wall.

"Now," she said, appraising the glowing room, "we just need the final touch." Nina followed Gladys into her room and watched her step behind the spinning wheel, bending to lift it from below.

"What is the wheel for, Gladys?" Nina's voice wavered with anxiety.

"For you, Nina. It'll be like the Fates. You can sit there, spinning out Athena's fortune. And you've really got to change out of your jeans before she gets here." Nina heard the sound of wood splitting. "Shit," said Gladys.

"You broke it."

"It's just a tiny crack," Gladys said from her half-bent position, her wild hair springing.

"Don't touch it."

"Nina, it's the perfect thing—"

"Put it back!"

Gladys stood up and placed her hands on her hips. "What on earth is wrong?"

Nina was trembling. A pulse beat in her head. "This was a mistake. You coming. I never should have asked you. I want you to leave."

"Now?"

"You're tearing everything up, you're destroying my living room, you're tossing my things around like they were just—pieces of garbage you don't even care about!" Nina's voice broke into a sob. "Now you broke my spinning wheel that was my mother's—and you! You act like you know so much about the world—"

"Nina—"

"You think you have some kind of sense about who I am. Well, don't assume, Gladys. Don't assume anything. You don't know anything about who I am. You don't know the first thing about me!"

"Well, for God's sake. Tell me what I need to know!"

Nina opened her throat—

And the wail came—thin at first, but grew broader. It echoed against the walls of the small room and keened out through the open windows over the small courtyard and into the neighborhood. It swelled with more fervor than ever, and in it were strains that the neighborhood had not heard before. Loss was there, like the whine of an oboe, and fear—a caterwauling soprano fear of loving and of dying. Despair echoed through it—a deep, hollow pitch—and some heard the sweet overtones of nostalgia. But above all, it was filled with the sound of loneliness, an ethereal moan of a melody that pierced the hearts of those who heard it.

It startled the earnest young yoga teacher, who was

teaching a class in his studio. He was in the midst of demonstrating the downward-facing dog pose when it began, and
he slipped and knocked the crown of his head against the
floor. He sat up, dazed, and looked out at his classful of students, who were frozen in various stages of the pose. He
rubbed his head and was surprised to feel the prick of tears
come to his nostrils, and before he could decide whether to
allow them to come, they came, and with them came a
sound that had never before come from his throat—an echo
of La Llorona's wail. The yoga teacher wept in front of his
Beginning Iyengar Technique class, and as he wept, he heard
his cries mingle with the wailing woman's in a sweetly dis-
sonant harmony. He wept more loudly, opening his throat
and braying like a saddled animal. Several members of his
class believed he was demonstrating the next pose, and they
watched, practicing his form—the eyes clenched closed, the
mouth yawning wide, the vocal cords stretched—a few of
them even wept with him, feeling as though they were free-
ing the demons that clutched at their hearts and choked
their most dear and limber thoughts and feelings and locked
them into cubbies of time and space, stifling compartments
of right and wrong and yes and no. The weeping welled up
in the yoga studio and joined Nina's wail, creating a tidal
wave of sound. It crashed into the evening traffic, making
drivers stop their cars, get out, and wonder at the echoes of
pain rustling through the leaves of the palm trees that lined
the street. One driver wondered if he was hearing the bells
ring in the tower of the Mission Dolores church on the corner, and it reminded him of his mother, who had come to
San Francisco from a small town in Italy, and how she used
to tell him of the church bells in her town, which rang every
morning and summoned the townspeople to morning mass
to pray and ask forgiveness, and he too began to cry—the
tears dropping onto his polyester pants, his hands gripping

the steering wheel—and as he leaned forward, resting his forehead against the wheel, his chest pressed the horn, which bleated out its own wail in accompaniment. The Colombian woman in the shotgun two-bedroom slipped in her ironing and burned her hand, and as she rushed into the kitchen to run cold water over the burn, she realized she had left the iron flat on her husband's last collared shirt, but as she ran back to save it from being singed, she heard her son call for her from his room, and finally she just stopped in her tracks and wept, letting the shirt burn and her hand pulse with pain and her son wander out into the dining room. He too bawled at the sight of his mama weeping. The newlywed computer programmers gripped each other tightly in the midst of their love-making, and the woman, in the throes of ecstasy, overcome with joy at the sweet gift of the man she held inside her, also allowed her wail to rise over the neighborhood, through the leaves of the lemon tree in the backyard, and mix with the general melee of sound that filled the air. Gladys listened to all of this, frozen, her eyes fixed on Nina's wide mouth and trembling tongue. Finally, Nina ran out of breath. The wail became a whimper, the wave of sound subsided, and Nina fell to the ground with a shuddering gasp. A sudden and deep quiet reigned over the small pocket of the city.

It stayed quiet like that for some time. Everyone who had heard or contributed to the wail rested, stunned. After a moment, the yoga teacher asked his students to assume the corpse pose, and he used the rest of the class time to speechify over their prostrate bodies, lauding the depth of the human soul and admonishing his students to remember what they experienced today—that the wailing woman embodied a humanity that was all but lost to society in its breakneck pace, that all of them, everyone in the neighborhood, in the whole city, all of them should follow her example and listen to the voices of their souls. The Colombian woman went to sit with her son, who had been frightened by the sound, and she brushed his hair off his forehead with her fingernails and rocked him back and forth, hugging him to her bosom, whispering to him "*Mi cariño, mi cariño,*" because she had felt in that one moment of deepest misery that her son was all she had in this world, all that was her very own, her flesh and her blood, and that her time with him would be entirely too short, that sooner than she could imagine she would be nothing more than the flicker of his eyelash, the flitting of memory in his consciousness. The newlywed couple lay in bed, holding each other, still entwined, still united, but shuddering now, trembling in voluptuousness and fear as to how deeply in love they were with each other, and how fragile and powerful it was. They lay, staring into each other's eyes, the woman dropping a silent tear now and then, the man stroking her shoulder, her hair, kissing each tear away as it fell. The traffic remained unmoving at the corner, as if stopped at the scene of an accident. The driver at the front of the line looked around, hoping to hear some kind of an explanation. None came, of course, only silence. Gladys still knelt by the spinning wheel, her hands clutching her knees, watching Nina.

Then the doorbell rang.

Nina raised her head. "Oh no," she whispered. "Athena."

Gladys did not move. "Jesus," she said.

A fist pounded against the door. "Nina! Gladys! Did you guys hear that? Unbelievable! Come on, open the door!" Tony.

"How did you do that?" Gladys whispered, leaning in toward Nina.

Nina exhaled sharply, a stunned laugh.

The pounding again. "I know you guys are in there. I

can smell you. Come on. I've got good news! Open up!"

"I don't know," said Nina.

"Gladys! Listen—I just saw Athena at the café. She was bragging about how she had found out where you were and was going to come rescue you or some bullshit like that—and by the way, I just want you to know that I do not know how she found out, because I did not breathe a word to anyone. I only mentioned it to Greg, who so wanted to know how you were doing. Anyway, guess what I did? You're going to love me forever. I told her that you and Nina had a fight, that she had thrown you out, and that you had decided to go back home to make up with your mom. Isn't that the most? She's on the Greyhound to Missouri, as we speak!"

"My God, Nina. That was you," said Gladys. She crept to Nina on her knees, flattened her palms against Nina's thighs, and rested her forehead against Nina's.

"Fine, you guys. I guess I'm probably interrupting something. I know when I'm not wanted. You can just call me later to thank me." Tony's shoes knocked against the stairs as he descended.

Nina sat, her forehead pressed against Gladys's. She closed her eyes, felt the warmth of Gladys's skin against hers, smelled the faint citrus flavor of her breath.

"Well, God," whispered Gladys. "Where on earth does it come from?"

Nina, who did not know, only breathed and listened deeply, joyfully, to the silence she had created.

the jew in bright red

orly brownstein

At the San Francisco Museum of Modern Art he
sits inside a painting, on a bench, one hand white,
the other green. Left eye open, right shut. His
red-black beard burns from his chin. His skin? Blue.

Yellow behind him, and inside that wash I see
the letters of my mothers, the starters: aleph and bet;
the whirling lameds; blooming gimels; sailing shins;
and the swimming ones, the fish, the pretty nuns.

Right here I find what is mine: the possibility
of my heart, the love I've hoped for but not let
in. And this sweet thing is tough and soft, moving,
not whole. It is in the consonants, the vowels, the few

women whose souls are giant and red and free,
those more than happy to offer me their skin, wet
with knowledge, their neshamas waiting like flint.

This is my job: to find her, to love her, a woman, a Jew.

potatoes, sex,
and security

sally bellerose

⟶

MJ is destroying geraniums in the cellar because she is anxious about the prospect of war. She insists that this makes perfect sense. Her plants have been over-wintering in plastic pots on the cold cement floor. MJ has always had a special place in her heart for the tough old-fashioned flower. For ten years now, the plants have survived from November until May with little water and scant light from a casement window. With only a few weeks left until they can be set in the warm ground outdoors, MJ bends at the waist, wrenches the flowers from their containers, and tosses the leggy remains into a big black garbage bag. She wants to sleep in the cellar in case of chemical, biological, or nuclear attack. There's not room for the geraniums, and the water, the canned goods, the battery-operated radio. Her girlfriend, Bonnie, leans against the cinder-block wall of the basement and watches.

MJ is a round-bodied woman. Unless provoked, she has a pleasant, no-nonsense demeanor. When provoked she is not pleasant. Every time another yellow, orange, or red alert is announced, she becomes more provoked.

When she is composed, MJ's looks and manner put her friends in mind of Barbara Bush during her glory days with George the First. But unlike Barbara, MJ has no big money men to prop her up or rein her in. Her cotton candy hair hasn't seen scissors since 1982. Her overalls are paint-splattered but freshly laundered. She is clean and, in her flamboyant way, tidy. Her look is not unkempt, just untamed. Next to MJ, Mrs. Bush looks like a bonbon fresh from a Tupperware container. Still, the resemblance between the ex-president's wife and the old dyke from small-town Massachusetts can't be denied.

Because Bonnie is small, friends joke that she's Nancy Reagan to MJ's Barbara Bush. The couple socializes with a crowd who likes to imagine the elderly wives of retired statesmen curled up in the same bed. Except for size, Bonnie looks nothing like Mrs. Reagan. She's a freckled redhead with a braid halfway down her back and furrows around her lips and eyes from years of sun and smiling. Her pink base-ball cap matches her Keds. Someone who spends a day with Bonnie and MJ might come away believing MJ rules the roost. But Bonnie's resemblance to Nancy is strongest in that Bonnie is a femme top who is happy on the sidelines staunchly loving her mate and, when necessary, calling the shots.

MJ straightens up for a moment to capture her great shock of hair in a bandanna, which she ties at the nape of her neck. "I don't need your help."

"You won't get my help," Bonnie answers calmly. "This bomb shelter you plan to build down here is insane. You know this."

"Stop calling it a bomb shelter. I'm moving the bed-room." MJ says mechanically. The argument has been going for days. It's all been said before.

MJ is a scrapper with a passion for words, for ideas, for being right. Nothing in all their years together has prepared Bonnie for this kind of anxiety in her lover. She was less worried when MJ was spending half her waking hours haranguing politicians and throwing *The Sunday Republican* across the kitchen. Bonnie has tried everything she can think of to get MJ to calm down. She has tried gentle persuasion, valerian tea, shoulder massage, and Michael Moore videos.

She tries again. "I don't want to sleep upstairs without you. I won't sleep in the cellar with you. I want you and a bathroom near me all night. I want to climb the stairs to our warm room on the second floor for another twenty-seven years. We have more than most people could ever hope for. You're willing to sleep in a cold, damp place because Katie Couric's voice cracked? You, MJ?" She shakes her head and frowns. MJ has already turned back to the geraniums, so this effort is wasted.

Bonnie says with real sincerely, "It's an insult to people who have to hide underground." This last bit gets to MJ. She kicks a bag of sprouting potatoes, bought in bulk and forgotten months ago. Three wrinkled potatoes spill on the floor. She kicks one at Bonnie and returns to the geraniums, sputtering something unintelligible. The potato lands at Bonnie's feet.

Now we're making progress, Bonnie thinks. She contemplates MJ's ass, which is back in the air, as MJ bends over the plants. MJ is sixty. Before they started to get old Bonnie did not imagine a person could move like that at sixty. Bonnie is sixty-two. She looks frail, but she is not, she is just size six. She can carry grocery bags and rake the lawn. More strenuous exercise has never interested her. But she's always admired her girlfriend's strength. If the panic behind MJ's behavior wasn't so disturbing to

Bonnie, she could happily watch her move by the hour. She particularly enjoys the way MJ's overalls stretch across her ample bottom every time she bends at the waist. Just the way her overalls are straining now. Bonnie is put in mind of other times MJ has taken this position: making love, moving the coffee table, caring for her mother when she broke her hip.

Swept by memory and love, Bonnie takes a deep breath and says, "You're becoming a coward." She picks up the potato. "Burying your beautiful self in fear."

"Fuck you," MJ says.

"Such a mouth on an old lady." Bonnie, still fondling the potato, removes a bag of old clothes from an unmade bed. The bed has been in the cellar since they converted to queen-size a decade ago. The mattress sags when she sits down. Her knees practically bump into MJ's butt. "The springs are shot in this thing. It's going to kill your back," she says, bouncing. "Remember that wooden cutout of a woman, that garden ornament, that used to live in the Reeses' flower bed?" The Reeses are their next-door neighbors. "That's what you remind me of, bent at the waist like that."

MJ, looking over her butt, cuts her eyes at Bonnie. "You hated that thing. All butt and bowed legs, no head, no arms, no upper torso. All our friends agreed—demeaning, objectification. Remember the fight you had with Mary Reese? I heard you say, 'Why does her ass have to blossom in full view of our bay window?' "

Bonnie grins. "I have a secret." She leans on her elbows. "You want to hear my secret?"

"No," MJ says. "You're trying to distract me from my work. You think I'm crazy, in need of distraction, because I happen to think we're safer in the cellar?"

"That's right." Bonnie agrees. "Tell me again, so you

can hear how crazy you sound, why exactly are you killing the tender perennials?"

"You hate scented geraniums." MJ, wielding a plant, walks to where Bonnie is sprawled on the bed. The naked root dangles an inch from Bonnie's nose. Bonnie slaps it away and the roots spit little black BBs of soil onto her sweatshirt.

Bonnie screws up her face and picks a heart-shaped leaf out of her hair. "They do smell like something that used to be pleasant. Like garlic on the breath the day after a good meal."

MJ says, "Nothing's all that pleasant if you get close enough. You are the coward. We aren't secure. Face it."

Bonnie studies the sprouted potato that's still in her hand. "We're going to die sooner than later no matter what. A bad night's rest isn't going to buy us one minute. Nothing's secure. Never has been." She tosses the potato in the air and catches it. "This thing is still edible." She takes a bite.

"Jesus." MJ grimaces. "There's dirt on those old things. They're raw."

"Gritty, but not bad." Bonnie concentrates and swallows. Her eyes widen. She starts to spit and cough.

"Stop it," MJ snaps. "You can eat the whole bag. I'm going upstairs to get some linens." Bonnie continues to hack and gag, and MJ makes no move to help.

Bonnie's eyes water. She exhales a squeaky wheeze and points to her throat.

"Damn fool," MJ says, and whacks Bonnie on the back. A piece of raw potato flies out of Bonnie's mouth. She sucks in a lungful of air and continues coughing.

MJ leads her upstairs, sits her on a kitchen chair, and feeds her a spoon of honey. She puts the kettle on to boil. They sip their tea in silence. Bonnie cries a little. MJ watches the birds outside the window and pretends she doesn't care that her girlfriend is crying, but there are tears on her cheeks too. "What was that, potato therapy?" MJ turns to face Bonnie.

"That's all I've got," Bonnie says. "I quit. If you want to go crazy, you're on your own."

MJ nods. "I'm not used to feeling helpless. I needed something to do." She pats Bonnie's wrist. "That wooden woman had a polka-dot skirt and frilly underpants, remember?"

"Pink panties and bowed legs," Bonnie grins. "She didn't care what the neighbors thought. She was hot."

"Remember what happened to her?" MJ lets out a big sigh.

"You backed into her with the Toyota." Bonnie's grin broadens. "You were hot too."

MJ's eyes narrow. "I know your secret. You've always been kinky in unexpected ways. You actually liked that big wooden butt staring at you from the neighbor's lawn. She didn't seem your type, but she turned you on. I owe you an apology." MJ doesn't sound apologetic. She sounds cocky. "I should have taken your feelings into consideration before I mowed that bitch down."

Bonnie says, "If you smile and stop killing the geraniums, I will accept your apology."

MJ smiles.

francesca

tzivia gover

→

It was Pride Day in Claremont, and from her perch on top of her best friend's shoulders D'vora watched people gather for the march. She could see the two women who rented the apartment above her art studio pushing their baby in a stroller; she could see her auto mechanic revving up her Harley in the Dykes on Bikes contingent; and she spotted the men who ran the florist shop walking their twin Scottish terriers on lavender leashes. She could see everyone, that is, except the one person she was looking for. The cute girl from the bookstore who'd sold her a biography of Romaine Brooks was nowhere to be seen.

Karen, who was bearing D'vora's weight, would have said it was just as well the Bookstore Babe, as she'd come to call her, was nowhere in sight. It was well-known in the community that in addition to selling books, she and her lover of eleven years were in the process of inseminating and that she was probably the least available woman at the march. But Karen was studying human behavior at the local college and knew the value of reverse psychology. So

174

she let D'vora sit atop her shoulders in hopes that by encouraging her to pursue this crush, her friend's enthusiasm would eventually wane.

Karen's experiment had unexpected results. The Scottish terriers got a hold of the baby's balloon and pierced it, causing an explosion that set off a wail from the child, which caused Karen, who had a phobia of loud noises, to lurch, which caused D'vora to topple from her friend's shoulders and into the arms of a well-tanned woman who took the mishap in stride.

"See," Billie joked, "women throw themselves at me."

But D'vora barely noticed her. "No luck," she said to Karen, as she dusted off the seat of her black jeans and gave a cursory "Sorry" to Billie, who looked disappointed to be taken so lightly.

Billie wasn't used to being brushed aside so easily. Granted, women didn't usually land in her lap in such an obvious way, but she was used to being pursued, and just as used to being the one to say "Sorry," as in "Sorry, I'm not looking to get involved right now."

So the fact that D'vora had knocked her, quite literally, off her feet didn't make Billie take notice nearly as much as the fact that the tall woman with red highlights in her curly brown hair seemed so disinterested.

And the fact that D'vora then took her companion's elbow as they walked off to line up for the march, which was about to begin, made her even more interested. As her roommate Claudia always told her, "You only want what you can't have."

The rally held little interest for D'vora, who finally spotted her crush just as the object of her affection wrapped an arm around her partner and climbed into their car. So she was just as glad when a burst of thunder interrupted the final speaker's talk about the importance of visibility and the crowd began to disperse. D'vora said goodbye to Karen and began her walk home.

Her apartment was about a mile from the common where the rally had been held, but she was glad to be trudging home in the rain alone; Karen wouldn't want to hear about her disappointment over not having exchanged two words with the unavailable bookseller.

Just as she was working up the argument she would use next time Karen tried to talk her out of this crush, a Chevy pickup splashed by and Billie leaned out the window. "Hop in," she said.

"Thanks anyway," D'vora answered, "I don't mind walking."

"In this mess?" Just then the heavens seemed to open and the rain poured down. Water was soaking through her sneakers, and her wet hair felt suddenly cold against her neck.

"Okay," she said, as Billie reached across and pushed the passenger door open.

The ringing phone greeted D'vora as soon as she stepped through her door. She grabbed the receiver and scooped Rembrandt, her overfed cat, into her arms in one practiced motion.

"I saw you get into her truck. How romantic! You fall into a woman's arms, then she whisks you away. Tell me everything."

"Karen, I'm starving," D'vora said as she opened a can of food for the cat. She fed Rembrandt then filled a pot with water as Karen continued. "You'll be happy to know her roommate is on my softball team, and I have the roster with her number on it right here."

D'vora fished around in the cabinet for a box of pasta. "You know I'm not interested."

"What I know is that you are suffering from a patho-
logical obsession with an unavailable woman, and in two
years when I have my degree I'll be able to treat you, but
in the meantime—"

"She offered me a ride because it was pouring. End of
story." D'vora settled into a chair by the stove. She
thought she might as well get comfortable, since she knew
she'd be in for a long lecture. Karen would remind her that
she hadn't had a girlfriend in over three years and that it
was time for her to find some happiness and that she had
to learn that not every relationship ended badly and blah,
blah, blah.

Instead Karen said, "I guess it doesn't matter, because
she lives with the shortstop and they're probably girlfriends anyway."

"Oh?" D'vora watched as Rembrandt licked his bowl
clean.

"That's all for now, I've got to go."

"You do?" D'vora was confused. Her conversations
with Karen usually lasted long enough to cook, eat, and
clean up from supper.

"Actually, there's one more thing," Karen said. "Five,
five, five, six, three, one, zero."

"Is that a lottery number?"

"No, but I bet it's a winning number. Write it down."

"You're terrible," D'vora said. "It's her number, isn't it?"

"Five, five, five, six, three, one, zero," Karen repeated.

"Talk about obsessed," D'vora groaned, as she scribbled the numbers onto a paper napkin.

She didn't need to write it down, though. D'vora had
already memorized the number, the same way she had
memorized how Billie looked when she was driving. How
Billie's gaze seemed to wander deep within herself, even
though her eyes were riveted to the road. "I suppose it's

worth a try," she told Rembrandt, as she lifted the steaming pasta from the stove.

♠

"Sorry," D'vora said, as she burst into the restaurant seven minutes late for their meeting. She refused to call it a date. She'd invited Billie to "meet" her for dinner.

Billie was dressed in chinos and a black shirt that had been meticulously pressed. D'vora smiled at the effort Billie had made as the hostess led them to a corner booth. The candles burning in netted jars on the tables bathed the room in a soothing light. D'vora felt comfortable here. And she was comfortable with Billie too. They talked about work: Billie's job at the photo lab, where she processed yearbook and wedding portraits, and D'vora's teaching position at the university, which earned her barely enough money to buy her canvases and paints but gave her a studio and time to spend there. While they talked, D'vora studied Billie's face as if she were preparing a composition. She liked how light grazed the planes of Billie's nose, cheeks, and slightly square chin, and how her cropped black hair seemed to absorb all the darkness of the restaurant. By the time the entrées arrived, she felt she had known Billie for a very long time and that dinners like this were common for them.

"You know," Billie said, "I don't even know if you're single. I mean, when I met you were straddling a woman's shoulders. That's fairly intimate, isn't it?"

"I guess we are pretty close," D'vora said. "Close friends. That's all."

Billie nodded and tore off a piece of garlic bread. Her hands were wide, her fingers short. And on the ring finger of her right hand D'vora noticed two gold bands. "And you, you're..." D'vora took a moment to try to piece together the meaning of those rings. "Are you divorced?"

Billie touched the rings with her thumb as if to hide, or maybe protect, whatever story they told. For the first time that night the silence between them was awkward. Finally Billie answered.

"Widowed."

D'vora nodded, not speaking. Should she say sorry? Should she ask to hear more? She wanted to know how long ago, but Billie's expression hinted that enough had been said. D'vora slid the sun-dried tomatoes from her pasta and gathered them into a small pile at the edge of her plate. Billie reached across and held her fork suspended above D'vora's unwanted food. She raised her eyebrows as if to say "Please?" and D'vora nodded.

"See, we make a good pair," Billie said. "Complementary tastes."

The waiter refilled their wineglasses and Billie raised a toast: "Cheers to queers," she said with a wink. Their glasses touched with a surprised, happy sound.

"Where are you parked?" D'vora asked as they left the restaurant.

"I walked," Billie said, zipping her jacket.

"Good, I think I owe you a ride." D'vora opened the passenger door to her slightly worse-for-wear Honda. "Hop in," she said, trying to imitate the way Billie had tossed off those same words just a few days before.

"No, thanks." Billie suddenly sounded all business. "I'll walk."

D'vora felt jolted out of the easy happiness of the past two hours. "Well. Good night, then."

But Billie didn't move. She just looked up at the wispy pink clouds that streaked the evening sky. Finally, D'vora walked around to the driver's side and unlocked the door.

"I guess I'm waiting," Billie said.

"Waiting?" D'vora asked.

"Waiting for a thunderclap or a downpour to make me change my mind." She looked at D'vora across the car's silver roof. "It worked for you, didn't it?"

"That was before we'd even met. You shouldn't need a storm to help you decide now." D'vora got into the car, pulled the door shut, and turned the key in the ignition. Just then, Billie opened the door and got inside. "Sorry," she said as D'vora pulled out into the street. "I guess I didn't expect to have such a nice time tonight."

"You make it sound like that's a bad thing," D'vora said. And maybe it was. She remembered the first time she'd ridden her brand-new purple bike. She'd gotten it for her birthday when she was ten years old. It had a white banana seat and pink tassels on the handlebars. She and her brothers were racing up and down the sidewalk, screaming with laughter. And then her tire nicked a branch that had fallen in the road. She lost her balance and flew off her bike and onto the curb. She cut her elbow and bruised her hip. It wasn't serious, but she never forgot how quickly laughter had turned into howling tears. And she couldn't help notice over the years how often good times would crash to a stop the same way.

Still, when Billie invited her inside, D'vora accepted. She thought they might at least salvage the closeness she'd felt earlier in the restaurant.

Billie's living room was cluttered with mismatched sofas, armchairs, and tables. D'vora tickled the fringe of a thrift-store lampshade and unconsciously thought of each item she'd remove from the room to create space and order. She sank into a settee that would be hauled out according to her interior decorating fantasy, and ran a finger over the spines of the books on the shelf nearby. There was a series of "how to" manuals, at least three years' worth of *Popular Photography* magazines and some adventure novels. She picked up the *Michelin Guide* to Italy and was thumbing through it when Billie walked in carrying a bottle of merlot and two glasses.

"Planning a trip?" She bent down to offer D'vora one of the wineglasses.

"I hope so—I mean, I'm applying for an art program in Venice next summer."

"Take the book," Billie said, working to open the bottle.

"That's okay. I don't want to jinx my luck." D'vora slid the book back into the empty space on the shelf. "Have you been?"

"To Italy?" Billie filled the glasses without looking up. "No, we never got there."

"Sorry," D'vora said again.

Billie put down the bottle and leaned so close that D'vora thought she was about to kiss her. Instead Billie plucked the book from the shelf and handed it back. "Luck's not good or bad. You can't jinx it."

D'vora held the book on her lap as they sat and talked and sipped the wine. She couldn't stop thinking of the feeling she'd had when Billie leaned across and she thought they were about to kiss. She wanted that kiss. But she didn't want to get caught in a relationship that would feel like this room: too close, too much.

"Refill?" Billie asked.

"No, no," D'vora said. "I need to get home. I hate leaving my cat this long. And he hasn't had his dinner."

"Easy on the excuses. I can take rejection."

D'vora stood. "No, it's not that, I had a wonderful time."

"Hey, don't sweat it. I'm not looking for anything either. To tell the truth, this date was my roommate

Claudia's idea. She's always pestering me to get out."

D'vora reached for her jacket.

"That sounded horrible. It's just...I'm not ready. I mean I've dated...I've had girlfriends since..." D'vora noticed Billie's thumb reach again for the rings. "I'm just not ready for anything serious."

"Serious?" D'vora buttoned her jacket. "I think you're jumping the gun. Who said anything about serious?" She was talking, but the words sounded like Karen's. It's what her friend would say on the phone when D'vora tried to explain why there would be no second date.

"So you're not looking to get serious either?" Billie put her hand on D'vora's, which was already on the doorknob. And then there was that kiss D'vora had been imagining. And it tasted as sweet as she'd dared hope. And it lasted much longer.

◆

Months had passed since that first date, D'vora thought, as she began sketching the first lines of a new painting. She started high on the right side of the canvas and drew a diagonal charcoal line. On the other side she made a similar but much smaller stroke. Billie called D'vora her summer fling, and when D'vora pointed out that the leaves were falling, Billie still refused to revise her definition of their relationship. D'vora referred to it as an affair, even when Karen pointed out that she and Billie saw each other every weekend and spoke on the phone every night. Besides, Karen had argued, an affair usually means someone is cheating on someone; there's a third party. D'vora added a form in the center of the canvas. She was selecting tubes of paint when she heard a knock at the door.

"I hope you don't mind the surprise," Billie said as she

stepped into the studio. "It's just such a beautiful day, and why would you want to paint it if you could be outside walking in it?"

"What are you doing out of work on a Thursday?" D'vora asked, taking in Billie's casual dress. She was wearing jeans, work boots, and a hooded sweatshirt.

"I called in sick," Billie said matter-of-factly. She stepped up to the canvas D'vora was working on. "What's this one going to be? The view between two mountains?"

D'vora smiled. "You know I don't do landscapes."

"Yeah, yeah, you paint abstractions. Light and shadow and form," Billie said, parroting an explanation she'd heard D'vora deliver many times by now.

"And emptiness," D'vora added. "I paint light and shadow, form and emptiness."

"Right," Billie said. "So why don't you leave the canvas empty and come out with me?"

D'vora didn't want to give in so easily. She'd been spending so much time with Billie on weekends, and now the classes she taught had started up again. She had to protect the little time she had left for her artwork. But, she really did want to go. "There's a story about a Buddhist artist and a Western artist who are painting the same landscape," she told Billie. "The Western artist steps outside to look at the trees and mountains and runs back inside to paint for days. The Buddhist artist sits outside and looks at the landscape for days, then goes inside and quickly paints. The point of the story is that the Buddhist is the true artist."

"So you're saying you're going to paint landscapes now?" Billie asked.

"I'm saying I'll go outside with you and I can still tell myself I'm working on a painting. I'll be observing light and shadow, form and—"

"And emptiness," Billie said as she took D'vora's hand. "I like the way you think. Let's go."

Outside, students rushed across the quadrangle like leaves swirling in the wind. "Where are you taking me?" D'vora asked.

"Who says I'm taking you anywhere? Maybe we're just walking."

"You have your determined look on. You have a destination in mind."

Billie slowed in front of an old stone house that was covered in ivy.

"This was her dorm, wasn't it?"

"You don't mind, do you?" Billie looked into D'vora's eyes as if the answer might be there. "It's just that no one else would understand. At first all my friends encouraged me to talk about what happened. But I wouldn't. I couldn't. And then when I was ready, it seemed like they didn't want to hear anymore. Work was the worst. Everyone at the lab thought she was just a friend. How long could I go on crying about a friend?"

D'vora pulled Billie down to sit on the stoop. "So talk to me."

"It's her birthday," Billie said. She looked down at the leaves piled around her feet, and started to move her foot from side to side, like a windshield wiper clearing away the rain. D'vora saw what she was uncovering. In the bald spot Billie had made, there was a heart carved into the cement. BILLIE LOVES FRAN, it read.

⚬

Above the Cream Puff Bakery the sky was a watery, nearly colorless gray. Seated inside, D'vora slid her cup back and forth along the shiny wooden tabletop, watching the clock. It was 8:38 when Karen pushed through the door, apologizing for being late. "I'll just grab a coffee and be right back."

D'vora forced a smile, trying not to show her impatience. She knew she needed to talk.

Finally, Karen sat down with a steaming mug of coffee in front of her. "So, what's up?" she asked. "It's not bad news from Italy already, is it?"

D'vora shook her head. "Billie's lover died."

"But you're Billie's lover," Karen protested.

"No—Francesca."

"Francesca? She died in a car crash four years ago. Claudia told me the whole story after practice one night."

"Right." D'vora picked at the cheese Danish on her plate. She was trying to uncoil the spiral of dough without breaking it.

"Does she talk about it a lot?"

"Not a lot, but—"

"Is she seeing anyone—you know, a professional?"

"What? Do you therapists get a bonus every time someone hires a shrink?"

"Okay, okay," Karen said. "You're right, I should be focusing on you, not Billie. So tell me, what's really bothering you?"

"Well, I had this dream."

"About?"

"Francesca."

"You know, everyone in your dream is really some aspect of yourself. So when you dream about Francesca, you're really dreaming about something inside yourself." Karen stirred her coffee in perfect rhythm with her words, slow and measured. "Do you think you might be upset about Francesca because it's easier than focusing on your own pain?"

D'vora shrugged.

"You know," Karen continued, "it makes sense you're having strong feelings. This is your first relationship since—"

"You don't listen to me," D'vora said, pushing her plate away. "Billie and I are not that serious. It's not a relationship."

"Of course," Karen said, putting her empty coffee cup down. "Look, I've got to get to school. I have a 9:30 class."

"I'm trying your patience, Doc, aren't I?"

Karen smiled. "It's good practice."

"I'll think about what you said." D'vora crumpled her napkin and put it on her plate with the half-eaten pastry.

Karen gave her a quick hug. "And I'll put your bill in the mail."

That night it happened again. The phone rang. D'vora picked it up. "Hello, is Billie there?" D'vora looked at Billie sleeping motionless beside her. "No, she's not in," D'vora said to the voice on the phone. It was the same dream she'd been having for weeks now. Except this time Francesca didn't give up. As D'vora lay in bed the door flew open and Francesca stood there, demanding.

D'vora would recognize her anywhere: a heavy black braid draped over one shoulder, copper-colored eyes, and a piano player's tapered fingers. She knew Francesca well. She knew her laugh came from somewhere deep inside her and that she couldn't carry a tune but loved to sing. She knew that the night Billie met her, Francesca was wearing a white miniskirt and yellow sweater, and that even though yellow wasn't good on her, Billie thought she was beautiful.

"D'vora, wake up." Billie was sitting now. "D'vora, please wake up," she was saying. It was 3:46, according to the digital clock. An icy rain slapped the window. "You're having another nightmare."

"Hold me," D'vora whispered.

Billie didn't move. "Dee, I have to get some sleep. I'm no good for anything else tonight."

"I didn't mean I wanted sex—I just wanted you to hold me." D'vora turned away from Billie. "I should know better than to ask you for anything."

Billie slid back under the covers and lay facing the window. "Nothing's ever good enough for you, D'vora."

"Nothing is all I get from you."

"You knew the deal. I never promised you anything."

D'vora willed the tears that were streaming down her cheeks to stop. She wanted to get up and leave, but she didn't want Billie to know she was crying.

"I get it," she said as she grabbed her turtleneck from a pile on the floor. "You can't love me." D'vora reached for her jeans. "You can't love anyone unless—" She slid one leg into her pants then realized they were backwards. "You can't love anyone who's alive, can you?" D'vora righted her pants and stood to go. But when she looked at Billie, she noticed her back was lifting and falling. She'd never seen Billie cry before.

"You're wrong," Billie said.

"No, Billie, it's true. This just can't work out."

Somewhere in the distance a siren whined, but inside the room there was no sound except the tsk-tsk-tsk of the radiator working.

Billie perched on her elbow and watched as D'vora put her boots on. "You're really leaving?"

"You expect me to stay?"

"Yes, stay," Billie said.

"I'm going," D'vora said. But even as she said it, she was lowering herself onto the bed and wrapping her arms around Billie.

"It's just hard. Scary. To try again. But I will try," Billie said. "Till it hurts."

As they were falling back into sleep D'vora heard Billie whisper, "Promise you won't die, Dee. Promise."

The next morning the ice on the trees magnified the sunlight, making the world look hopeful and delicate. Billie was already up; D'vora could hear the shower water pounding in the bathroom. Still wearing the turtleneck and underwear she'd thrown on during their fight, she got out of bed and walked into the bathroom. "That you?" Billie stepped out of the shower, grabbed a towel, and gave D'vora a kiss. "Look," Billie said, peering into the foggy mirror, "It's like one of your paintings. It's a composition all about light and shadow," she said, and gave D'vora a squeeze.

"There's emptiness, but no form," D'vora said. "I'll fix it." She reached out a finger and drew a circle. Inside she made two dots for eyes and a downturned crescent for a frown the way she used to do on fogged-up car windows when she was a child. She liked how the watery eyes would run like tears.

"No, that's not right," Billie said. "It should be a happy painting." She leaned past D'vora and traced a heart in the steam. Inside she wrote: "BRJ loves DBR." Billie kissed her neck. "Come on, I'll make some coffee."

While Billie was in the kitchen D'vora looked for music to put on. As she flipped through Billie's collection she knew which selections to avoid. The Wynton Marsalis always reminded Billie of the time she and Francesca heard him perform at an outdoor concert and they huddled under the blanket they'd brought to picnic on because they hadn't counted on the cold night in the middle of August. She didn't put on the Dave Brubeck album because that was the one

Francesca had given Billie for their last Christmas, the one when Billie had gotten sick from the eggnog and Francesca had strung cranberries on the tree and Claudia's cat crawled up to eat them and toppled the whole thing over.

"Hey, I thought you were putting on some music," Billie called from the kitchen.

D'vora settled on a tape by a trio she and Billie had heard play New Year's Eve. That was the night Billie had looked into D'vora's eyes and told her how happy she made her. And D'vora was sure Billie was going to say I love you, but instead she gave her a long sweet kiss that was just as good or even better, because D'vora thought those words were overrated and overused and should perhaps be as mysterious and cloistered as the name of God. She no longer believed anyone when they said them, anyway.

♠

D'vora was just about to press the buzzer to Billie's apartment when the door swung open and Billie came out. "Hey, I was just going to pick up some food for dinner."

"I have a better idea," D'vora said. "Why don't you take me out? It's a special occasion."

"Your birthday was last month, so that's not it," Billie said. "It's not our anniversary, is it?"

"Don't be ridiculous." D'vora clutched her heart with an exaggerated expression of shock. "We don't mention such things, let alone celebrate them. And besides," she said, taking Billie's hand, "it's not for six weeks."

"What is it, then?"

"First tell me where you're taking me—and don't say Burger King."

"Okay, McDonald's," she said, ushering D'vora into

the truck. D'vora let out a groan. "Just kidding. Let's go to the place where we had our first date."

Billie got inside and reached across to hug D'vora. "So what is it?"

D'vora pulled back and reached inside her jacket pocket for an envelope. Billie took it and pondered the elaborate air mail stamp.

"Good news from Italy?" Billie asked. "I guess I always knew you'd go."

"How could you have known?" D'vora snatched the letter back and held it in front of her as if she were seeing it for the first time. "I mean, I kept hoping, but I never for one minute thought it would really happen."

Billie put the key in the ignition and started the car. "I guess I just always knew you'd leave."

"It's just two months. That's not leaving—that's going away and coming back."

Billie tapped the gas but didn't shift out of park. "You might not come back. You might meet some handsome Italian butch and start a new summer fling."

"So you're jealous?" The creases D'vora loved so much at the corners of Billie's eyes seemed to be etched deeper. "It's not about that, is it?"

"Okay, maybe you won't meet someone. You might just love Italy and not want to come back."

"Then I'll send for you. We'll find a little villa at the edge of a vineyard and settle down."

Billie put the car in reverse. "Look, two months is a long time. Who knows what we'll both be feeling by then. I just don't want you to expect anything, that's all."

D'vora stared straight ahead as they turned onto Main. "You're threatening me. If I go to Italy, you'll take up with someone else."

Billie reached over for D'vora's hand. "Hey, I'm sorry.

I'm really happy for you. It's just that you never know what will happen with something like this. You'll be far away. You'll meet new people. It's a long time—"

"I never know what will happen tomorrow with you, let alone two months down the road."

Billie massaged D'vora's neck and shoulders with one hand. "I said I'm sorry, I really am. It's just, you know. I hate goodbyes. I don't want to lose you."

"But you don't want to keep me either."

Billie brushed D'vora's hair back with her fingers. "Let's start over. Tell me again and I'll tell you how proud I am of you."

D'vora was silent. She took the letter from her pocket again. Billie took it from her. "Good news from Italy," she said, as if she were learning it for the first time. "Let's celebrate."

They ate dinner outside on the patio, and when the waiter poured the wine Billie lifted her glass and looked at D'vora for a long time. "You know," she said, "it would be kind of nice to come home to you."

"Kind of nice?" D'vora asked.

"Really nice," Billie said.

"But you would never," D'vora said.

"I don't know, maybe I would." Billie touched her glass to D'vora's and took a sip.

"Maybe I would too," D'vora said, doing her best to sound detached, as if she hadn't already made up her mind.

Karen would tell D'vora she should be angry with Billie. Why should Billie keep her at such a distance? Why couldn't Billie just say outright she wanted to live with D'vora? Why should D'vora be happy with these scraps of affection? But D'vora knew better. She knew why Billie was scared.

She knew about the night Billie had woken up and Francesca wasn't in their bed, and how she'd found her in the living room slumped into an armchair reading some novel she'd already read a half dozen times before. Francesca had had a nightmare. Someone was coming after her and she was running away. It was just an anxiety dream, Billie had told her. After all, Francesca was getting ready to graduate in just a few weeks.

Then a few nights later Francesca was going out with some friends from school. Billie stayed home because she had to get up early for work the next morning. She went to sleep and woke a few hours later to the sound of the phone ringing. Then Claudia's footsteps stopping at her door. Billie's heart froze even before she heard her say, "Get dressed, we're going to the hospital."

D'vora understood why Billie was scared, but she'd misunderstood something too. She must have, because the week before she was going to leave for Italy, Billie said this really couldn't last and they might as well face it before D'vora's trip so she could keep her options open.

D'vora said she didn't understand, and Billie said she couldn't explain.

The next day she arrived at D'vora's door holding a shopping bag. "This is some stuff you left at my place. I thought you'd want it back."

All that was left between them fit inside a single bag, D'vora thought, as she gathered her cat into her arms. The gesture forced Billie to walk into the apartment and put the bag down herself. D'vora left her waiting there while she made a quick survey of the apartment, looking for anything that might be Billie's. She found a sweatshirt, a couple of CDs, and the travel book.

There was no fight. There were no accusations. The word "breakup" sounded like something shattering, but their ending was quiet, clean. Empty, D'vora couldn't help thinking.

As soon as Billie left, the cat jumped onto the couch and sniffed at the bag. D'vora began to sort through its contents. There was a T-shirt, D'vora's green sweater, her beach towel, toothbrush, and robe. There were also a handful of books she'd lent Billie. She picked up a lesbian detective novel Billie had been reading and flipped through the pages. Not one was folded down. No passages were marked. Billie had left no evidence that she'd once been there.

⬧

It was the night before her flight, and the phone rang and rang. D'vora didn't want to pick it up. She knew who it would be anyway. But it kept ringing and she couldn't sleep if she didn't answer. It was Francesca, of course. "Is D'vora there?" she asked.

"Francesca, is that you?"

"Is D'vora home or not?"

"No, she isn't here," D'vora said, and hung up the phone.

The dream haunted her all the way to Italy. She thought about it when she walked among olive trees marveling at the twisted wedges of sky between their branches. She thought about it as she set up her canvas in a studio crowded with artists from around the world, and with each day it became more difficult to fill that square of emptiness. And finally she realized that what she'd said to Billie wasn't true. She'd said Billie couldn't love her because she was alive. But she wasn't really alive. D'vora had become the absence of her own pain. She was disappearing into her own shadow.

The professor was saying something, and D'vora

began to listen. The next assignment would be a self-portrait, he explained.

After class D'vora would enter a shop that sold scarves and jewelry and beautiful gilded boxes. She would find a mirror shaped like an upside-down teardrop and she would take it back to her studio. For the weeks that remained she would look into it and she would discover who was there. And when she picked up her brush to start over she would paint with layers of color and intricate detail.

play money

elizabeth sims

I couldn't believe they used real money in class. I'd
expected to get trained on play money—not the kind for
children but adult play money, near-real money with the
basic markings that's regulation-size in order to fit into the
cash drawers properly. Plastic coins I expected too.

But there we were, a dozen brand-new teller trainees,
up to our elbows in the real thing, 10,000 dollars of it. The
trainer, a bored veteran of the Human Resource
Development department, had counted it out before our
eyes. This was the job for me, finally. I believe that was the
bank's first mistake.

Moreover, though, I thought I'd forgotten how to flirt.
Lord, it'd been years, my prime sliding away from me like
a wad of bacon grease across a hot skillet. But I hadn't forgotten. No, I sure hadn't.

I'd been unable to take my eyes off Giselle Brigsby from
the minute she set her sleek little butt down in the chair kitty-
corner from mine. Unlike the rest of the class, women who
were dressed as if for hooker tryouts, Giselle wore black

195

slacks that just missed the category of "jean styling" (forbidden), a black turtleneck, and this spring-green leather belt that slithered around her hips like a friendly cobra. The shoes? Well-worn Doc Martens, black of course.

She was a dewy little baby dyke whose attempts at looking and acting tough made my the tips of my toes ache. And on top of it all, her parents had had the miraculous sense to name her Giselle. Alva Johnson, the trainer, butchered it: "Jizzayel? Brigsby?"

"President," answered Giselle, little smart-mouth.

At break I staggered to the washroom and sat whispering, "Giselle. Giselle." On leaving, I avoided my eyes in the mirror, my accusing eyes that would have asked, "Who in God's name do you think you are? You've got fifteen years on her at least. Your tits sag and your bangs are crooked."

Yeah, but I had a new job, one I wasn't going to blow, a job that could lead to something. My self-esteem was at a high level.

So next break, lunchtime, Giselle happened to be right ahead of me going into the cafeteria, holding the door open, and I happened to place my warm, loving hand over hers for a moment. My lips are full and sensuous, and I sort of swirled a smile right into her startled face as I went by.

From then on I noticed her noticing me. She brought her tray to my table, where I and three other trainees got to know her a little bit, mostly because I asked her questions about herself. The other trainees would just as soon have discussed their hair and *Survivor XIX*. Giselle had gone to community college for one and a half semesters, then dropped out. She lived with her mother, who worked as salad lady at Sven's Family Place but was angling for hostess because her hands were starting to react to the lettuce. They rented an apartment in The Pines, a downtrodden place next to the railroad switching yard where the price was right but the incessant ringing of the crossing gates tended to turn brother against brother. Giselle's mom was thinking of going on disability if she didn't score hostess.

I was dismayed to learn Giselle hadn't had more advantages in life, but deep down I exulted: more leverage for me.

"I would so love to get out of that craphole," Giselle told our table.

Then she did an astonishing thing. She went over to the vending machine, bought a package of Famous Amoses, opened it, and placed it in the middle of the table for everyone to share. "These basically suck," she said, "but oh well." A generous girl. A girl who wanted to be liked, all the while pretending otherwise.

I knew what it was to want to be liked while pretending not to. That was pretty much my life. I'd pretended not to want to be liked so expertly for so long that most people took me literally and simply didn't like me.

They had a whole fake training branch set up in Main Office. It had counters and teller windows and panic buttons, plus a lecture-seating area. In the morning we'd learned to handle cash, to double-count and stack and band. We'd learned to align the presidents' heads with the right-hand edge of the cash slots, and so much more. Riffling through wads of the bank's cash felt luxurious and surreal. All this jack right in your hands: a down payment for a PT Cruiser, a winter in Orlando, a complete Pro Logic Surround Sound system. The means to all of it right in your hands, only it's not yours.

After lunch we practiced basic transactions like cash deposits and check cashing. Not until tomorrow would we be taught the complexities of third-party checks, inter-account transfers, and utility payments.

I saw it; I saw her do it.

It was the end of the day, and Giselle and I were working at windows side by side, and Alva Johnson had just told us to turn in our drawers when I saw Giselle's hand slipping from her drawer to her front pocket, and in it was a bill. She licked her lips. Just as she glanced toward me I looked away. A thrill ran through me. This kid's got guts.

Who knew the day's routine would end with Alva Johnson consolidating all our cash drawers and counting the money again while we watched? She counted it once, looked up, pressed her mouth tight, then counted it again.

She sighed heavily and said, "A twenty-dollar bill is missin'."

No one spoke.

"Everyone remain seated." She pulled her chair from behind her table to sit facing us squarely. "Whoever has the twenty, bring it to me."

Silence. From my side-view seat I watched Giselle run her tongue over her teeth. She was trying to decide whether to be amused or scared.

"Class, this is disappointin'," said Alva. "We all have to wait here until whoever has the twenty comes forward."

My classmates, except Giselle, shifted and groaned. We sat in silence for about six years, then I had a sudden thought. My wallet was in my coat pocket, which was hanging on the back of my chair. I made a loud, real-sounding sneeze, then fumbled in my coat pocket as if for a Kleenex. A minute later I bent down to look under my chair. "Oh, what's this!" I cried, holding up a twenty. "What the heck!"

Giselle's head snapped around. She gazed at me in complete awe.

Alva narrowed her eyes. "Everybody waits until I check the serial number."

Shit.

We went back to waiting. Eventually the people spoke out.

"I have now missed three buses."

"My baby-sitter leaves at 5:30, and I mean 5:30."

"Come on! Which idiot took the money!"

Alva shouted, "Don't shout!"

"You don't have the right to keep us here!"

"I most certainly do."

After ten more years of silence, Giselle rose and casually walked over to Alva. All eyes followed.

She plucked the bill from her pocket and held it up for all to see. The class as one heaved a sigh. Alva said, "Put it on the table."

"I won't do it again," said Giselle.

"You're damn right you won't," said Alva. "We'll do your termination paperwork now. Everybody else, you can go."

I couldn't believe they fired her. What if she'd had a good reason? Alva didn't even ask.

I passed the training and went to work in branch oh-five, at Connelly Avenue and Third. It was an old branch, designed in pre-computer days, with cramped teller stations and a massive vault straight out of Marvel Comics. Also an endless wall of safe-deposit boxes. Banks are getting out of the safe-deposit business, I was told by the branch manager, Joe Cool Boss. His name was Joseph Kulbosi, but he tried to get his subordinates to call him Joe Cool Boss. I couldn't do it, and started using "Mr. K," which he decided was all right.

"Safe-deposit is labor-intensive," he said. I understood: I'd been trained to escort a customer to the boxes, do the horseshit with my key and the customer's key, then escort the customer and their box into the privacy cubicle. If I were a customer, I wouldn't be happy with the privacy cubicle; the walls were barely chest-high. If you wanted real privacy, you'd have to pitch a tent inside it.

I got to know the other tellers, a sensible bunch of women plus one guy, who hosted a monthly potluck at his apartment. His name was Clarence, and by night he was a drag queen, a pretty good one, I guess. He and the head teller, Penny, were best friends, swapping makeup secrets and low-fat recipes on breaks.

I quickly got to know and despise the regular customers. The women who would come in to make cash deposits, drawing crumpled bills from their cleavages, the money damp and hot. The crabby old-timers who distrusted ATMs or who just liked to check in on their money every week.

The most morbidly fascinating of them was Nasty Patsy, a stooped witch with BO who would slap down an endorsed check with two hands and say down her nose, "You owe me. You owe me 173 dollars." As if we'd been withholding money that was rightfully hers and only now had she deigned to jump through the hoop we had so hatefully imposed on her. She'd stand there with her arms folded, stern and angry, until you finished counting the money out. If you went too fast, she'd yelp, "I can't follow you! Start over slow this time."

Nasty Patsy had a checking account, but she only kept the minimum in it so as to have the privilege of renting a safe-deposit box. It was a big one, and according to Penny and Clarence, who had both peeked over the wall of the privacy cubicle while Patsy and her box were in it, that was where she kept her bundles of money as well as an eye-boggling stash of jewelry. She came in every Monday morning to visit her money and jewels. Penny and Clarence said that every month or so she changed small bills for a hundred and added that in.

To help the tellers deal with difficult customers, Penny and Clarence had worked up an official sheet with important information on it. Each piece of information was numbered. When you were dealing with a real asshole, you'd say "Excuse me for just a second" and leave your window. You'd go over to the next window—where the teller was well aware of what you were going through—and ask that teller for, let's say, Form Sixteen. That teller would pull out the information sheet and read number sixteen, which said, "This customer got blown out of Hitler's ass a long time ago."

That teller would have to keep from laughing and say quietly, "No, I don't have Form Sixteen."

And there would be this moment of relief and solidarity, and you would gather enough strength to return to your window and finish the transaction.

Exciting though my new job was, it wasn't enough to make me forget Giselle. There was only one Brigsby in the phone book. Giselle sounded flattered to hear from me. "So you made it through the training," she said. "Amazing."

I told her about my job at branch oh-five.

"And just think," she said, "that could be me, working over there at branch oh-five."

"Well, I just wanted to say, you were screwed."

I don't know why she laughed just then.

"Everybody in the whole class thought so," I insisted.

"Well," Giselle said, "the beat goes on." I could hear her trying to hide her hurt.

"Well," I said, "what are you doing now?"

"Watching Lucy on TV Land."

"Yeah? Well, I thought maybe we could get a cup of coffee or something."

"Okay."

I picked her up from her and her mother's apartment and took her over to The Clock.

"Are you hungry?" I asked as we settled into our booth.

That got a smile. "I'm always hungry." Dear girl.

Watching her put away a bacon cheeseburger, a whole order of fries, and a Coke, I fell more solidly in love with her than ever. The girl could eat. "Aren't you having anything?" she asked.

I was too thrilled to eat. "Coffee's fine for me."

We fell to talking about the main thing we had in common, our day of teller training.

"So did you plan it from the beginning or what?" I wanted to know.

Giselle, it turned out, had been thinking all the same things I had about all that money we were handling. "You know," she said, "you're standing there with this tiny pack of twenties and it's a thousand dollars."

"What would you do with a thousand dollars?"

"Oh," with a crooked little smile, "I can think of lots of things."

We expressed anger at the bank.

"The sons of bitches," I said, "with all that money. Paying us shit. Firing somebody for a lousy twenty bucks."

"And I didn't even do it." Giselle wiped up ketchup with a fry.

"What do you mean?"

"Well, I mean, I didn't leave the building with it, did I? I never took that money off the premises."

My God, she was right. "You never even stole that money and yet they fire you. I could just take Alva Johnson by the neck and make her eat dog shit. I'd like to do that, I would."

Giselle sipped her Coke. She gathered up her hair, a crazy clowd of chestnut tresses, then let it fall. "Well, you know, she's just a puppet."

"Huh?"

"She's as innocent as you and me. What choice does she have if she wants to put shoes on her kids' feet?"

"You mean—"

"I mean, there are forces out there that are beyond you and me and fucking Alva Johnson. I mean, we're all a bunch of dupes. All that money in the bank? Where do you think that money goes? To the people who need it? Right. Take a look around you. Take a look at America, Red!"

My name, since I haven't mentioned it, is Red. My hair on my head is reddish. On my arms it's blond.

Giselle went on, "How long do you think it's gonna last before it all comes crashing down of its own weight?"

I'd fallen in love with a prophet.

I said, "I have some marijuana at my place."

And that was the beginning. You're wondering, How does Red do it? How does she get this gorgeous young prophet into her bed not once, but repeatedly over the course of the next two months?

I'll let Giselle speak to that in her own words:

Unh...ayah, ayah, ayah, don't stop, oh please don't stop, pleasedontstop pleasedontstop pleasedontstop, ayah, ayah, iiiiiiiiiii!

When she asked how I did it, I played coy. The answer was: with a lot of careful prep. I circumvented the arthritis in my neck by using a special three-inch foam mat under her bottom and another under my chest. That way there was hardly any strain on my neck and I had all the staying power I needed. More, in fact. Giselle was so full of hormones, I could taste them. The flavor? I'd describe it as halfway between a Chessmen cookie and a good grade of malt liquor. Plus, orally speaking, I'm very nimble. I'd say my chief talent is pressure control. I begin very softly, and build gradually to a sustained crescendo.

And...? You're wondering. Well, I don't ask for much. "Oh, I am so okay," I'd say. "Later, my sweet. Later. You rest now, I'll order us a pizza."

Thus did Giselle become my own. I felt fifteen years younger and acted it.

We talked up a storm. "My mom is such a wage slave," Giselle said. "She thinks her job at Sven's Family is the real deal. She says, Well, I'm paying our rent, and what have you done today? When she's dead I'm going to have them carve on her tombstone SHE PAID THE RENT."

I muttered, "That ought to make her happy."

"Yeah." Giselle gnawed a pizza crust. "My ex-girlfriend used to take forever."

"Oh, yeah?"

"She was very dependent on me."

"Yeah?"

"Plus, she never had any money. The thing about you, Red, is you're fun and you're not a tightwad and you don't act like you think you're so great all the time."

That was true. I let Giselle talk. Over time I kept gently leading her to bed and I kept buying pizza, beer, and dope.

It was so good to not be lonely.

When I looked into the future, though, things looked slightly grim. I probably could convince my goddess to move in with me, but the thing was, my second Visa was approaching max-out from all the cash advances I was taking to keep us in Afghani Thunderfuck and Canadian psilocybin, which is so much better than the regular kind.

She kept talking to me about big business running our country and American corporate-military hegemony ruining the world. I started to get into it. The more I thought about it, the more I realized how little I'd thought about that stuff before. To think I'd actually wanted my job at the bank. I'd competed for that job, taking my binder home and testing my memory at night. Giselle helped me understand that the reality of my life was that my job had been shoved down my throat. Every job I'd ever had had been shoved down my throat and I hadn't known it.

One night after yet more great sex, Giselle rose up on an elbow and said, "Red, it occurs to me that we should teach the bank a lesson."

Now, that was a tremendous coincidence, because lately it had occurred to me that staying out of trouble wasn't enough of a life goal.

"What do you mean?" I said. I knew what she meant, but I wanted a little more convincing.

She said, "How loyal do you feel to that bank? What does that job give you?"

"A paycheck."

"And what does the paycheck mean to you?"

"Well, it pays my rent, and—"

I saw the look in her eyes. We were both thinking the same thing: *She paid the rent.*

No way did I want to be categorized in the same slot as Giselle's lettuce-chopping, brainless mother. And I realized Giselle and I could really work for change, significant change that would make a difference to people.

"I'm a trusted financial professional now," I told her. "I'm on the inside." But I'd learned in teller training that most stickups don't yield much money. You've got your exploding dye packs, you've got your panic buttons. Plus, computers have helped banks trim the amount of ready cash at tellers' windows.

I thought about Nasty Patsy. "Her jewelry is fabulous," Clarence had told me one night at potluck. "Have you seen it yet?"

By then I had.

He went on, "Pearls the size of grapes, those pearl earrings? It's vintage Tiffany and Cartier."

"Really?"

"Tons of diamonds."

"How do you know it's real?"

"The settings. I used to work for a jeweler who did a lot of estate appraisals. I don't know where Patsy got all that stuff, but there's probably half a mil in diamonds alone in that box. Art deco settings. Platinum. Rose gold, green gold. Piles of stones."

Penny said, "And yet she looks like such shit." Patsy wore appliquéd sweatshirts and stretch clam-diggers with loafers, topped off with an acrylic Tam o' Shanter. And no jewelry.

"Yes," said Clarence, "she does have issues with presentation."

Nasty Patsy trusted no one, but her problem was that she was trustworthy. You could trust her to come in every Monday between 10 and 11 o'clock, request access to her box, then hang with her treasure for about fifteen minutes.

I studied the near flawless complexion of Giselle's belly. "Do you have a firearm?" I asked.

"Um-hmm."

"Is it big? I mean, does it look big and threatening?"

"Not really. Maybe I should get another one."

"Can you work on that?"

"Yeah. I might need some money."

"All right."

Giselle and I cooked up a simple plan. The Sunday night before we carried it out, we did no dope at all.

Patsy betrayed herself on schedule, coming in a few minutes after 10. As soon as she was alone in the privacy cubicle, I stepped over to the drive-thru window and pretended to swat a fly.

Half a minute later a masked gunperson dressed all in black stormed in, shouting for everybody to lie down. I obeyed with the rest. I heard nothing from the privacy cubicle.

"You, get up!" Giselle kicked my foot. "Put the money in this bag, and don't give me any marked stuff. I'll kill you if you do."

It was thrilling to be ordered around by Giselle. She used a growly, tough voice that I believe she intended to sound guylike.

"Faster!" she commanded. I scurried through all the teller drawers and picked out the good cash, bypassing the dye packs. She stuffed it into her pillow case, then turned toward the privacy cubicle.

"No!" I cried. "No!"

Giselle boosted herself over the chest-high wall and dropped down on Nasty Patsy. I fumbled with my key, knowing Patsy wouldn't give up her shit without a fight. My role was to prevent Patsy from beating the hell out of Giselle, who didn't want to shoot anybody.

Giselle and I were pacifist people on a mission to get corporate America to take a look at itself, not rid the world of miserly old women.

Patsy yelled, "No, you son of a bitch!" and flung herself on top of her box.

"Ma'am!" I screamed. "Get back!" I grabbed her shoulder and pushed her into the corner.

"Let go of me!" she shrieked. "Goddamn you!" She shoved me with all her might but, outweighing her, I stood firm.

I hollered into her face, "You'll get killed, it's not worth it!"

Giselle was gone. We'd planned it for speed, and it was done. Somebody had hit their button while we were in the enclosure. The cops surged in, but the gunperson in black had been away for about four minutes, I guessed. She would now be walking casually up Connelly Avenue, a young imp with fluffy hair wearing a bright orange poncho, swinging a D&D Grocery bag.

What a high. The cops questioned the hell out of me, but I played just as coy as when Giselle wanted to know about my sexual technique.

Joe Cool Boss and everybody else was awestruck by my selfless protecting of Nasty Patsy. Not that she was ever going to thank me. She shrieked at the cops, Joe Cool Boss, and me for two hours.

My whole world had changed, from dull puppetry to meaningful action.

That night Giselle and I met up in a room at the Super 8 next to the expressway. We kissed. We laughed at our audacity. We did it. Nobody got hurt. We got the money. We did it.

Giselle upended the pillowcase onto the bed. The bundles of money were there, but instead of the jewelry there was a freezer-weight Ziploc bag filled with sparkly stones.

I asked, "Where's the jewelry?"

"That's it." Giselle lit a cigarette and rubbed the back of her neck. "I spent all afternoon prying the gems out of the metal."

I was shocked. "Why'd you do that?"

"Because we weren't going to take it to Antiques Roadshow. Because the bare gems can't be so easily identified. Outside of their settings, they could come from anywhere. Belong to anybody. Be sold to any jeweler."

My crotch had been damp all day, but now it positively dripped.

Giselle said, "I threw the settings away, and if you don't know where, that's better for you."

"I love you."

"Now, look, I'm getting nervous. Let's divide this stuff."

"Divide it? Okay."

The cash came to 17,450 dollars. We sorted the stones into piles and divided them one by one. Even the murky light of the motel room lamp couldn't make those stones look dull. There were sixty-six pearls, including the two grape-size ones. There were a hundred and nine diamonds, twenty-one emeralds, and six rubies. I insisted Giselle take the odd diamond and emerald.

"All right," she said. "We'd better get out."

I rose. "Where to?"

She looked at me. "Well. I don't think we ought to tell each other."

"What?"

"Safer for both of us."

"I don't understand."

"I'm going."

"You mean, we're going."

"No. Red, come on. This is it. We have to separate."

"The fuck!" My knees more or less gave out and I sat down on the bed. I stared at her, and after a minute I started to understand. I said, "I thought...this was just the beginning, you know? I thought we were going to pull more of these, and more and more, and finance operations against more corporations, that would get the people to wake up. Or at least begin to question their shallow lives."

"If we were together and got picked up, they'd use one against the other."

"But we wouldn't—"

"Bullshit. I can't believe you didn't get this from the beginning. This was a one-shot deal. The stars lined up for us here. Now it's over." Lifting her arms, she gathered up her chestnut tresses, then let them fall. The gesture made my eyes sting. "Look, Red," she went on, "You can do whatever you want. Buy those speakers you want. Sponsor a kid in Honduras. Join PETA."

"You mean you never thought we'd...you know...be...together?"

She was getting unnerved by my intensity. She edged away from me. "Red, it's been fun. I needed a fling. But—"

"A fling! I love you!"

"You do not. All right, I can see why you say that. A drowning person loves the life ring that falls in front of them. You only love me because I went to bed with you and made you think about something more than the view off the end of your own nose."

Crying now, I said, "It's a start, isn't it?"

"You thought I was a kid you could manipulate with dope and your tongue. Well, lady, there's plenty more tongues out there waiting for the likes of me. And I can buy my own dope now."

"You're just trying to act tough. Come here."

"Get away from me!"

I sobbed, "Why are you so mad at me?"

"Because you're stupid. You think two dykes can convince anybody of anything? Bullshit! When the world gets changed, people change it for themselves. I've changed my world as of today."

She tucked her bundle of cash and jewels under her arm and walked out.

She was right, of course. I loved her exactly for the reasons she said. She went to bed with me, and she opened my eyes to how the world really works. But she thought I didn't love her. And she had no idea she loved me. I repeat: She showed me the way the world really works. That isn't love? You tell me.

keep your fingers lost

jenie pak

He calls to me every night from the street beneath my window. It's almost as if he's singing a song full of the mantra of my name: *Yoon Ni. Yoon Ni. Yoon Ni Yah.*

The strange thing is, I don't go by my Korean name anymore. Not since the third grade, when I had finally had enough of the mispronunciations, the bastardizations of my name.

Yoon Ni Yah, he calls to me nightly like a loon who has grown tired of wearing its moonlit feathers and rose one morning in the form of a man. You would think I would call the police, maybe. Help! Come over quick! A man is calling out my name.

But the thing is, I look forward to it. I rush through my dinner, unplug the phone, position myself by the huge picture window that looks out onto the street an hour before he's scheduled to appear. I turn off the lights and sit on my zafu cushion with my eyes closed.

He's coming. He'll be here soon. Won't disappoint you. Never.

◆

I live on the F Market line. Every twenty minutes or so, the streetcar comes by, announcing itself with a bang. They come in various colors and shapes. But the orange one, so rickety I expect its wheels to pop off any day now, is the one I wait for most. It assaults my nerves, but I've grown used to it, how it makes my blood grow brighter. And crisscrossed wires undulate outside my window—a web of thick black lines that will not compromise anything. I have the urge to disconnect them, let them free. But someone, I suppose, would notice. At the very least I might rearrange them—a new order, a slightly altered composition.

And people. Always people getting on, people getting off. Where do they all go? There aren't enough rooms and windows in this city for them all. Some nights I get out my Mini-DV camcorder and shoot without them knowing. I shoot in super night-shot mode, and slow shutter speed so that every motion seems exaggerated. Every step taken, like some monumental thing.

And I wait, always, for someone to catch me in the act. A look of surprise, a finger pointing, a shout. *Hey, you! What do you think you're doing? Who do you think you are?* But no one ever notices. Everyone's too wrapped up in a haze of to-do lists and busy moving one foot in front of the other. Later, I rewind my tapes and play them. Because you never know. There might be something I may not have noticed the first time.

◆

She could never remember my real name. *What is it again?* She'd ask every two months or so. *And how do you say "I love you"?*

213

Sahranghae. Yoon Ni Yah, nuh sahranghae. Almost like those Korean soap opera videos.

The boy and the girl sitting on a bench at night. Cherry blossom petals drifting onto their shoulders and laps, a warm breeze brushing their cheeks. The boy turning to the girl, saying, *Sahranghae.* The girl looking not at him, but instead at a lamppost, the falling honey-colored light.

Except we were always in real life, and we were two girls sitting on a twin-size bed with too many pillows scattered around us. And don't forget, I never had the luxury of a lighted storefront or a passerby on his bicycle to feign distraction. So I looked at her.

I looked right into her and beyond the lines of her smile. I looked and looked into where it was bright pink and orange and warm, so warm like a big pot boiling over with oxtail bones, and though I kept going, and though I waited, in the end, there was nothing behind the voice, the stumbling words, the sound of my name about to become something unbearable.

♠

I watch TV with the sound turned off. But I make good use of the special caption feature. White words scrolling up within a black background. I only watch the news. Because I care about what's happening in the world? Not really. I like to fixate on the words. How they come out messed-up sometimes. I'll be sitting there, reading the story of a kidnapped six-year-old being reunited with her mother. There will be close-ups of happy tears and shots of relatives flocked around the girl. Then, all of a sudden, the sentence will read something like: *The unarmed girl is crappy, now wrestling safely at comb.* And an error like that, once you read the sentence over again, doesn't really seem in any way wrong. And the words become small pieces of the world, every combination you can come up with equally plausible.

Last night, for instance, there was a story about conjoined twins. They had just undergone a surgery that had separated them at the head. I watched clips of doctors in gowns, the twins before and after, and the mother whose only words, as the camera slowly zoomed in on her, were: *Please bray for them. Keep your fingers lost.*

◆

In the end it came down to sorting out CDs and books, returning clothes to their rightful owner. What's mine is mine, what's yours, yours. How had we accumulated so many things? And why had I bought so much junk? *Do you want this?* I'd ask her, holding up an ice shaver in the shape of a polar bear. And she did. She wanted everything, anything I offered her. A juicer with carrot bits stuck in the grater, a set of gondola-shaped nail clippers I had bought at a street market in Italy, photos of us I didn't want to keep.

Like the one of us each holding a pumpkin, those lighted faces staring out endlessly. That was the first time I had carved a pumpkin, and I still remember the smell of the orange meat, the sight of our hands and forearms clinging with wet seeds. Later that night I pulled some more seeds out of her hair, where she had hid them like little mysteries for me to find.

But only the necessary things, those I'd keep with me.

In the end she still had fewer boxes than me. The room looked so empty. I said, *Hey, look, now we can take inventory, now we can see what's ours.*

And she began to look small, like a knickknack of sorts, like she might crawl into one of those boxes and stay there until the van arrived and hauled away my stuff. Her skin took on an odd tone; she was saying something, but I heard nothing but the sound of feet shuffling around next door. And low voices coming from inside my head, a dull chorus of drones deeply rooted in a recurring dream I used to have as a child.

◆

Last weekend she stood in front of me And asked me to dance. *Dance with me.*

We were smack in the center of the club. I thought I heard someone call out my name. So I did. Dance with her. For a long time, like swimming in a warm pool. There's a world down there, and all of a sudden your body's speaking to you. And she became fragments, fragments of light dependent on the strobes overhead and what glimpses I caught from the corner of my eye. Her hips repulsed me somehow. I kept my feet at a safe distance. We danced in that endless hole that narrowed and narrowed till we were a single point in time, and when she smiled at me I swore I had become her last meal, clamped between her teeth, at their sharpest points.

And then the song was over. Our shoulders turned toward opposite corners of the room. Though her sweat lingered for hours like the smell of fish on your clothes long after you've fried it. Like a memory that always brings sadness along with it. All the rooms within me stayed dark, closed, as she held me. I could smell wood fading somewhere.

◆

Yoon Ni Yah, he calls to me. And when I look out the window I almost bang straight into the glass, because for some reason this time he's not alone. There's someone else with him.

I look closer. They're holding hands. I press my nose to the window. Dust blows through my nostrils. *No*, I say. *No, no, no. He's mine! You can't have him.*

Yoon Ni Yah, he says just like always, but I can detect the change in melody.

He's going to leave. This will be the last time. And like one of those passengers, he'll step off the platform out into the blah-blah of streets. He'll walk in a rational line and head toward the skyline.

And then, one last time, he calls me by name. And by then I've got my camcorder out. I'm shooting him at the slowest speed there is. Drawing out those two syllables like pollen dust floating in fog, like clouds breaking in air. And there they are—the two of them—uninvited, purposeless, standing outside my window in that grainy square patch, inside that infrared green world.

He knows I'm watching as I focus on his elbow. It resembles a mouth, the inside of a hungry mouth. For all I know it could have been his elbow calling to me all along. Then he moves and the lines blur. And in a small panic, I zoom in. Zoom in all the way, blurring the picture even more. So I zoom back out ETH-slow, controlled, regulating my breath. He has his arm around the other figure. He whispers into its ear. He points at my window. Points at me. Then, just like that, he's gone, leaving behind a single moving streak of light.

♠

I've been dreaming the same dream for the past three months. Except a bit of variation here and there. But always the same main players. Me and the shadow-man who sits at the foot of my bed. We have conversations though we never make eye contact. I just lie there, in my bed, eyes closed and let my lips do the moving.

Are you halfie? He asks me. *Have you found what you're cooking more?* And I feel a deep silence spreading outward from my lungs. Out to my chest bones, my arms. I try to flap them, but they won't move at all. *I still steal you*, I say. You're like a ghost-twin. My alter ego. Like you've never been gone.

Sometimes the shadow-man isn't so nice. Sometimes he's managed to inch his way toward my face. And before I know it, he's there, breathing down on me, his mouth a few centimeters away from mine. *Tell me you still glove me*, he says. *Tell me I'll always beep in your heart.*

homeschooling

carol guess

If you've read the Bible, you know about violence. The woman planting tulips in my front yard had to know this, at least: One human can stop another's heart like a clock held underwater. Her name was Laurel. She promised me the tulips would come up golden. She was homeschooling her children, all six, and lived in the dark-green house across the street. I was new to the neighborhood. She knocked on my door, very good-neighborly, and asked if she could plant tulips in my yard to welcome me to the Hall of the Slain. The name of our street—a Norse myth. Valhalla. She knelt out front on a gardening pad.

Her last name was Watson. The Watsons' car, which took six children to church and possibly other places, was bigger even than an SUV. It was like a moving van or a bus. Their house was the biggest on the block and yet simple. It was all about square footage and not about beauty. All of the houses on Valhalla were a little like that.

"Thank you," I said sincerely. I had blood running down my right leg, underneath my jeans, because I'd been

219

stung by a bee and was allergic. I wasn't sure if I should now do something in return, and if I did, whether she'd do something in return and we'd be stuck forever in a circle of exchange. If that was what being good-neighborly meant. She was beautiful but gaunt. The husband seemed to be away all the time. By the looks of it, homeschooling was about letting each kid do their special thing. One of the boys dug up worms and one of the girls played softball. I was a little confused about the softball angle, since I'd assumed they were fundies and would reign the girls in. Maybe they were hippies instead, but I didn't think so, because of her smile. It's strange to have a grown woman knock on your door and then kneel. This seemed somehow about Jesus, but my life was so different, I thought, what do I know.

I offered to help. When she said no I made small talk. It would've been rude to shut the door and go inside while she was out there working on my barren yard. But the dogs were barking like crazy, and after a while I excused myself to go in and calm them down. When I came out she was gone. The earth over the future tulips was smooth and flat, scuff prints the size of her palm, the plot the size of a bathtub. I hadn't the heart to tell her nothing would ever grow there because of the dogs. Three or four times a day I opened the door and the dogs shot out of my gun of a kitchen. The younger dog, Bucket, was blind. He'd stumble around in circles, trampling everything the older dog, Barney, didn't trample first.

Barney and Bucket are my kids, although I didn't say so to Laurel. Some people get mad when you compare your dogs to their darlings. I'd just bought the house, so it was glowing. Inside was a girl—a warm stone in my bed. I thought of Laurel looking at dirt and wondered how she'd feel if she knew about that. Then I stopped thinking of Laurel and thought of the girl. Then I smelled her on my fingers and then I was gone.

My house was a paler shade of the same green as Laurel's. All the houses on our street looked the same, just larger or smaller, dark-green or pale. Pacific Rim Ridge Ranchettes. One thing Laurel had told me besides stuff about tulips was that her husband wanted this particular house. She'd liked the house three doors down from me— smaller, a paler shade of my pale. But we agreed that how clean they were was an amazing thing. I'd always said if I could ever own a house it would be new, with a dishwasher. Ugly, because beauty takes too much trouble. This was my dream house—mine, Barney's, and Bucket's. To think that I owned it made me shiver inside.

When I moved in I didn't feel out of place. I thought I'd be part of things, buying Girl Scout cookies and stuff like that.

Turned out every kid on the block had their own fund-raiser. I ended up with two tubs of cookie dough, a coffee mug, and three boxes of yogurt-covered pretzels. These kids were either budding entrepreneurs or mooches. It wasn't like being one of the family.

Laurel genuinely seemed to like doing things for other people. When she drove off to Save Mart in her big white van she'd roll down the window and call out my name. She'd ask if I wanted anything—lumber or milk. I always said no, although I could've used both.

Later that day the girl in my bed sat up and reached for her glasses. She'd never see me again, so she didn't need them. Unwashed and in disarray, she ran down the front steps, toward me and toward the street. Her dress was blue. My dogs barked behind her. When she reached the bottom of the steps she looked around as if she'd forgotten where she'd parked her car. She had. I wanted to tell her not to worry, that Bellingham was too small to lose anything except her heart. But she'd found it already, blue like her skirt. She got into her car and drove away.

♦

One thing I knew for sure about Laurel was that she knew less about cars than bulbs. Or dirt. That big white van was always breaking down and she was always asking me to look under the hood. But that isn't how it is in my life.

She had the tomboy thing going on, Laurel did. Jeans and T-shirts. Sweatshirts and boots. Nothing cute—no felt puppies or appliqué kittens. Solid colors, the kind I like. Her hair was long but in a thick braid down her back, so plain it looked functional: a leash or a whip. She started stopping by sometimes, just to chat. Still, there was always this space between what we said and didn't say. Surely she had a lot on her mind, home alone with six kids all day. The youngest in diapers and the oldest in heels. Her husband's face stone when he got off work.

Every morning Laurel did this weird thing that didn't seem to go with the rest of her life. She'd stand out on the porch, bend at the waist, and brush all that long hair. The first time I saw her do this I felt sick inside, remembering some sex ed narrative about a virgin on her wedding night, undoing her hair for her husband's pleasure. But this seemed to be Laurel's time for Laurel. She'd groom her fur like a cream-fed cat.

Sometimes a girl would leave my house while Laurel was outside untangling her hair. The girl would be daze-y and sloppy and sheer. Laurel would smile and give a Princess Di wave. She never asked about the girl later.

♠

Some of the things the Watsons did in homeschool: play basketball, paint, go jogging, read and mess around on the computer, cook, learn German, learn French, dress up and act out plays.

Some of the things I did at home: play basketball, develop photographs, go jogging, read and mess around on the computer, cook, have sex with girls I met in bars, not drink or smoke anymore, brew three or four pots of coffee a day.

♠

Later, Laurel with a huge umbrella, two or three kids folded into her body. Sometimes all six would follow her outside, a circus cookie parade, but more often the oldest girl tended to the littlest ones while the others played catch. Drizzle had no effect on their games, and for this I admired them. The tomboy was genuinely talented, with a killer pitch. I'd given up worrying they might crack one of my windows. The lower level of my house was mostly garage, and wasn't that what childhood was for? Cracking things open to see what's inside. I wondered if her kids knew they weren't normal.

♠

But what was sacred to her?
The palest green?
The seventh child?

♠

223

Sometimes my lovers left things behind. I won't say "forgot things," because it was usually on purpose. Once a girl with a wheelchair left candles burning. I'm lying when I say it was a romantic gesture.

♠

She was beautiful at night. Laurel, I mean. Surrounded by things her husband had bought her. I could see through the windows—thin white curtains. A wooden table. One hundred chairs.

Laurel's job was teaching, but it was more than teaching. She had to love them; what choice did she have? I wondered if she ever felt the strange things I felt for Barney and Bucket. Liking their belches. The smell of their farts.

Maybe it was inappropriate, but one day I asked her if she'd actually given birth to all six of her children. She was so thin and young-looking, it was hard to believe. But yes she said. She said she had. Her husband, she said, was the disciplinarian.

♠

Laurel knocked on my door the first Friday of the rainy season. I was playing with Barney and Bucket, dragging a stuffed toy back and forth on the carpet. Yeah, okay, I was on my knees. On my knees only for my gods and my dogs.

She wanted to know if I had a bike. What does this mean? I thought to myself. If I say yes, will she ask me to ride with her? Or does she just want to borrow my toy?

She wanted to take the trail to Lake Whatcom. "The two of us" was what she said. She wanted to get to know me a little. Some hair in her eyes when she said this to me.

Why am I suspicious? I asked myself later. Why does this not feel like friendships I've known?

Sometimes people are shiny for me. There's no other way I can think to explain it. Take Laurel, for example, or my ex-girlfriend Clea. It's not always about sex, but with her it was. If I'd kneel for anyone, I'd kneel for Clea. Not that I would. Especially now. Shininess is never scary, but it isn't always hearts and flowers. Not the same as attraction. A sense that the person has something I need or that I owe them something, although never money. Clea cheated on me, and then I left Nebraska. That's all I have to say about Clea.

It was driving me crazy, my friendship with Laurel. She had to be nuts—all those kids, that huge house. I was trying to figure out if I was attracted to her and so maybe uncomfortable from that kind of angle. But it wasn't that. It wasn't some kind of eerie desire for a woman whose body belonged to a man. She was a slave and I was free. It was fascination, sick on my part, really, with what it would mean to give up your will.

spit and polish

zsa zsa gershick

On the day that was to change my entire life, I remember one thing clearly: the softness of Elizabeth's skin and the sweetness of her scent. A clean, light smell, like strawberries just in season. And also something wild and damp and only recently disclosed. I remember feeling content, the way you do with your face buried between a woman's breasts, hearing her heartbeat, like nothing ever could go wrong if you just stayed right there. We lay in each other's arms, talking, kissing, laughing, our bodies perfectly molded, falling into each other with no barrier of muscle and bone.

We nibbled on the plate of *pane dolce* that had just been delivered to our room. Well, Liz nibbled. I don't say I'm that dainty. I wolf. I gobble. It's my nature. But she does nibble, taking impossibly crumbless, ladylike bites. We washed the sweet, moist cake down with steaming coffee, and the sun streamed through the blinds, casting thin, shadowy bars across our crumpled bedsheets.

And then the MPs came, thundering down the hallway

that led to the half-dozen hotel rooms in which we and the others slept.

We thought it was an earthquake.

The pictures on the bleached stucco walls rattled, the floor shook, and the still morning at once was filled with the shouts of men and the shrieks of women. The air was flush with the sounds and smells of leather and gunmetal, of deep, pungent man sweat, polish, and oil.

We heard a series of crashes. A woman screamed.

We sat upright, toppling our tray, as a Marine burst through our door with his M16 drawn. Terrified, we drew the sheets close.

It is difficult to conceal a weapon between two plump, bare breasts, but they made us stand in formation, bare-assed, in the hallway anyway.

"Fucking dykes," said one Marine, guarding us. Were we going to bolt butt naked down the stairs and into the streets, where curious onlookers had already gathered? "I'd like to take that broad-ass on the end and fuck her silly," he said.

He was talking about Elizabeth.

He glared at another woman, a corporal from supply I didn't know too well, and grabbed his crotch.

None of us was allowed to dress fully. Not fit to wear the uniform, they said—as we shuffled, disheveled and wary, into a paddy wagon for the long ride back to base. My handcuffs rattled as I reached for Elizabeth's hand. The other women whispered worriedly.

"Shut up back there, you bitches!" said a seaman through the window that separated the cab from the cage.

As we passed through the guard post and the main gate of the base, a platoon of Marines double-timed past our van, singing in cadence, sixty pairs of black leather boots stomping out a familiar rhythm.

♦

I'm seated in a small, sterile cubicle. Two men in ill-fitting civilian suits stand over me.

"What were you and those other women doing in that hotel, Ensign?" says the first.

"May I smoke?"

"If you got 'em, light 'em," he says, pulling my personnel file from a battered Samsonite attaché with a GO NAVY! sticker plastered on one side.

"Did you have genital contact with that woman? Did she touch you? Do you know the other women?"

I smoke.

"You can save yourself," the other tells me. "Just tell us the names of the other lesbians on base. There's no reason for you to take the rap. Your lover is singin' in the next room."

I grind the butt into the tin ashtray and light another.

The second man, who had been leaning against the door, walks over. He stoops so his mouth is level with my ear, and I feel the bristles of his mustache.

"You know, I could fuck you right here and nobody would know. That's what you need, isn't it?"

I think about that time when I was about seven and my mother had made a chicken, browned the onions, stuffed it up the ass with carrots and cabbage. Afterward she asked my father to do the dishes.

"No," he said. "I'm gonna read the paper."

She never got upset about the big stuff: Nazis undercover in Argentina, Cuban missiles inching toward Miami. It was the chickenshit, built up, that set her off: imperfect vacuum tracks on the shag carpet, a chipped coffee cup, telling the truth.

She went to the cabinet, opened it coolly, and

smashed every piece until all that remained was a single plate. She carefully removed it from the shelf and, walking across the room to where my father stood in shock, smashed it over his head. I remember taking cover, terrified, beneath the kitchen table. But at some point my terror rolled over, and I watched the scene with a kind of detached calm.

The same icy calm I feel now.

"Do you recognize these women?" asks the first man, sliding a grainy photo my way. One of the women pictured is the public affairs officer, Lieutenant Arroyo.

"No."

"Do you know what lewd and lascivious conduct is, Ensign? That's what we're charging you with. That and conduct unbecoming an officer." He pauses to see if I am listening. "Those are federal offenses. You're going to Quantico if you don't take some fast action. You just can't lay with another woman like that in this man's Navy and get away with it." He pounds the table for emphasis.

Lie, I think. You can't lie with another woman.

When the men leave the room, I find myself thinking about Seaman Ermine. We'd met in boot camp. Nineteen years old and she'd never been away from Michigan. One night the petty officer who was her drill instructor called her into the duty office and raped her. At four foot eleven, she was the smallest of us. Nobody ever saw Ermine after that. But word got around. We heard she'd been shipped off to psych then sent home. The drill was transferred to another assignment, and no charges were filed.

♠

How long have I been left alone here? There's no clock on the wall, but it's dark outside and the ashtray is overflowing. When the men return, the first one is kind of clucking. He struts in waving an official-looking paper.

"That's it, Ensign. Your girlfriend's said it all. She's signed a statement. I think you'll need a lawyer."

He places the paper in front of me and pats it for emphasis. I see Elizabeth's signature at the bottom and feel the floor beneath me slide open and suck me into some dark, despondent place.

◆

Dear Elizabeth:

The women's brig is on the second floor of a surprisingly modern building, and there are only five of us occupying it. One of the women, a Pfc., is doing seven years for vehicular manslaughter while driving under the influence; one is in for going AWOL; another for making unauthorized long-distance calls on her duty phone. The fourth is in for assaulting a male Marine who called her a cunt.

Then there's me, awaiting my hearing. At first I thought they'd return me to duty pending the proceeding, but evidently I'm too big a threat to good order and discipline. Imagine the amount of muff I might eat in 90 days.

The floor, laid out barracks-style, is an open bay with racks and lockers precisely lined up along the wall. A glass window fronts the bay. Female guards—"bull-ettes" we call them—can look in and watch their charges around the clock. Even the latrine is fronted by a large glass pane so there's no privacy, even while peeing. We can have PT from 0800 to 0930, but most of the girls just want to sit around and knit for Navy Relief. We can use the prison library, and we're permitted twenty pieces of stationery per week. That's what I'm writing you with. We can receive mail, but it

arrives opened, read by the prison censors. There is no talking permitted, except during smoke breaks.

I can always tear this up.

♠

Dear Elizabeth:

I tried to do push-ups the other day; I knocked out
only twenty before I had to stop. I'm smoking too much.
The brig commander, Major Phelps, a Marine, runs at
0600 every morning. I see him in his OD shorts and white
T-shirt. His calves are lithe and cut. I'm going to ask per-
mission to run with him.

Last night alone in my rack I closed my eyes and felt
your body against mine, the round fullness of you pressed
into me, my breasts to your back, my arms around you,
our hands clasped. Did you really give me up?

♠

Dear Elizabeth:

I still starch my cammies and shine my boots, which
the other women find amusing. Sergeant Washington, the
Marine mechanic who busted her Gunny's jaw with a
wrench after he used the C word on her, sometimes has a
smoke with me before lights out. She would have killed
him if the other Marines hadn't restrained her, she says. I
admire her.

One night she plopped herself down on my rack, pat-
ting her chest pockets, cigarette dangling from her mouth.

"Got a light?" she said, spotting the glint of my Zippo
beneath a blackened boot rag.

"Help yourself."

"That's your life raft, ain't it? Holdin' onto it for dear

231

life," she said, taking a drag and pointing to the glossy boot I sat busily polishing with a tight circular motion over the toe, just the right pressure, just the right amount of polish and water.

"I don't care how much you put yourself together, baby. You're still a queer to them. Just as much a nigger as I am." She paused to inhale. "You think all that starch and shit's going to make a difference?" She slapped my shoulder good-naturedly. "You still here, ain't you?"

And, of course, I am.

♠

Dear Elizabeth:

Lt. Commander Sabastiani, my military counsel, sits in his bland beige office, shuffling papers. My case, he said, is open and shut. He is a bony little man with two tiny service ribbons unevenly pinned to the linty black fabric of his Class A's.

"Well," he told me, "we should definitely plead coercion. You had never had a lesbian relationship before and were seduced by Lt. Garrett into performing unnatural acts, possibly under the influence of drugs and alcohol. Do you have a drug problem of record? I mean, have you ever undergone treatment?"

"No," I told him.

Sabastiani's lips are thin and his feet are small.

"Pleading coercion, coupled with supplying the names of other lesbians on base, should get you a lighter sentence."

"I want to return to duty," I said, crossing my legs and glancing down at my resplendent Corfam pumps. "Aren't you going to argue against this regulation? Aren't you going to present my record?"

Sabastiani has a comb-over, the kind with an unnaturally low part, and just then a long, oily strip was losing its grip and falling off to the side of his head like a wilting blade of bear grass. He quickly pasted it back on top and gave a little hairball cough.

"They caught you cold," he told me. "There's not a lot I can do."

He paused.

"Think of the bright side. You're a nurse. You'll have no trouble finding civilian work." Then he rose, signaling the end of our meeting.

"We'll be in touch," he said, extending a pale, wan hand. "Try not to worry."

◆

Dear Elizabeth:

I ran with the commander this morning. His face is deeply creased and weathered. His hair is buzzed to a quarter inch on top. I had a hard time keeping his pace, but I didn't let on. He kept stealing sidelong glances at me. He was probably thinking, What a waste.

"Those women up in the bay are some tough customers," he said to me nearing our run's end.

"Some," I said. "They're all right."

The women's brig is peculiar because even though it's for women, it is not of women. There is nothing womanly about it. It is cold, antiseptic, angular, gray. Our lovemaking lies a million miles off. I long for something lush, something soft and curvaceous. Something wet.

Something that doesn't smell like Brasso.

Sometimes at night I stroke my head, gently tugging my short hair the way you did when you were revved up and wanting me to fuck you. I feel your full lips on my face, magnetizing me, insistent. You order me not to stop, knowing that following instructions has always been my strong suit.

◆

Dear Elizabeth:

The NIS guys, the pricks to whom you confessed your sins, told me you cried a deep, broken, little-girl cry as you were signing the paper. They felt sorry for you, they said. Such a pretty girl. And blond. Like a model. They don't know that the sweater girls, the ones who look made for the boy next door—but would rather have his sister—are the queerest of all.

◆

Dear Elizabeth:

Emma Schwartz, for my money one of the best ER nurses in the unit, is the only person not afraid to visit me while I await my court-martial hearing. She is "short," she likes to remind me, with a scant six months remaining in her final tour of duty. She's sick of the bullshit, she says.

"Listen," she practically shouted, "if the NIS got rid of all the queens and lezzies in this hospital, the patients would have to take care of themselves." Schwartzie, bless her, is one of the few straight nurses on staff.

"Let 'em try to come after me," she told me. She's fearless: Her fiancé is Walter Eastman, the hospital's chief orthopedic surgeon, a real bone man in and out of surgery, she says. "We'll send Walt down and have him show them the bite marks on his weenie if they want evidence of my credentials."

So far, Emma and Walt are the only two who've agreed to offer character testimony on my behalf.

♠

Dear Elizabeth:

I stood rigidly at attention before the bench as the lead judge read my sentence yesterday: two years at Quantico, suspended in consideration of my service record, and immediate dismissal. It was over, just like that.

I half expected to see you. Maybe it was better that you signed the paper. But because you did, I know we can never be together.

I was hustled back to the brig, where I packed a few belongings but left my uniforms and boots in the locker. Sgt. Washington sat on my bunk, watching me. When I'd gathered everything, we shook hands, a hard clasp, and half-hugged. In an instant the intercom snapped on.

"There are no physical displays of affection on the floor," said a female voice, the same one that said "Fuck me, baby, harder" to her girlfriend at the Super 8 last weekend, probably.

"She's just jealous," I whispered to Washington, who shot the bird behind the woman's back. We stood apart.

I wonder where you are, Liz. Maybe even you don't know.

♠

On my way out I passed through a series of high-security steel doors and stepped into the late-afternoon sunshine. Uniformed men and women marched by. The first few notes of "Taps," heralding day's end, began to play. Marines and sailors stopped dead, came to attention, pivoted toward the flag, and saluted smartly. I walked on, weaving between them.

At the curb, my new attorney, a woman from the

235

ACLU, leaned against her car with the passenger door standing open. Her ankles looked impossibly fine.

"Captain Schwartz told us your story," she began.

"If you don't mind, I can't talk for a bit," I said, throwing my duffel bag into the backseat.

Once inside, I could smell her perfume, a kind of jasmine. My head met the pillowy leather neck rest, and I closed my eyes.

We drove through the gate to the bugle's last strains.

an order, a dispute, a burning

gina schien

Suddenly it's gone from warm to cold. Just dry cold, but snow has started falling in tiny flakes that melt as soon as they hit the road. We are looking for lunch—not a big lunch, because we had a large breakfast, but something. In the fish shop three women struggle against waves of cold air coming through the screen door.

"Shut the door, please," someone calls.

Frying is an art. Keep the wind from the flame.

Megan and I stand and look at the chalkboard menu, forced in from an active day of scenery and walking. We've been squeezing gum leaves, smelling the stink ants crushed against granite rock, but now the slight snow has sent us back through the bush up the escarpment to the main street to here, where fish has been frying for centuries. My body is still hot from fighting through scrub to see the perfect view, find the perfect rock, achieve the perfect kissing point, but my face and fingers are chilled.

The fish shop is caught on the steep slope of the mountains, held in and tucked up as if the mountain were rolling, pushing against a fierce sea gale. The salt smell is a forlorn, fish-laden dock; the sweet tang of vinegar is the pitch smell of dank tar.

Three workers weave their way along the deck of the shop's innards.

A young girl, called Natalie by the older one, grins at us and bashes the life out of the deep baskets. She flings a handful of onions on the grill while her mother—-it has to be; look at the similar dip of the brown hair across the forehead and the same lips and disappointed chin—catches up white battered fillets between large metal tongs and submits them to the fat.

A girl with a nest of fire engine–red hair is squeezing the very devil out of the phone she whispers into. At her elbow, half-floured calamari and chunks of fish fill a stainless steel bowl bigger than the town hall clock.

"Sandra, get off that phone."

Sandra rolls her green eyes at us, but I ignore the complicity because the mother-daughter team is overworked and they don't have the romance of a phone call. She relinquishes the phone with a loud click and a sigh. Her wrists plunge into the floury bowl.

"Up for the weekend?" the mother asks. She hasn't looked at us properly.

"Yep. From Sydney."

Natalie suspends a deep-fry basket above the oil and then turns with it in her hand, facing us and then lifting it as if she has a good mind to spatter us with chips. Something has clouded her eyes, made her hands forget what she's holding. "I've never been to Sydney," she says.

Never. Two hours' drive east. In my shock I laugh. "Well, Sydney's not that great, really."

But then she spins briskly back around to the fryer and the chips crash and plunge to their doom. As we watch objects bubble in oil, Natalie gazes at us intently, as if for instructions: *How do I get to Sydney? How do I get to the ultimate shore?* Up here on the cold sea-blue plateau, the mountains roll on and on like wasted time.

Even as she opens her mouth, even though she's smiling, I know what she will say.

"Mum won't let me go yet."

She's examining Megan and me in our denim and corduroy jackets—heavy and stupid for walking through scrub but great to wear when drinking caffe lattes in Oxford Street—and our black boots and our hair. She's wearing an apron that says KATOOMBA FISH. She lifts herself on her toes to look over the counter and—ah yes, as she suspected—our fingers are linked and held between us.

She's still smiling at us. I smile back at her. I shift from one foot to the other, worried Natalie will ask for our numbers. She leans over the counter, saying sotto voce, "Do you know any good lesbian bars?" as though it were opera bouncing around the shop, bouncing onto the two new customers who've walked in.

I imagine her mother's life without the enthusiasm and good nature of Natalie. Life with sulking, flame-red Sandra and chips and fish and pineapple fritters and spring rolls.

The older woman is silent now. She has become our mother as well, radiating disapproval and hurt. She has taken our measure and glares at us, a thorough glare that hits us as a couple and then one by one. Won't let you go yet? Forget "yet." "Yet" is fast becoming "never."

There's no small chat about the snow; there are no communal laughs about the breasts-bubbling-over mermaid carved in wood like a figurehead (a 1970s addition for sure). Behind the shop counter the storm is gathering and the sails flap and crack.

I sense and respect Natalie's vision of Sydney. I fear for her future.

Our purchase is parceled and bound with a terse slap of tape. "Six dollars thirty," the mother says. She almost sucks it back as she says it, wanting to expend as little energy on us as possible.

Through the net of wire screen the snow falls on in mid-spring madness. We are schooled out, free to go back to Sydney, blatantly encouraged to, and the screen door bangs shut behind us. The mother has fish to fry.

But I know Natalie is watching us walk down Katoomba's main street to the car park. We cross over, touching shoulders, brushing hips. The spine of the road is tilted like a roller coaster so that the side we walk down is higher than the other. Every movement feels electrically charged under Natalie's gaze, and as we stand and fuss for the car keys I look back. Once. Twice. She's pushing a cloth across the glass window in front of the bream, the dory, the redfish, and the off-white mounds of cut chips. Then with her free hand she waves at us. And stops. She looks back inside, diverted by an order, a dispute, a burning, and her face disappears altogether.

mrs. frye

s. o'briant

I'm not sure how old Mrs. Frye was when we met. Married, she had an incredible number of children—six, I think. They were old enough for her to leave them at home so she could do graduate work in anthropology. That made her pretty old in my twenty-year-old mind—at least forty. Maybe even fifty, my mother's age. Wiry and tan, Mrs. Frye wore her dark hair cut in a practical buster brown. I don't think she used makeup. She looked like she'd been to plenty of PTA meetings, maybe even been the president of the PTA.

I'd moved into this place near campus that boasted dormitory-style apartment living. That is, you had a private apartment, but there was also a cafeteria downstairs. I'd lost ten pounds from my already lean frame by trying to cook for myself. For me it was an oasis of culinary delight. I was to learn that for Mrs. Frye it was a sexual smorgasbord.

I first noticed her at the pool talking to a plump redhead in a pink bikini. She talked and the girl listened. They sat on the coping, dangling their feet in the water. I wasn't the only one watching them. A group of guys around my age sat together off to my right, sneaking peeks and snickering.

The girl pulled her knees up to her chest and crossed her arms around them protectively. She lowered her head and, without actually moving, withdrew from Mrs. Frye. I could tell she was uncomfortable but too polite to get up and leave. She sat there—cringing. Mrs. Frye continued unaware, laughing and gesturing. The girl lifted her worried eyes to mine at one point.

Watch out! they seemed to say. Maybe it was just the glare from the pool making her squint and deepening the circles under her eyes. Mrs. Frye followed her stare and smiled open-mouthed, her teeth glinting in the sunlight. She waved at me. I lifted my hand, ignoring the masculine snorts off to my right.

I became her best friend after that. She'd set her tray across from mine in the cafeteria and regale me with stories of her life. Her husband was a nuclear physicist, and I got the impression that when she wasn't busy having kids, she had a lot of time on her hands. She'd had many affairs, and her husband knew about them. They shared everything. She made Los Alamos, home of the Manhattan Project and the A-bomb, sound like a swinger's paradise. Talk about afterglow.

"She is aberrant, that one," Vinkesh, my friend from India, said, and shifted his eyes to Mrs. Frye. We were in the noisy cafeteria, which was filled to capacity. She sat across from the redhead, who no longer cringed in her presence but didn't look particularly happy either. They were deep in conversation, and at one point Mrs. Frye reached across the table and squeezed the girl's hand.

"They're just talking," I said. "She's married. She's into guys."

"Yes, as many of the men here can attest to, but, my friend, I caution you." He shook his forefinger at me, and then shrugged. "Well, you'll find out if you're not careful."

I laughed, glanced at Mrs. Frye, and once again thought of my mother.

In addition to the usual childhood warnings about not taking candy from strangers, Mom had a certain paranoia regarding public bathrooms, especially those in movie theaters.

"Watch out for the queers," she'd warn. She never gave an exact description of who or what I was to avoid, so in one of those twists every parent dreads, she aroused my curiosity instead of creating fear. In those bathrooms, I searched each child and adult face for the telltale mark or nervous twitch that would reveal the female demon my mother feared. In return, adults asked me if I was lost, and children thought I was creepy. Like a diligent bird-watcher in pursuit of a rare species, I was on the constant lookout for this exotic breed but never managed to spot one. Mom, on the other hand, was eagle-eyed.

One summer she helped me move out of the dorm and into an apartment with a girl I'd met on campus. Several women helped my roommate move her stuff in, and one of them winked at Mom.

"I don't think you should live here," my mother said. She lowered her voice. "I think they're lesbians."

"Really?" I laughed, and looked the women over again, trying to see what Mom saw. She frowned, pressing her lips into a tight line. I tried to reassure her. "Even if they are, it doesn't mean I'll become a lesbian," I said. She didn't look convinced. "Even if they held me down and forced me to do stuff doesn't mean I'd turn into a lesbian."

"Yeah, but you might like it," she said.

♦

Mrs. Frye continued to seek me out, her sexual pecca-dilloes the usual topic of conversation. For Mrs. Frye sexual pleasure was the cultural collateral, the pinnacle of her artistic and intellectual expression. An American college campus was the perfect site to practice her obsession.

So I wasn't surprised when she flopped down across from me in the community lounge late one night. In her usual ebullient mood, she wore a short dress, or it might have been a long shirt—I couldn't decide which. She'd created a fashion dilemma in my mind, not made any easier when she kept crossing and uncrossing her legs so that the whole outfit rode up, raising the new question of whether she wore underwear. I wondered if she was trying to seduce me. I'm not an idiot—I'd seen *The Graduate*. So what if I wasn't a guy; she'd already done all the guys. And so what if she wasn't Mrs. Robinson, with her fancy bras and martinis. She was a horny old broad, and I was…well, I was curious.

It occurred to me she hadn't come looking for me in the lounge—she'd been restless and decided to troll the night waters. I just happened to be there. I laughed at her jokes, and pondered her innuendos in my desultory way, and didn't volunteer too much information about myself. After a while I said good night and returned to my apartment.

Just as I got out of the shower she knocked at my door. I put on a robe and peered through the peephole. Mrs. Frye smiled and held up a bottle of champagne. Taking a deep breath, I opened the door.

"What are we celebrating?" I welcomed her in with a sweep of my arm. She said nothing.

"I'll get some glasses." I moved toward my tiny

kitchen, but Mrs. Frye blocked my path. I hadn't realized before that she was shorter than me. She looked up at me with melting PTA eyes and slid cold hands inside my robe. I shuddered and took a step back but didn't stop her when she filled the space again and opened my robe further. She dropped her eyes to my body and grazed her fingertips lightly across my breasts and down my stomach.

"So tight," she murmured. She laid her cheek against my chest and floated down to her knees.

I didn't resist her tongue. I stood there in my living room, looking down at her helmet of shiny black hair moving with the thrust of her tongue and head. She slipped a finger into me without losing the cadence of tongue-head-hair, and I came immediately, reaching out to the wall to steady myself. She remained kneeling and smiled up at me, the skin around her mouth glistening, minimizing the wrinkles there.

We moved to my bed. Now my turn, I just couldn't bring myself to return the favor. She wasn't a good kisser, and her breasts were flabby. Her clitoris impressed me, though. It was huge, and I rotated it with my hand like a tiller on a sailboat, hoping for the best. Finally, much to my relief, she gave up on me and left.

I avoided her after that. Toward the end of the term I ran into Mrs. Frye and her husband on the stairwell. Running up the stairs, I almost crashed into them. They stood on the steps above me, holding hands while she introduced us. She looked sad, disappointed, not her usual effervescent self. That she'd told him about me was obvious. Her husband's eyes roved up and down my body...speculative, but his sympathies were with his wife. I'd displeased her, but I was probably not the only one. Poor thing. Poor Mrs. Frye. All that youth around her and no talent whatsoever.

♦

At lunch that day I set my tray across from the red-head. "Hi, I'm Alexis." I held my hand out to her. Face-to-face, she was pretty, not so much plump as zaftig.

She squeezed my fingertips. "Carly." Her green eyes swept the room. "Where's Paula?"

I blinked, and then made the connection. "Oh, you mean Mrs. Frye? She left this morning with her husband." Carly smiled, one side of her mouth higher than the other.

"I guess we have her in common," she said. "Did she tell you I'm a lesbian?" she asked matter-of-factly. I blinked again.

The person my mother had warned me about sat across from me and lowered her eyes to her salad. Her eye-lashes were incredibly long. When I didn't answer she looked up. "I don't mess with married women. Next thing I know she's following you around." She waited, looking me in the eye.

"I didn't know," I managed to say, my words tumbling out. "I mean, that you're a…" I looked to my left and then to my right and whispered, "a lesbian."

She laughed and shook her head. "It's not a secret, Alexis. You can say it out loud." She leaned back in her chair. "Say it. Say les-bi-an." Her full lips wrapped around each syllable.

"Lesbian, all right? Lesbian, lesbian, lesbian!" I always face a challenge head-on. "Look, it was a lark for me. Well, not exactly a lark. I've always wanted to do it, but I couldn't really get into it, you know, because she reminds me of my mother, so it was more her than me, and I think she wasn't happy, and anyway she's married, and maybe with someone my own age it would be different." I stopped, and felt the heat rise up to my face.

A smile spread across Carly's face. "Maybe," she said gently. "Maybe it would be different." We held each other's eyes.

"Mrs. Frye." She shook her head, laughing. "That's what you called her?"

plato's fish

kathryn ann

I truly can't believe this. Nightmare. When I finally
made the contact it seemed more like a coup than a crime.
How should I have known he was a cop? I guess I knew it
was a bad idea, sorta, but I didn't think the police would
make such a big deal out of it, especially after I
EXPLAINED this was just part of my sorority initiation
and I wasn't actually going to SMOKE the stuff.

I can't believe they put me in here with all these
women! They're so hard-looking, most of them. And
the way some of them stare at me makes me very, very
nervous. I tried to explain to one of the guards—McVey
is her name—that they made a mistake putting me here.
I mean really, I'm an honors student at college and,
what's more, I am a National Merit Scholar! But she
just looked me up and down, slow, and told me to shut
my yap.

I said at least let me use a telephone so I can call my parents. Even though they're going to KILL me! She said that
wasn't part of her job description, and tough luck, because the

warden won't be back until after the Labor Day weekend.

That's five days away! I don't know what to do.

♦

I notice her immediately at dinner. Even with her head bent over her tray, she seems to emit something that surrounds her, almost like an aura? But that's ridiculous. Her hair is silvery blond, short curls tousled around her head, so maybe it's a trick of the overhead lights.

There are women on either side of her; but as I pass with my tray, she moves her legs together and pats the bench, and now there's just enough room for my little self. Somehow she was able to take up more space than she needed—that aura thing again.

I sit down. Something about her—my eyes sting and I can't swallow my food. She doesn't look at me or say anything, but she presses her knee against mine, comforting me without drawing attention. And when she gets up to leave, she puts her hand on my shoulder for balance and squeezes a little.

Maybe I could have a friend here?

First night and it's hours before I fall asleep. But at least I'm alone in my cell and the bars keep me safe from the other prisoners.

♦

The gunk at the bottom of the kitchen sink drain when you scoop it out. That's what McVey's breath smells like. She's leaning over me, and at first I think I'm still dreaming.

I wake up completely when she sits her fat butt on the edge of my bed and JAMS the blanket between my legs with her hand. I'd yell—because it hurts like when you go over a bump on your bike—but she clamps her other hand over my mouth. I try to bite her. She bears down harder and laughs.

"Think you're special. Educated." Sneering. She whips her hand away and bangs her mouth against mine, and that's about the most disgusting thing yet. Then the buzzer goes off to get up. As she stands to leave, she says, "Those big bulls in corridor three get a hold of you, you'll be wishing it was me instead."

At breakfast a bunch of women start, like, playing some stupid game where they bump into me in the lineup and rub up against me and laugh. When I say CUT IT OUT they only laugh louder.

I sit down at a table with nobody there, and wouldn't you know they all sit down around me. One of them sticks her foot in my crotch from across the table and they all yell "Woo-hoo!"

This is insane!!

When they shut up all at once, I wonder why. I'm afraid to look up because that might get them going all over again. But I finally do. And it's her, standing there with her tray. Cereal and orange juice, as if this were a normal place and not a prison. There's obviously some sort of pecking-order thing here, because she just, like, NODS at them and they get up! And take off!!

I smile in thanks. She doesn't smile back. She sits down next to me, props an open paperback against her bowl, and starts to eat her corn flakes. So I wonder if maybe she hasn't done anything special for me but just wanted to sit here in peace and quiet, or something.

The whole meal passes like that, without us saying anything. Nobody else sits down with us, and for that, at least, I'm grateful. This whole thing is so crazy. When I get out I'm going to have some letters to write and they will really regret...oh, forget it. I'm on nervous overload. When I try to take a deep breath, the inhale gets stuck at the top and kind of hiccups out like the sound when you drive on a flat tire. For some reason, when I'm near her I feel like crying.

She leaves without saying anything. I want to thank her for rescuing me, if that's what it was, but she might not even know what I was talking about.

Back down the hall to my cell. I curl up on the bumpy mattress and multiply random numbers until I doze off. I dream I'm back at school trying to study for an exam, but I'm frantic because all the pages in the textbook are filled with gibberish.

◆

On the way to dinner those women are in a clump in front of me. I usually walk pretty fast, but no way am I going to pass them. So I walk slow and try to do the head-down thing.

The littlest one, with her dried-apple face, says, "Oh, if it isn't little Miss Priss."

They all start laughing and saying "Woo-hoo" again, until one of them looks around, nervous-like, and says, "You can walk the wild side, ladies, but not me. I seen what she can do."

What's she talking about? She's never seen what I can do.

The rest of them kind of mutter. AppleFace tries to keep it going by making a big show of slowing down so I almost bump into her, but she gives up when no one laughs.

Dinner is macaroni and cheese. And iceberg lettuce. Which does nothing for you, nutritionally. When I feel someone brush against my back, at first I think it's AppleFace. I pull away so fast, I bash my ribs against the edge of the table. Before I can turn around, a voice close to my ear says, "Take it easy," and someone slides into the space beside me. It's her. She arranges her plate and utensils, then pushes her tray off to one side.

She doesn't seem like much of a talker, so I guess it's up to me to break the ice.

"I don't know if you helped me on purpose at breakfast," I say, "but I really want to thank you because there was some kind of demented gang thing, or initiation, going on."

She nods and opens her book. I consider asking what she's in for but figure that might be some kind of breach of prison protocol, and besides, I don't really want to know. Instead I ask how you get access to a telephone around here.

She picks up her fork and starts to eat. I'm just about giving up when she turns to look at me and says, "How are you holding up?"

The first time I see her eyes close up and it's like a deer caught in headlights, is how I feel.

"Well, I shouldn't really BE here! It was just that I made a screwed-up decision when it so happened someone was looking. They put me in here by mistake. I'm sure I could clear things up if they'd just let me use a phone!"

She goes back to eating and reading, so I figure she doesn't want to hear about my problems, and I don't blame her. As soon as she's cleared her plate, she returns her stuff to her tray and gets up without looking at me, which hurts my feelings. What is it with her? But I'm not complaining because, after all, no one bugged me during dinner.

"Ten A.M. tomorrow," she says, glancing back over her shoulder. "Meet me at the gym." And then she's gone. Maybe she'll help me? I feel a little bit hopeful for the first time in two days.

As I'm leaving the cafeteria, I see McVey standing near the door. I figure she hasn't noticed me, until she shouts, "Hey, new fish! I got me an appetite."

And I feel my macaroni rising up.

◆

Someone comes around with a book cart after dinner. Mostly Harlequins and other junk. I end up with an ancient *Vanity Fair* magazine with a picture of Cindy Crawford on the cover shaving k.d. lang in an old-fashioned barber's chair!! Freaky.

I can't sleep for a long time because I'm so keyed up. Someone nearby is kicking her bed or something. Sounds like she's getting madder and madder. She stops finally and just groans loud. I kick my own bed a few times, lying on my back, until someone yells out, "Baby's got the hots!"

Laughter, like it's some joke I don't get. I hope to God I'm not "Baby."

I dream that AppleFace and her gang are holding me down and taking my clothes off. Cindy Crawford is watching and is all shocked but she can't help me. The whole time McVey is saying "Fresh fish, fresh fish…" in a sexy voice.

◆

Breakfast. I have zero interest in food. Or anything, really. I don't even care when AppleFace walks up behind me in the lineup and butts against me with her sharp hip-bone and sings a verse from "Nobody Does It Better." On key, which makes it even more bizarre. When she's done, the others cheer and snicker. I don't react. She pinches my butt and sashays off. I stare straight ahead.

Orange juice made from crystals, and Wonder bread toast. It's a miracle everyone here doesn't die from malnutrition. I don't care where the heck I sit. Paste in my mouth. Ball in my stomach. Back to my cell. I lie down and rest my cheek on the *Vanity Fair* magazine because it's cool and smooth.

"What, no rec for you?"

Oh, God. McVey's in the doorway. Just stands there, leering. I slide my cheek back and forth on the satiny cover of the magazine and shut my eyes. Just get it over with, lard ass.

"Not a lot of privacy here, but maybe you like it that way."

I wait. I wait more. What the hell is she doing? I open one eye enough to peek through my lashes. The shape in the door is wrong. Taller. Broad shoulders, tapered hips. I open my eyes all the way. It's her!

"Ten," she says. "It's now 10:15."

"Sorry." Why should I have to say I'm sorry, after all this? But I'm so glad to see her there, instead of—

"Um, was McVey here when you came up?"

She strolls in. I didn't know visiting was allowed. I look past her nervously, but the corridor is empty. I suppose because of rec time. She sits on my bed without asking. I get up so fast, I'm light-headed for a second.

"I asked about McVey because—"

"As we speak, McVey is rousing up her fellow screws for a poker game. She unexpectedly came into a bit of good fortune." She hasn't been looking at me, but now she does and I'm caught again in that gray-blue. They're so clear, her eyes.

"See, she misunderstood how I am and she—"

"You're lucky, you know. McVey treats her favorites quite well."

She picks up my magazine, glances at the cover, then sets it aside with a slight smile. I want to explain that I don't normally read magazines, and before this I was studying *Heart of Darkness* by Conrad, in my Classic Lit class. In fact, writing a paper on it about—

"Things could be worse," she says. "Much worse. Trust me on that."

"No, they couldn't!" And damn it, I'm crying. Not just tears either, but hiccuping like a baby. I know my face is red and I must look like an idiot and what a strange thing to be caring about right now.

"You'd better quiet down. Unless you want company."

Yes. The corridor is still empty. I'd like to keep it that way, and try to swallow the sobs.

"Breathe in through your nose, out through your mouth. Unhunch your shoulders."

I'm so glad she's here. I look at her, willing my gratitude to show because I don't trust myself to speak without starting to cry again.

But she's gazing at my shirt, not my face. I'm not wearing a bra, but surely she couldn't be looking at that. She's not McVey! Then she looks up at my face and I see something kind there and I relax just a bit.

"Listen. McVey is taken care of for the time being. But she'll be back. And she does like the new fish." The term makes me shudder. "Quite a few of us do."

I wait for her to go on, but she doesn't. And that last thing she said sort of hangs there.

After a minute she stands up and stretches. Long-boned and lithe—I can't help noticing. A little past her prime, I'm guessing, but she'd be a natural at tennis.

"It doesn't have to be her," she says. "The choice is yours to make." She pauses for a moment, smiling at me, then walks out of the cell.

Quite a few of us do.

My God. Is this whole place full of them? Did they screw up and send me to a special prison just for them? If so, they made a BIG mistake. I'm not like THAT! I shouldn't be like anything, to tell the truth, at this point. Of course I practiced kissing with my best friend when I was in high school, but I've heard practically everyone does that. I never had time for a real boyfriend, what with junior tennis league and keeping my grades up and all.

But her eyes. Windows of the soul, they say. And hers seem so clear, and what's inside so...I don't know. Good? Of course, who would be in here if they were so darned good. Stupid, stupid, stupid.

I have to pull myself together or I'm going to go nuts.

Deep breath. Like she said: in through the nose, out through the mouth. And again. Okay. McVey is not an option because I would never stop barfing and I don't care if she treats her "favorites" well, because "well" in my book does not mean scaring the bejesus out of someone and laughing over it.

And if not McVey, who'll protect me from AppleFace and her crew?

Which leaves *her.* I know she can't be any worse than the others, but for some reason the thought of her touching me scares me breathless.

◈

Saturday morning. Three days to go.

I don't see her at first. Not until I've looked twice, all the way around the cafeteria, and the woman in back of me says "Shit or get off the pot, honey" in a cigarette voice. She's got her head buried in her book, is why I didn't spot her right away.

I deliberately pick a table at the other end of the cafeteria. She should know I'm my own person and not just some loser you can order around. I don't normally need protecting. I'm top-seeded in our tennis league, thank you, and I finished out an important doubles match despite a bad case of flu. Which took a lot of fortitude.

"You like living dangerously?"

Her voice makes me jump. Cheerios leap off my spoon and plop onto the table.

For the first time, I notice her hands—surprisingly small, almost delicate, the nails clean and clipped short— as she places her tray on the table without a noise and slips into the seat opposite me. She's like a cat.

"Sitting alone sends a perilous message," she continues, using her knife to scoop the last of her scrambled eggs onto the back of her fork. She holds her utensils as if she took a course in table etiquette, fingers extended down the handles. Only it doesn't look affected when she does it.

Okay, I'll talk.

"What message?"

She tilts her head a little to one side and studies my face. I can't help shivering. It's strange: I'm so mad at her because first she fooled me into thinking she was on my side, and now I know it's that she wants something from me, but I just feel so...so funny inside when she looks at me. It's that she's paying such close attention to me. I feel, well, I feel important, or something.

"In here you're either predator or prey. And if you're the latter—"

"I'd like you to know I'm not a total pushover. I have the hardest serve in my college tennis league. And I'm not as naive as everyone here seems to think."

One of her eyebrows flicks up. I wonder if now is

maybe the time to mention *Heart of Darkness,* but she goes on.

"Perhaps not in your world. But right now you need someone to watch your back. You'd best decide who it's going to be. Soon."

I nod. But I'm thinking if I can just keep to myself until Tuesday when the warden gets back, maybe I can get out of here before I have to do anything.

♠

I skip lunch. No one makes me go, and it's safer here in my cell. I keep checking the clock at the end of the hall. It's so insulting that they took my watch. Like, what was I going to do with it? Use the glass face to cut my wrists?

Sometimes when I look it's been five whole minutes. I'll do sit-ups. Keep my strength up. I get out sixty and then I'm all trembly. At least now I have a good reason to be trembly. Other than this nervousness. Geez. I just don't get her. Mostly she seems like this kind person, and nice. But after she said that, about liking the new fish, I don't see how she could be.

A hot shower would feel pretty good after the exercise, so I get my towel and a bar of soap and peek into the locker room, and yay, it's deserted. As I unbutton my shirt, a stall door swings open. AppleFace steps out.

The way she grins at me you'd think we were old friends. I wish like everything I'd just stayed in my cell.

Okay. I'm going to walk out briskly without looking up. But as I pass her, she grips my shoulders and shoves me against a sink. I'm more physically fit, but she's tougher, like an old chicken. I start to scream, but she rams her mouth over mine, and it's all I can do to keep my lips together against her tongue. I try to turn my head away from her. She grabs my hair and yanks.

When her weight vanishes, I almost fall down. A gasp, like hissing in breath. My ersatz protector has appeared out of nowhere and has AppleFace down on the concrete floor on her stomach with her hand twisted behind her back. She's squirming from the pain, but she can't squirm too much, it looks like, or it hurts worse.

"Motherfucker!" AppleFace yells. All of a sudden she shrieks, really high and short. "Awright, I'm sorry! I didn't know!"

"After this, perhaps you'll pay closer attention."

AppleFace takes a big breath then scrambles up and out, and I can't believe she can move so fast.

She's watching me now, and I'm crying. Big sobs and trying to be quiet. I smell clean, warm cotton as she puts her arms around me and holds me while I cry into the front of her shoulder. She stands perfectly still. I like her holding me. I can feel the muscle of her arms and back, cushioned a little.

"Good decision," she whispers. "They'll stay away from you this way."

I shrug. I guess I have decided.

She moves her hands side to side across my lower back where it still aches from the sink. Maybe she's just comforting me? Then one hand slides up my stomach and cups my breast. Well, if it has to be somebody, I'm glad it's her. I wait for the kiss and figure I'll accept it but not really kiss back because a) I don't think I could; and b) I don't want her to think I'm like that.

But the kiss never comes.

She nudges her hips up against mine and kind of circles around. Slow. And keeps fondling my breast. She rubs her thumb over my nipple and I'm kind of embarrassed because I can feel it stand up. She presses it back down and massages it in circles like the ones she's making with her hips. I'm almost sorry when she moves her hand away but don't have time to be sorry because it's sliding under the waistband of my pants. She must feel the indents the elastic made because she kind of smooths them out. I smile because that's sort of a nice thing to do, you know? And then she's kneading my butt. Pulling me into her hips.

She spreads her legs farther apart and presses herself against me, going faster and harder and still holding onto my butt. And I guess she's just not a kisser. Well, I suppose that's good. Then she says "Oh" into my ear and presses really long and hard.

After a few seconds, she steps back, and I'm in those headlights again. Her eyes just keep going on and on, like the sky when I was a little kid.

"Later," she says, giving my shoulder a pat before she walks out.

That's it??? For just a second I think she should've said thank you or told me she was proud of me for not falling apart. Anything! But then I remember AppleFace grinning at me, and I guess she doesn't owe me any thanks.

◈

On Sunday morning I'm conscripted to work in the laundry room. It's sweltering and stinks of Pine-Sol, but the worst part is the racket, which gives me a headache. My job is pulling out big armloads of wet sheets to stuff in the dryer, which is boring. But it's probably better than sorting the dirty laundry, which is what AppleFace is doing.

My pants, which are too big and make me look like a little girl, are wet at the hems from the sudsy water on the floor. When I hitch them up, AppleFace says, "Awww, now, isn't that cu-u-ute?" I can't believe she dares to say anything after what happened in the locker room yesterday. But I guess my viewpoint has changed some, because I figure words, those I can stand.

I'm shoving in a load when I practically fall in because McVey heaves into sight and leans her forearms on the dryer. Her fingers look like pink sausages. There's flab hanging down from her upper arms, which I can practically hear gloop back and forth, and big sweat stains in the armpits of her short sleeves.

"Got a honey, I hear. She doin' you yet?" she barks.

What the hell is she talking about?

"Plato has a way with you young 'uns," she says, sniggering. "Word to the wise: Don't get too comfy with her cuz she's a bad 'un. Be scared."

So *that's* what they call her. Figures.

I peel my eyes from McVey's once-biceps and finish pushing the sheets in.

A hawk of mucus, swallowed, and she swaggers off.

♠

When the buzzer for dinner wakes me from my nap, it takes me a few seconds to remember where I am.

Oh, yeah.

Geezus.

If I knew for sure the others would leave me alone now, I'd almost be okay with this. Right. How can I be *okay* with someone touching me without my consent. But that isn't exactly right, because she did ask me to choose. Ha! Like I had any other option. Getting killed, maybe, by AppleFace. Or going nuts—really, truly, I think I would— if smelly old McVey got hold of me again.

I'll be able to tell at dinner, I think, if I'm safe now, and I'm more nervous than I've been since coming here. Is she going to look after me? Or act like nothing happened?

♠

The tap on my shoulder startles me. A paper napkin flies off my tray and she catches it midair. Weird thought: those hands yesterday under my clothes. Weirder thought: how easy it seems to catch a dollar bill as it floats in the air but how hard it really is.

She grasps the nape of my neck with her fingers and thumb, just like we were a doubles team, and steers me to the table where she was. I try hard not to smile because I don't want her to know how badly I need her to be nice right now.

"What's new at academe, college girl?" she says conversationally.

Finally!

"Well, before *this* happened, I was working on an essay about the moral implications of *Heart of Darkness.*" I'm reasonably sure she hasn't read it. I'm hoping she'll ask me to elaborate.

Instead she says, "To be able to think in another language. That's why Conrad's English was so...effective. You know, most of us have a Kurtz deep inside. Though few dare to admit it."

"What are...were you?" My astonishment is plain. "Did you teach? Or write? Or what?"

"Amateur philosopher," she says thoughtfully. "Life is the only teacher. And God is the only writer. I just try to understand."

Well, there's a conversation stopper. Maybe she's a religious fanatic. First Church of The Holy Rapist. I can hardly hold in my laugh, so I take a drink of the watery tomato juice and swallow it the wrong way. She pats my back as I cough.

It actually doesn't bother me that much when she touches me, even though she did what she did.

❧

It must be after midnight when I hear a key turn in the lock. The cell door slides open. It occurs to me someone must've used WD-40 on it, because it sure was a lot noisier before.

Who is it?

Quiet steps, so I know.

All at once, I'm so tired and worn out I don't think I can stand it, being here, anymore. I close my eyes and feel myself sink into a still, dark place inside.

The mattress creaks as she sits down.

It's a long time, seems like, and I can't believe it but she's humming?? Not only that, but I know the tune. If I could only remember it—"Me and Bobby McGee"! I swim back out of the dark and open my eyes.

She's looking at the floor, not at me, which strikes me as a classy thing to do—you know?—giving me some space. I take a deep breath and let it out, kind of loud, because I want her to hear it. And she does and stops humming.

"Forgive my directness, but time is, well, inexorable—especially in our current circumstances."

She rests her fingers on my cheek and runs the ball of her thumb lightly over my lips, which are dry, and when she gets to the corner she puts it in a little so her thumb is wet, and rubs back the other way. Maybe she's planning to kiss me this time?

"Sorry. No time for niceties," she apologizes, as she lies on top of me.

The springs are squeaking, and I'm so-o-o embarrassed. My face is stuck in her neck, so I turn the other way and stare at the wall, and I can't believe it but my feelings are hurt that she didn't kiss me.

Her breathing, which starts out slow, gets raggedy,

and then she gasps and I feel her body relax. Makes me feel kind of funny, actually, like I have to pee, which I tell her in order to remind her that I, too, am a person inside this body.

She lifts her head up to look at me, one eyebrow cocked.

"I see," she says, and it seems like she knows something I don't. So what else is new.

If it weren't for her weight on me, I would've hit the ceiling when the door at the end of the corridor rolled open then clanged shut again. She peels herself off me and is on her feet, one move, and reaches the door in a second.

I pray the lock to be silent, but it sounds like a sonic boom instead. Moments later I hear her laugh softly, as if she's relieved.

"...could use another twenty." A mucousy cough like an old woman smoker. Definitely McVey.

"... adequate for services rendered," she says.

Darn! I can't really hear! I crawl to the bottom of the bed. I can't see, but now the voices are clearer. I'm dying to know what the deal is with those two.

"C'mon, Plato! You never been stingy before."

"True. But more, uh, persuasion would be redundant."

"And what if I tell you no? You and your pal already get away with too much shit around here."

Long pause.

"And you think that's your doing? Keep in mind, our shit is lucrative to quite a few of you. Busting us wouldn't be in your best interest. You know how people feel about their drugs."

Whoa.

A grunt from McVey. Then footsteps, and then nothing except the buzzing of the fluorescent lights in the empty corridor.

♠

On Monday afternoon there's basketball in the yard. I wouldn't mind joining the game, except it looks dangerous.

The court is just a scabby old asphalt rectangle and two hoops without nets, and some of the players body-check, which you'd get a penalty for anywhere else. The only foul shot I saw so far was when this woman who resembles an ex–sumo wrestler whacked someone in the face with her elbow. On purpose, I'm pretty sure.

I caught her eye by mistake, and she gave me the finger. So now I'm just walking fast around the edge of the yard, keeping my eyes to myself.

When all of a sudden Plato is walking next to me, I'm startled. I hate that! Always letting her have the upper hand. I wonder if she does it on purpose, this sneaking-up thing. I'm also a little excited. It's strange, but it's kind of flattering she picked me, her being such a big shot and all.

I'm curious to know what the bribery thing with McVey is all about. I should probably mind my own business, but since when could I keep my mouth shut.

"Awesome, how you handled McVey last night. Are you paying her to stay away from me? Or what?"

Well, she could say *something* back. It's so rude to ignore me. Each step we take I feel redder and hotter until my scalp tingles. She could at least tell me she'd rather not discuss it.

The impact to the side of my head makes my teeth rattle. For a second I think she hit me, but then I hear the basketball bouncing away and see sumo woman snatch it up. She doesn't say sorry, but I don't expect her to.

I can't believe it when she throws it at me again. This time on purpose. I manage to raise my arms in time to block it. When she scoops the ball up and looks like she's going to nail me a third time, I yell, "Cut it out, fatso!"

I definitely feel braver with *her* standing beside me.

Then I'm on the ground and sumo woman's on top of me, and there Plato is with her fingers in the woman's eye sockets, wrenching her head back. Something shiny slashes upward and blood patters down onto my face. I hear feet trampling, then McVey's voice bawling, "Break it up!"

Plato lets go like a shot and starts walking backwards with her hands in the air. There's a crack of something hard hitting bone. Sumo woman goes limp and topples off me. Then Plato is helping me up and brushing me off.

⚬

I can't remember how on earth we got here, in this little room with a cot and one of those bar fridges and a sink. Everything hurts!

Plato is holding ice cubes in a towel against the back of my head where I fell. It makes my head ache worse than it did before, but at least this is a pain with an outline drawn around it.

I notice my elbow is bleeding and there's dirt all around the gash—little pebbles of crumbly asphalt—and I'll bet it's going to get infected if we don't clean it with some hydrogen peroxide or Betadine. I point to it because I don't want her to hear that soprano quavery voice I get when I'm trying not to cry.

When nothing happens, it strikes me she hasn't said anything at all since we've been in here. Well, I think I need some disinfectant for my elbow now more than the ice pack. And maybe a couple of Band-Aids.

So I turn around and forget about crying because there's blood all over her shirt front, and her ear is crusty with dried blood. Oh, God, and she's been standing there holding the ice for my head.

She's just looking at me, not saying anything. I feel an urge to wipe away all the crust and the dirt. It would at least give a chance for a clean scab to form. I take the towel from her and wet it with hot water from the sink, and start to clean her up as tenderly as I can.

Pretty soon the crusted stuff is all off and there's a trickle of fresh blood coming from her ear, where it looks like a nick came out, and she says the first thing.

"Pressure."

I didn't realize she reacted to the pressure in this place, and I'm surprised.

"Is it getting to you?" I ask.

"Apply pressure, if you would. To stop the bleeding."

Oh.

She sits down and smiles at me—little, tired smile—then pulls me down so I'm straddling her thigh. I brace her head with one hand and press the towel against her ear.

It still makes me squirmy when she gazes at me with those eyes, the color of faded blue jeans. She's warm and soap-smelling, and I've done a good job of tidying her up and stopping the bleeding. It's kind of nice just sitting here.

I'm not even all that surprised when she puts her arms around me and pulls me closer. For a second I wonder whether this is friendly or what, but when she takes the towel from my hand and drops it on the floor, I know. And know what? It's all right. It doesn't take that long, and at least she smells good. And, okay, maybe I like the attention. I don't know why she picked me, but it wasn't to be a bully or hurt me, like the others.

So when she lifts me off her leg, at first I'm a little disappointed, but I decide she probably wants to lean me up against something, like in the showers after she rescued me from AppleFace.

But she's still sitting there, so I can't figure what she wants me to do. She reaches under my shirt and brushes her palms across my nipples, which sort of tickles. Not tickling, exactly. More like an itch?

It's like she knows, because she grazes her fingernails over my breasts. At first it feels like she's rubbing the itch, and that's nice, but I have another feeling, like the itch is spreading.

When she takes her hands away I almost say something. My chest sort of misses her touch, and I *really* want to sit on her leg now. She nuzzles her face into my tummy, and I feel her tongue probing into my belly button, and little thrills play around lower down.

I guess she wants me undressed this time, because she pulls my pants down around my ankles. I step out of them, and then my panties, which, thank God, are clean ones, and while I'm wondering what comes next, she leads me over to the cot and pushes me—none too gently—and down I go.

She wedges her hands under my butt where I'm sitting and sort of shrugs my thighs over her shoulders and—oh! She really goes straight for the gusto!

Prickly heat where her mouth is pressing. The warmth is spreading into my belly and thighs. I weave my fingers through her curls and pull her face into me harder; this time I'm making sure she doesn't move away. Her nose is kind of smooshed against my pubic bone, but what she's doing has me too fired up to worry much about whether or not she can breathe.

And then *sweet Jesus*—the spasm of pleasure is so fierce it almost hurts.

I fall back on my elbows and take a deep, shuddery breath. She looks up at me, and I see her eyebrows are raised like she's asking a question. But I don't know what the question is, so I just lean forward and kiss her mouth, a light kiss, and then again, longer. And she lets me.

I don't want to say anything, like break the moment and all, but I'm really curious why she never kissed me before, so I ask anyway.

"Because that's the most intimate part," she says softly. And I see what she means.

◆

I stare out my dormitory window, watching the campus clock creep toward midnight, trying not to think of anything, most of all her, and wishing I could sleep. Yeah, right. My parents never even knew I was missing, at least, so thank God for small mercies. Maybe if I keep staring I'll get hypnotized and forget the last five days ever happened. I just want everything to be normal again, though I wonder how that's possible now I know what's out there, and how things can change on a dime.

Hard to believe only this morning I was in a whole other world. If I close my eyes, I can still see the way she leaned into my cell, casually, holding onto one of the bars. And I can still feel the little buzz of excitement in my stomach.

"Warden wants you. You're out of here" was all she said. Oh.

Mostly I felt relieved, but there was something else too. Maybe it showed on my face, my confusion, because she came over and hunkered down, balancing with her hands on my knees.

She looked at me, and what was it? Resignation? Maybe tenderness? I couldn't read her. As usual. One thing for sure, there was nothing sappy in her expression, like she was going to miss me, or poor her being in prison while I get to go have a life.

She cleared her throat as if she was going to say something, but before she could, AppleFace poked her head around the cell door.

"New arrivals," she said, grinning. "McVey says move your ass. Your turn to play bad con."

It was like the world stopped, and then started again. And while it was stopped, everything got shifted around. I mean, what did I *think* that "new fish" business was all about? Hook, line, and sinker.

Plato winked at me, fast, like she was blinking something out of her eye, then stood up and followed her *pal* down the corridor.

Well, she told me the truth about one thing, at least: It *could've* been worse. *A lot* worse. Like, what if it had been AppleFace's turn to get the girl?

.

howling: a story of woolfs
lana gail taylor

———————————→

The first time I spoke to Erin—not the first time I saw her in the bookstore buying *Mrs. Dalloway*—my words weren't fantastic or even vaguely inspired. I said the usual. "Did you find what you need today?" and rang up her purchase, a three-ring notebook, and almost dropped it. She said, "Maybe. You remind me of someone."

That could be fantastic. Or it could mean bad news. I had to ask her, "Who?"

Erin shrugged. "I don't know yet."

Until this moment, I observed Erin from a distance. This was the third time she had been in the store and the closest I'd come in proximity. Her hair looked wind blown. Two weeks before, I illicitly snatched her name of a credit card receipt. It sounds gutsy, but really I wasn't. Not lately. I pushed the notebook into a bag.

Erin placed a tube of lip balm on the counter. "I'll take this too."

Something about her voice, but I missed it, missed something. Otherwise, I might have gotten excited, thought she was flirting, but instead I worked out the math in my head: Ninety-nine cents added to four dollars and fifty-nine cents equals five dollars and fifty-eight cents plus tax.

Erin passed me a twenty, then said, "When I noticed you staring, I thought right away, She makes me think of someone."

"I wasn't staring." I gave her back change.

"You have a noble expression."

I caught her half smile showing two teeth. "Isn't 'noble' a word you use when you can't call a person 'attractive' or 'pretty'?" I held her bag out to her.

"Your face is better than pretty." Erin titled her head and showed more teeth. "What sort of face do you think I have? Since you stare at me every time I come in here." She hadn't taken the bag yet.

I tried to feign nonchalance. "Maybe I thought you were shoplifting."

"You didn't think that." Erin took the bag. "How about coffee sometime?"

◆

At 7 A.M. every morning (except Thursday when I did nothing) I clocked in at the bookstore, downed a half pot of it-was-so-strong-it-was-almost-espresso coffee (guaranteed to shake the sleep off the fur) and then accepted a semi-satisfying vegetarian something from Dynna (who worked early too and was always baking, always bringing me food.) Then I stalked the aisles and straightened books on the shelves and read author biographies on the inside flaps. Sometimes, I noted awards. I won an award once: best short story by a lesbian author. Matthew framed it for me. It wasn't up in the new apartment. Every time I posted *The New York Times* Best-Seller List, I never imagined my name there.

Dynna asked me, "What's your story?"

I didn't answer right away, but seeing as we worked together and she would probably ask the same question until she got a response (which she would consider her right since she fed me), I decided to tell her, "I got a BFA at a college back home then started an MFA. It wasn't what I signed up for."

"What'd you sign up for?"

I answered Dynna by shrugging.

"I got a couple friends in the workshop here," Dynna said as she rearranged Dorothy Allison on the shelf. "I like to put them in the order I like them," she explained before adding, "My friends say writers go for the throat."

Workshop for me was a headache, a weight lowering itself down my forehead over the bridge of my nose, my whole face. Matthew said my peers were jealous of a "wolf in sheep's clothing" and tried to nurse me back with enthusiasm and insight. "The weakest always try to bring down the strong," he insisted, "and that's what's going on in your workshop." But the workshop put a bullet in my brain. Every time I approached the computer, I felt a shot to the head, and then the weight that finally sunk like a stone in my stomach. When I left the program and then the town, I moved into a new place, and the computer stayed in the box. I unpacked it later to check e-mail, but there were too many to deal with. I got a job at the campus bookstore and observed the comings and goings, students and faculty, with mild interest to none. I wasn't hungry for socialization or inspiration. I worked and went home.

When Erin came into the store my second month here, I thought she was pretty but would have left it at that if she hadn't bought *Mrs. Dalloway*. First, it was the smell of rain-washed sidewalks that followed her into the store. Outside, the sun had ripped through a thick hide of clouds and streaked through the windows, and now it was almost too warm inside where I stood at the register. The woman wore jeans and a woolly lamb sweater; sunglasses dangled from one side of her mouth like a rabbit. She streaked past New Releases to Classic Literature. I made a bet with myself about what she would come out with: Ernest Hemingway, a sort of irony that would fade to no consequence. She was just another maybe-lesbian writing about Hemingway's homophobia or his sexism, and maybe such an attack was noble or even necessary but it didn't feel like it anymore, so I was ready to brush her off.

She came out of the books with Virginia Woolf. I recognized the cover of *Mrs. Dalloway* even from a distance. Five years ago I plotted my own *Mrs. Dalloway*, my own magnum opus, but that was mute anymore, so I ducked behind Self-Help while Dynna rang up the book. The maybe-lesbian paid with a credit card, and for a moment I thought she looked over her shoulder and caught me between the shelves; I wanted to stay with her eyes one more moment—bright, dark eyes—but she turned her head and said something to Dynna. As she left the store, I felt the hairs on my skin lifting.

♠

Obsessive-compulsive behavior is often observed in animals held captive. I saw a hyena in a zoo walk in a circle, sniff its own butt, sit down, and then start over. It did this for close to an hour. Workshop every week for three months reminded me of the hyena. I was also hyenalike slinking between the shelves of Classic Literature after the woman in the woolly lamb sweater left with Woolf's book. I snapped the other copy of *Mrs. Dalloway* off the shelf and read the first line several times: "Mrs. Dalloway

274

decided to buy the flowers herself." Who the fuck cared? I carried the book to the register and went through the credit card receipts; I did this while Dynna wasn't looking. I found the maybe-lesbian's name and recorded "ErIn" on my palm—just like that, big E and big I—and for the rest of the day, I picked up the pen a few more times and scribbled on the notepad by the register. I opened the book and read "Mrs. Dalloway decided to buy the flowers herself," a few more times.

When I got home, I ate prepared chicken from the grocery store and finished two beers. In bed, I curled the hand with the name ErIn under my chin and plunged into a dream-pocked sleep. I dreamed that, with two hands, I lifted a dead chicken over my chin and drank blood. Once upon a time, I swore writing was in my blood. It couldn't leave me. At this thought, I shuddered out of sleep and flipped on the lamp by the bed. I had kicked the sheets to a ball at my feet. I got up and wrapped a wool blanket around me and wandered down the hallway and stared into space. In the kitchen, I stared at the counters and thought, "She decided to buy the flowers herself. Herself, herself; she'd do it herself." Then I worried about my sanity.

Virginia Woolf wrote letters to friends describing the voices in her head, the depression, the nervousness, and admitted she thought she was crazy.

I picked up a beer and went into the living room: The alcohol tasted cold and biting and good. I set down the bottle and scratched my palm. I used to write like an animal dashing into a stretch of dark woods, never knowing when and where I'd come out. I grabbed the notebook off the table and noticed where I'd scribbled, "Don't forget to take out the trash" and "See if Dynna wants to go for a beer Saturday night," and then flipped to a new page and wrote: "She sat Indian style on the floor of my bedroom closet with the single light on, the naked bulb with the string that you pull, and she signaled me with a flick of her tongue through her lips. She wanted me to join her. No, she wanted to come out. Her eyes were as cobalt-blue as a night sky over the house when I was thirteen and climbed the roof because I wanted to swallow the moon."

I pushed the notebook under a newspaper and sat at the edge of the couch. Virginia Woolf suffered migraines that kept her in bed. I touched the pain in my forehead and nose as I retreated to the bedroom.

♠

The second time Erin came to the store (and I didn't talk to her that time either), she was with a couple of guys. The three of them sat at a table by one of the windows, and the guys held hands. Clouds muffled the sun overhead. The store felt cool. Erin's hair looked almost silver in the gray light. Her bangs fell over her eyes like branches. Erin propped her head in her hands, elbows jabbing the table, fingers holding the bangs off her face. Her brows pulled together. She wore thick, black eyeliner and nothing else on her face. I wrote on the notepad near the register: "Her eyes were planets divided by a belt of freckles, cheeks like a milky way of skin."

Erin and her friends stood up and hugged, and made their way toward the door.

Before I left home, before I quit the MFA program, the local paper ran a headline: "Fifth-grade teacher investigated after teaching homosexuality in school." All Matthew said was that homosexuality wasn't like getting a cold unless you considered oppression a runny nose and high fever. "We don't like oppression," the kids said, and then drew sketches of people with red noses and thermometers hanging out of their mouths.

Some kid's parents had a fit. Who knew in a college community? After all, it wasn't Wyoming. But there it was: another battle. I laid out a map and drew a line from there to here, and the spread seemed wide enough. I asked Matthew, "What do you think?" and he shrugged.

"We could go. There's room enough in the car for both of us." I held Matt's face with my eyes, and for a second we exchanged a soulful wish, a gentle nudging, and then his eyes said something else: You don't live by running away. But I couldn't move in captivity either: I hated this hypocritical college community now; I hated the workshop, what I wasn't doing in there. Later, when I called Matthew from the new place, the long-distance hum made him feel far away, and suddenly I panicked: I had abandoned us both.

I asked him about the allegations.

"I think it's turning," he said, and his tone was optimistic.

"God, I hope this goes away." I was tired.

"Then it will be something else."

"Right. How do they say it? 'Win a few battles but never the war'?"

"Doesn't mean we give up."

Matt wanted me to say something else, maybe admit that's what I did. But he stayed quiet, forgiving, and patient. Maybe he thought if enough time went by, I'd make another dash at the woods—start writing again—because Matt believed I could fight. But I barely kept hold of the phone now.

Even at her weakest, Virginia Woolf wrote, not novels but in her journals and letters, and it was only when she determined an awful truth—she couldn't write anything anymore—that she dropped the stone in her pocket.

"I should go," I said after a moment. "I got this new job."

"Yeah, what are you doing?"

"Nothing really. Just a bookstore."

Matt didn't chuckle or sigh or even say You know how crazy you are? He said, "I'll come see you. When you're settled."

♦

A chick came into the bookstore almost every week. She had a small, flat nose and wiry hair. One day she pounced on a couple of undergraduates reading a passage from a book. "Dig the fucking dykes!" one of them had chortled as the chick with the flat nose walked by. "Yeah," the other one laughed, "carpet snappers!"

The chick shouldered into both of them and then started shoving books at their faces. I recognized the covers: Willa Cather, Audre Lorde, Paula Gunn Allen, and Jeanette Winterson. "Here you go, here." The chick frowned and shoved harder.

The one laughing stopped. "Fucking crazy lezbo."

"I'll have her call security," the other one said, looking at me while fielding another book with his arms.

When I didn't say anything, he said, "What are you waiting for?"

Nothing came out; I didn't move. The chick snorted, shoving past the guys and then straight past the register before leaving the store.

I gathered the books later: They weren't biting.

♦

Two nights after Erin came into the store with her friends, I went to a bar with Dynna. Woolf was a sublime hostess, witty in conversation and sometimes a tease. She liked talking openly of things she never experienced. Dynna told me she was bisexual but more inclined toward men and had never had sex with a woman.

"I read lesbian sex scenes in books, and I like it."

I drank martinis and quoted Philip Larkin: "Get stewed. Books are a load of crap."

Later, Dynna asked me if that was why I gave up.

I didn't know what she meant.

"You know, writing."

I started in with excuses. Dynna jerked me toward the dance floor. When I protested, Dynna called me a chicken-shit. I retorted, "You'll just leave with a man," and Dynna loosened her grip. I sat down. "Don't hook up with a frat boy, okay?"

"But if it was a sorority girl, you'd think that was cool?"

I took her response as insensitive. Dynna left me alone with the rest of the slovenly drunks.

♦

When I met Erin for coffee, I found it difficult to talk. Finally I asked, "How's Mrs. Dalloway?"

"I bought a copy of that in the store not too long ago." Erin smiled. "You must have been there."

I held my coffee mug, inhaling the steam. "How is it?" I asked again.

"It's one of my favorite books. I bought that other copy for a friend."

I wanted to ask what kind of a friend.

Erin made a small, audible sound of pleasure. "That's it. That's who you remind me of, Virginia Woolf."

I shook my head.

"Yeah," Erin said. "That's it."

I felt my wry smile. "You know she wasn't pretty."

"Her face was better than pretty."

I watched steam rise from my cup like long strands of fur in the air. "There was a time when any comparison to Virginia Woolf would have thrilled me."

"Not now?"

I shrugged.

Erin rested her chin in her hand. Her bangs were held back by a barrette today and her eyes were open and dark and blue. "Tell me why not."

I thought about it. It wasn't simply that I had aspired to Woolf's greatness and the workshop shot me coming out of the woods. It was (I realized sitting across the table from Erin, admiring her eyes and smelling the coffee and wanting to touch her, boldly proclaim my attraction to her) the realization that Woolf's literary prowess hadn't done much good.

"Her bark was worse than her bite," I said.

"Whose afraid of the big, bad Woolf?" Erin smiled.

"No one," I said.

"Really?" Erin sipped her coffee. "Have you read *Orlando*?"

"Maybe. Who cares?"

"Did you know Woolf modeled the main character after a woman, another writer, Vita Sackville-West? Woolf had a lesbian affair with her."

The steam from our cups started to mingle. I showed Erin a small smile. "Are you a writer?"

"I'm terrible at it. How about you?"

I didn't answer.

"Why do you look like that?"

I tapped the side of my coffee cup with a finger. "I think I was remembering when I was in the MFA program back home."

"You *are* a writer." Erin looked pleased.

"Not really."

"How's that?"

I explained it as briefly as possible. "I quit."

Erin didn't look convinced. "You think that's why you remind me of her, because you're a writer? It's subliminal maybe, the genius, the intensity."

"I'm not a genius."

Erin smiled. "I got a feeling about you."

"I just wish Woolf had done more for lesbians. I mean, she could have; the stuff in *Orlando,* it was all a fuzzy, vague subtext, wasn't it? And she never came out; she never admitted her lesbian desire publicly."

Erin turned her face toward the window. Sunlight scratched at the clouds outside until a leg jut through and came in as a slant of light through the window, rubbing our faces and necks. "This is all mysterious, you know it?" Erin placed a bag on the table between us. "I got this for you."

I didn't know what to say.

"Open it."

It was a copy of *The Hours* by Michael Cunningham. It was a Pulitzer Prize winner, a tribute to Virginia Woolf's creative prowess, and a parallel to Mrs. Dalloway's story. At least that's what I had heard. I stared at the cover. Finally I said, "Thanks."

Erin leaned close like she was getting ready to tell me a secret, an amazing, eye-popping secret, and her voice was a conspirator's, a romantic's, an optimist's. She explained that the kiss in *The Hours*—shared by Kitty and Mrs. Brown—was a pivotal, self-discovering moment that paralleled Clarissa Dalloway's desire for Sally Seton in Woolf's book.

"It's the kind of kiss that causes a quake in a woman's

core," said Erin. "Like surreal clarity. It probably saved Mrs. Brown from killing herself."

"It didn't save Virginia Woolf," I said.

Erin thought for a moment. "Sometimes it doesn't. I mean, not if the moment goes unrealized."

I thought Erin would touch my hand now; our fingers were so close. I glanced out the window: People passed by in a hurry, not seeing her or me. And that's when Erin touched me, three fingers resting on the line of my knuckles. I felt the hairs on my skin lifting.

"Tell me about your pivotal, self-discovering moment." Erin said this meeting my eyes. I tried to read hers and couldn't.

The waitress came to the table with more coffee. Erin's fingers laced through mine. The waitress didn't appear to notice. I told Erin about Leah, my best friend during freshman year in college. We were in Leah's dorm room, sitting on the one bed in the place, and I got drunk enough to consider telling her I was a lesbian. But then Leah passed out. She was drunk too. Her legs sprawled over the bed into mine, and the sheets with the flowers all over them, flannel, were bunched up and damp from spilled beer.

Then I noticed Leah's sweater was pulled up; I could see her navel. Without giving myself time to reason it out, I lowered my head and held my lips to her belly button, the mouth of skin, the den to the inside of her body. It occurred to me this was the part of Leah that had held her to the womb. It held us all. I was overcome by wanting her, was warmed by tenderness, by the recognition of my desire, but then a paralyzing heaviness settled into my limbs: I couldn't move.

"I wrote about Leah," I admit to Erin, "and the workshop said it was typical: a lesbian wanting what she can't have. All this self-loathing and blah, blah."

"Maybe you just need to try it again. Write it again," Erin said.

"Maybe." I kept hold of her hand as a shadow outside the window caught my attention: a guy pulling money from the ATM and a pretty girlfriend who hung back. She wore a gray wool sweater. Her arms crossed over her chest. She stared down the street, which made me wonder if what she longed for was any easier. I decided it probably was.

"It got hard in a room full of heterosexuals," I said, caressing Erin's fingers. "You know, the workshop. I was trying to figure out my politics, my emotional mistakes and fears, my desire—not to mention grammar and syntax—while a bunch of straight writers passed judgment. It was like I'd never do any good. It was like they didn't want me to. I got scared, all right? I just couldn't fight anymore."

"Is that what it is to you?" Erin asked. "Fighting?"

"I had this friend," I said. "A black writer who said no matter what, everything she wrote would encompass the politics of identity because she was black. It's the same for me as a lesbian."

Erin smiled. "So every sentiment has a bigger subtext, huh?"

I met her eyes and then turned her hand over in mine. I lifted Erin's palm to my lips and kissed it with my eyes closed and then opened, lingering. A sound rose between us—a sigh or a moan—but I heard it like howling Woolfs.

♠

The last workshop was worst. My passion was buried by politics. I attacked the status quo and ostracized (heterosexual?) readers. Lezbo. It wasn't exactly like that. Academics prided themselves on their liberal views, but the view became shortsighted once flushed from the fields of heterosexual complacency. They would fidget and squirm and ponder a brilliant analysis and then at last just bristle. That was how it was in the workshop.

I might have declined a third date after that. No matter how much I longed for her initially, it became clear from that point forward—no, it was clear at the very beginning—that Erin's discussions about Virginia Woolf were not limited to just that, and also, she brought out that old copy of *Orlando* out for a reason; I was supposed to know or guess. She was patient. This morning I duck under the covers and rest my head next to Erin's thigh. Right beneath the pattern of the inhale-exhale is a whistle barely concealed. She hasn't shaved in several days. I hear her stomach churn. I could make breakfast. One of her hands rests in my hair, but the other hand, I hear it, flips the pages of *Orlando* with purpose. I imagine the book, because it's old and fragile, falling apart, but this book, I think, stays together for her. And it's going to stay together forever even though I could crumble.

Erin is a college professor. Her students come into the bookstore and whisper to each other. "That's Erin's wife."

"We're not married." I say this fast.

On our second date, I told Erin I quit.

"You don't need it," she said.

Erin left.

After we moved in together, Erin attacked my good cause. She said hanging out in animal shelters because I felt sorry for the surplus of abused and unwanted pets was irrational. When I got ready to leave on Friday mornings, at the door preparing, pulling on gloves and a hat so I could walk emaciated dogs and shovel their kennels free of crap, Erin said, "Do you remember why the little boy shot

Old Yeller? The dog didn't recognize him anymore. It was rabid and sick and in pain."

I told her to make love to me gentle.

But Erin was anything but that. On our fourth and fifth dates, she kissed me ferociously. In class she banged podiums and beat blackboards with an eraser, and after we moved in together, came home with chalk in her hair, smelling like energy, like wire, and when I twisted her hair with my fingers until she held her mouth close to mine, almost bumping, she said, "Boo."

The third time Erin came to the bookstore, she wore heavy boots that left behind prints. Later I watched one of the guys mop them off the linoleum along with pats of mud and spilled coffee. What I thought was the woman of my dreams would never stroll into the bookstore, in broad daylight when I'm sober (because I'd only be brave enough to approach a woman like her under the low lights of a nightclub with a cigarette hanging out of my mouth and a tall scotch in my stomach—boo, hiss). You see what you want in bars. You can see very little in low lights. That's when I like to kiss her. Or we make out in the apartment. On our third date, in the dark street, I kissed Erin on the mouth, felt its vastness against my lips quivering, making my core quake almost to the brink of something that would eclipse me but I didn't give over to it fully; I stopped. I waited for someone who would barge through a door and find us with a flashlight and call out some names with that face and I'd cringe away, scared.

This morning, under the covers with my head near Erin's leg, I think that gray isn't a color. It's faded black, darkened white, not really a color. In between one thing and another. I hear Erin turn another page of the book. She said I had a stone in my pocket. Almost as if so I move head and it's heavy; I move between her legs, and they're muscled and the hairs are like bristles against my cheeks. What would it be like to kiss each of her legs, the insides of them, with tears stinging my eyes and blurring, with snot down my nose and a hiccup in my breath that's a silent whistle?

Last night, Erin was up in her sleep. Sometimes, she sits up in bed with her eyes wide open but her consciousness shut, and she talks. Last night, she said, "Get up." I patted her leg, groggy, mumbling it was time to sleep. She said it again, "Get up."

"Erin," I said, more awake but still groggy, "we're sleeping."

Her head was someone's else's for just a moment, falling sideways with the eyes fluttering drunk and slightly snoring and slack and it's vulnerable to everyone else but me. It's a head and knotted hair visible against a backdrop of our bedroom, white spots and dark shadows. "Erin, I don't want to get up."

The mattress bounced softly when she fell back on the bed.

This morning, I think I feel the weight of the book beside her on top of the covers over my head. She's waiting for something. I jostle and the book falls with an audible thud on the floor. I make my way up to her navel. I press my mouth there and she sighs, cradling the back of my head with her palms. The covers fall off as I lift myself, my face upturned, hers lowering for our kiss. It's bright in the room. I imagine a thousand places I'd like to kiss her. I see now how she faces the world face-first. And I've ducked mine behind my hand.

Later, she'll pat *Orlando* in its space on the shelf. She'll wear a satisfied smile. "Finished at last," she'll say about the book but directly to me.

She wanders down the hallway humming, and I pull the cord that opens the curtains above my desk and sit down to a familiar warming-up, the glow of a third face and then the patter of steadfast typing. "Erin has gray eyes beneath her cola-colored bangs that fall forward while she reads a secondhand copy of *Orlando* by Virginia Woolf."

This morning, she presses back on two pillows and reads with the book on her knees. I don't glance at the clock to know that it's early: crust in her eyes, then a yawn, and light just after sunrise passing over her face tells me how early it is, and I'm not up now usually. Erin reads with sleep knots tucked behind her ears. She doesn't keep her hair butch-cropped: just down to her chin. Sometimes she combs it back with pomade.

I'm buried in sheets that smell like my breath, like our sleep and an interchange of dawn's sweat. I hug a pillow and gaze up at Erin, and her expression changes, not for me, for the book. The first time I spoke to her, when I worked up the guts I said something amazing. I walked up and said hi. A sound rose between us—a sigh or a moan, but I heard it like howling Woolfs.

false creek ferry

cheyenne blue

———————————————————→

The man who faces forward as he rows on False Creek passes Beth, as she waits at Granville Island for the ferry. She watches his quiet movements, the gentle splash of his oars, and tries to duplicate his motions in her head. Try as she might, Beth can't figure out the play of muscles in her body that could make that happen. She never learned to moonwalk either.

The morning is calm, a rare Vancouver October morning when the sun sprinkles the wide inlet with patterns of light filtered by the scudding clouds overhead. Only tattered rags remain of the mist that normally hangs over the mountains north of the city. The day is a bursting one, springing fully formed into the world with the abruptness of a siren, no gradual ascent of light and birdsong this morning. Beth pushes her hands into the pockets of her overcoat and waits.

She can see the passenger ferry approach: Gaily bedecked in the brightest of colors, the jaunty boat scuds over the water toward the landing. It races toward her, then pulls up and turns on a dime, like a horse in a western, settling alongside the dock. The pilot jumps out, a young man with a ponytail, and he helps out his only passenger. "Watch your head," he cautions, and the woman ducks instinctively.

"Going to Yaletown?" He smiles at Beth.

"No," she lies. "The Aquatic Center."

He checks his watch and points to a little yellow boat, far out on the water. "That one's yours; it'll be along in six minutes." He secures his ferry with deft loops of rope and sprints up the walkway to the café, returning in indecently quick time with a muffin and coffee. No passengers wait, but he frees the boat and skates out to his next destination.

Beth imagines she can smell the coffee curling back to her through the shining morning.

Two other ferries come and go, and she smiles her lies to the pilots. No, she's going to Stamps Landing, to the Aquatic Center. Such young and glowing people, she thinks, bursting with life and promise like the morning. Not even a decade separates her from them, but she feels dull and faded, a static sepia picture in a Technicolor world. Then she sees her ferry approach, a red one, the maple leaf fluttering from the stern, and her heart expands and color washes into her fingertips. Love can do this to you, love really does make the world go round, and love really does give you life.

The pilot swings out onto the dock, her blond braid swaying. Beth watches her help out a man with a walking cane, handing him onto the dock as if he were the most precious thing in her life. Then the girl turns to Beth. No need to ask where she's going, of course.

"How many ferries did you let pass while waiting for me?" The grin is white and confident. "You'll be late for work."

Beth wants to stoop and kiss her cheek, feel her turn into
the caress so that their lips meet briefly, but she does nothing. It's only been two hours since she saw her last, when
they lay close in bed. Even after all their time together, she
still feels the urgency to touch. But Leigh takes her work
seriously—this funny, not quite real job piloting a False
Creek ferryboat—and she doesn't allow any distractions.

"Three," she allows, and she knows her grin is foolish
and glowing, but she's in love, and unlike Leigh, she doesn't
care who knows it right now.

There are two other passengers for Yaletown. Beth
settles into the stern of the boat, where she can watch
Leigh without being obvious about it. Leigh is swift and
efficient as she releases the turn of the rope, swings herself
up onto the central chair, and turns the prow toward the
open water. Beth studies her, cataloging the small pieces
that are part of the whole. Today, she watches Leigh's
ankles, golden lines of flesh and bone emerging from her
blue jeans and disappearing into her canvas shoes. Leigh
never wears socks.

She disembarks at Yaletown and watches for a
moment as Leigh's ferry chugs its way to the Science
Center. The color magic leeches from her slightly, the
vibrancy she felt in Leigh's presence seeps through her
shoes into the wooden dock, and she is once more merely
Beth the nearly middle-aged accountant. She belts her coat
more firmly around her and walks to her office.

♠

Leigh calls her mid afternoon. "My turn to cook," she
says, without preamble. "I'll shop on my way over to your
place."

"Cooking" is a misnomer; Leigh never cooks. She

arranges sprouts and green things on a plate, which is probably why she's so skinny. Beth indulges her cravings for real food at lunchtimes with slices of pizza and hamburgers, which, she knows, is probably why she's so stocky. But Leigh likes raw food and the color green, and it's a small price to pay.

Beth arrives home as the sun is bleeding into the water and climbs the stairs to her apartment as penance for lunchtime pizza. Officially, she lives alone, but Leigh has a key and they spend most nights together in Beth's bed with the primrose-yellow sheets. After circling her apartment once, to see if Leigh has been and gone, she settles at her desk with her textbooks; she's studying for her master of business administration. It's a worthy subject, responsible and practical, and it will keep her moving up the corporate ladder at a steady pace.

At 7:30 she realizes Leigh has been distracted again. She imagines her flitting through the cafés on Davie Street with her friends, her bright braid swinging as she gesticulates, spending her money on friends and acquaintances with careless disregard for her pathetically low bank balance. Beth has seen the statement, the alternating lines of red and black, and she knows. She shuts her mind back into break-even analyses.

Leigh arrives at 8, and the waspish words Beth had planned to say are swallowed up by the soft lips opening over hers. When Leigh's tongue flicks over the corner of her mouth and delves inside, she's lost, and she sinks into the kiss. She can taste white wine; slightly sour now, the cheap wine all Leigh's friends buy.

Leigh's eyes are glittering and bright, and she whirls around in the small kitchen, pulling green things from supermarket bags and rummaging in the fridge for salad dressing. "Madison and Eva have broken up," she reports, the words muffled by the vegetable crisper. "I'm sorry I'm late. Eva's taking it rather badly. I couldn't leave her in that state by herself, so I walked with her to Brad's place."

She chops a tomato fiercely and the seeds splatter onto the countertop. "Madison cleaned out their apartment and took most of the furniture, the TV, all the books…" She turns, and Beth is surprised by the sheen of tears in her eyes. She doesn't care that much for Eva, thinks she's silly and pretentious, a prettied poodle in a rowdy crowd of mongrels, but Leigh's heart is as soft and convoluted as a warm pretzel.

"Eva will need a lawyer." Beth is thinking ahead, her mind shifting to find the practical thing to do.

Leigh's mouth forms an O of surprise. "She will? Why?"

"To get her stuff back. To figure out who will take over the lease on their apartment, who gets the cat. That sort of thing."

"I guess she'll just ask Madison someday, and they'll sort it out between them." She slices a cucumber into thick, translucent chunks.

So linear, Leigh's life. The innocence of a Girl Scout and unquestioning belief in a greater good. She gives money to street people and simply shrugs when Beth tells her they will spend it on booze.

Beth chews the simple food without tasting it. Her mind spins though several topics: a project at work, her brother's birthday—would Leigh mind if she signed the card from both of them, they've been together nearly a year now—the chocolate doughnut she ate at Granville Island, the excess padding on her hips. With a start, she realizes she's missed Leigh's words.

"Still three days until payday," she says, and Beth understands she's out of money.

Leigh never asks for funds; when she has money she shares, when she doesn't she shrugs and eats lightly. The ferry company doesn't pay her too well, certainly nothing like Beth's own comfortable salary. Yet, Leigh has a degree in marketing, relevant experience, and computer skills. She doesn't have to live this hand-to-mouth existence.

"When are you going to get a real job?" The words are out of Beth's mouth before she's aware of their formation, and she winces at their bitterness.

Leigh shrugs and picks a mung bean out of her salad. "I have a real job," she says mildly.

"You have work," corrects Beth. "I wouldn't call it—"

"Call it what?" Leigh isn't angry, she seldom is, instead she's wide-eyed and analytical. Curious as to what her lover is thinking.

Several options present themselves as an answer. *Important,* maybe. Operating the ferries can't compare with manipulating figures, lining up the zeros in spreadsheets, calculating differentials and returns. It doesn't have a lasting effect. Leigh's passengers disembark and blend into the world. Where's the tangibility in that, she thinks, where's the accomplishment and achievement?

Achievement—another word. Leigh doesn't come home at night and relate stories of acquisitions and profitable mergers. She tells tales of dogs with their paws over the prow of a boat and the wind blowing their ears flat against their heads.

Or *ambitious.* In ten years' time, will Leigh still be a ferry pilot? Older maybe; the blond hair salt-crusted and dulled; her strong, capable fingers red-knuckled from winters on the water. But will she still be doing exactly what she does now?

And what of herself? Beth has quiet ambitions: a corner office with a view, vice president before forty, seven years away. She can do it; she has the drive and the intelligence.

She doesn't answer Leigh directly. The words curl and die on her tongue; she doesn't want to crush this fairy-child, she just wants to guide her, help her become the person Beth knows she can be. "You can do more with your life," she says instead. The evasive answer, a lover's answer, a lover who doesn't want to quarrel over the butter lettuce and alfalfa.

Leigh fiddles with the pepper grinder. "I like my life exactly the way it is," she says. "I love skimming over the water in the mornings, the view from this apartment, and the crunch of leaves under my feet when we walk out to the ocean. I love it when you take my hand and tug me toward you." She looks up, at once wistful and avaricious, and Beth catches her breath at the longing in her eyes.

Her heart thumps once, loud and off-key, then resumes its steady rhythm. Reaching a hand over the table, winding through the maze of condiments and plates, she entwines Leigh's fingers through her own, tugging them into place one by one. Leigh's hand is dry and curls trustingly against her palm. The touch of her fingers ignites the warm, coiling sensations of love and sex, twin angels of desire. It's not even 10 o'clock, but Beth thinks of the bed with the sunshine sheets and what they will do there, together, not so much later.

She takes Leigh's hand and pulls her closer.

◈

Leigh starts later on Thursdays, so there's morning-time loving, fresh and sweet—damp, mossy sex in the wide, soft bed. Leigh's hand rests lightly on the curve of Beth's waist. Solid it must feel, stodgy marble-white slabs of flesh. Beth never feels her body is anything special, it's just the space she occupies, but Leigh makes her feel beautiful. Leigh holds her as if she's fragile, Leigh loves her as if she's truly something special and seems to genuinely delight in her explorations. She hums as she traces Beth's body with her tongue, mumbling her way over freckles and small imperfections, worshiping her breasts, stroking her inner thighs, up, slowly up, until Beth is wound tight as a spring with anticipation and need. She comes under her lover's fingers, sweetly arching into an orgasm that leaves her limp, like a floating leaf. Then she parts Leigh's thighs and loves her just as tenderly.

They lie and cuddle for stolen minutes afterward; Beth should be getting up, carefully putting on her professional face for the day, finding a pair of dark panty hose with no holes in them—at least none that show—and making sure she has all her papers in order. Instead, she presses her face into Leigh's shoulder, smelling the sleep-soft skin, feeling Leigh's hair tickle her nose like hay fever.

Reluctantly she leaves their bed and does morning-time things with toothpaste and body lotion. Leigh sits naked on the toilet, reading short stories. She does this every morning, a page at a time. She says the slowness allows her to savor the writing. Beth doesn't understand that; she reads a book in a single gulp, grabbing the words as they spring off the page. Leigh's blond hair is loose, swinging down to cover her face, feathering over her small breasts, hiding the shell-pink nipples. Translucent, her body; ethereal, even in the harsh light of the bathroom. Beth pauses momentarily just to absorb the moment.

"I have to swing by my place this evening," Leigh says. "Eva will be there—I gave her a key. I said she could borrow a few things for a while."

"Will you be over later?" Beth tries hard to remain casual since they don't live together. She doesn't want to be a grasping, clinging sort of person, but an evening without her lover is a gray one.

"Yeah," Leigh turns the page, places the bookmark carefully, and closes the book. "Will you wait for me before you eat?"

The warmth of being wanted again. "I'll cook," Beth says. "Maybe chili?"

"Lots of cilantro," Leigh agrees, and uncoils herself to say goodbye.

On the days when Leigh isn't working the ferries, Beth takes the bus. More mundane, it was her normal way of traveling in the days Before Leigh. She can see one of the tiny ferries below on False Creek as the bus crosses the Cambie Bridge; it chugs purposefully to its destination, one small part of the fabric of life in this city. She imagines the pilot; is it just a job to them, something to do until college is finished, until the acting break comes along, or is it an integral part of their life, like it is for Leigh? Suddenly she wished she had taken the ferry this morning. Although the morning is gray and subdued, the city drifting in a low mist that hides the mountains, those few minutes on the water would have given her something that a bus ride never could. A small lift of freedom to start her day. Beth disembarks and walks to her office, her head full of meetings, and profit and loss.

She takes the ferry home, missing two until Leigh's blue one swings into the dock. She is the only passenger, so once they've cleared the yachts anchored by the marina, Leigh points the boat forward and goes to stand with Beth, drawing her up, into her arms, mussing her short brown hair, kissing away her professional lipstick. The noise of the diesel engine makes talking difficult, but she hears the words "Eva" and "love you" and "lots of cilantro" in her ear.

There are passengers waiting at Granville Island. She watches Leigh for a moment, sees her sharing a joke with a middle-aged woman laden with shopping bags then receiving an enthusiastic lick from her terrier. Leigh laughs, pets the dog, then turns to assist a young mother with a stroller. The mother smiles gratefully; she looks harried, as if life is a string of petty annoyances, something to be tolerated rather than enjoyed. But as the ferry swings off into False Creek the passengers are all smiling. At that moment, Beth sees, and understands, just a little.

She buys cilantro at the market, big damp bunches of it, and on an impulse, hard green tomatillos to make the salsa Leigh likes so much. When her lover returns, bringing her tenderness and enthusiasm with her, there will be a large pot of simmering chili waiting, and the air will be warm with more than the cooking.

what the hell do you know about music anyway?

jane summer

——————————————→

It just doesn't happen. Certainly not in a world-class orchestra. Ask any performer. Ask your neighbor in 2B, the kid who does stand-up, or your aunt, the former prima ballerina. They'll both tell you: Even if a performer has chosen your knobby head as a focal point, it's not you she's looking at; you, in fact, may as well be the exit sign.

You know this. You remember your third-grade Christmas pageant, remember looking out into the gaping jaw of the audience, searching for your mom the way a man overboard searches for a thing that floats. But you learned when houselights went down, the audience couldn't be seen from the stage, and certainly not individualized. And a good thing it was for your mother, who was beached in bed with a migraine. I told you then not to panic, I fed you your lines. (What a darling lamb you made, you with your innocence and eyeglasses.) After the finale the roar from the audience took your breath away—such a feeling of discomfort that you never acted in another school play. It's your life, I said. But you just covered your ears. You can't live your life with a paper bag over your head.

Possibilities frighten you. Though you reside in a great city, you rarely attend live theater, preferring the known outcome of the movies. On the occasions when you do purchase a seat for the ballet or concert hall, maybe even an off-Broadway matinee, you're aware of a pleasurable sensation, your brain awash in Culture. But you always pack a Valium in case the possibilities inflate your anxieties so much that you jump out of your skin: What if the conductor falls from the podium, the bassoonist suffers a heart attack, the pianist loses her place? What if the lead actor develops the stomach flu or trips over a prop? What if you find yourself, as in a dream, urinating in your seat? What if there's a lunatic in the audience, a blind man weeps uncontrollably, the usher dives off the third tier? Possibilities cause you anxiety. You have seen some of these possibilities become reality—a ballerina (not your aunt) fell flat on her butt, an actor tried to exit stage right but the doorknob came off in his hand. "These things happen," says your ballerina aunt. "That's what makes live performance snap with electricity. One simply picks oneself up and continues on." But not you. A Valium under the tongue and you're calm as the Dalai Lama.

What about the Beatles at Shea Stadium? you say. How can so many girls have been wrong? You're referring to the fact that nearly every girl in the audience believed Paul (or John or George or Ringo) had smiled right at her, directly at her. Don't you realize I made that happen? I make fibbers believe in themselves on the witness stand. I falsify lie detector tests. I make adulterers relinquish responsibility for their actions.

But I swear I have nothing to do with what happens tonight.

Like eating fish, concertgoing is something you ought to do regularly. And here you are, in line at the ticket counter, flush with cash, calendar cleared. It's one of the rare holiday concerts without a whiff of "Messiah," that pervasive treacle.

The tickets in your wallet elate you, you feel you've pulled off a coup, been taken for someone you're not—a sophisticate!

What the hell do you know about music anyway? Can't read it. Can't write it. Can't sing on key. Can't tell a viola from a violin. You even have to listen to it with your eyes closed. Music is your pornography. It drives you out of your mind. You're crazy about the way it breaks your heart one minute and the next you're grinning over one of Mozart's jokes. You say music is untrustworthy? That's because you don't understand how it works. The education system in this country stinks.

Whatever happened to that singer girlfriend of yours? You were in your twenties, full of self-loathing and fat with sexual desire when you met in a downtown coffeehouse. She looked as healthy as Katharine Ross in *The Graduate,* and until she cut her hair people often made the analogy. Her sense of humor, full lips, and her interest in you were irresistible. She opened your world the way the sidewalk opens a watermelon—splat down the middle. Oh, the masses you learned, the Schubert, Bach's *Coffee Cantata,* the *lieder*! There was music always between you, even pop radio songs when you drove beyond the range of the FM reception. There were her travels wide and narrow—Vienna, Buffalo, a cathedral here, a YMCA there—while you stayed home and cared for the cats.

It was two years before she let you hear her in performance. The minute you heard her sing, you understood the cruelty of which she was capable, the cruelty of surgeons and soldiers and hopeless cases. You'd heard her vocalize in the shower; she'd sung along with James Taylor in the car. But the first time you heard her sing for good, it was here, in this same music hall. The B Minor Mass. She sang soprano and it immediately cooled your passion. Her voice made you feel terribly small and ordinary, a tenpenny nail.

For years you scoured the newspaper reviews, certain her name would appear, critics noting her emerald gown. I'll tell you this: Her voice is unpleasant now, but her lips remain red as rubies. She runs an animal rescue in a forbidding part of the state, up near the Canadian border. She lives ascetically, and not alone, and believes in no god but Richard Strauss. She used to say she didn't give a flying fuck about the audience: She sang for her father. (She was making a joke, you know, that Robert Anderson play.) She rarely thinks of you.

So you've bought symphony tickets. Being in the sixth row, you've worn velvet and put your hair up. You check your identity like a hat with the usher; once seated and handed a program, you're nothing more than an audience member; the only way to distinguish yourself would be to sneeze or go mad. It's unnerving, it's anarchic, and yet it's what you've always wanted, isn't it, a socialistic personality, a world of equals, the old paper bag over the head.

Once everyone is settled and has ceased showing off their bare shoulders and glitter, the audience becomes one, this expansive beast, sometimes breathing metronomically, sometimes bored as hell, and in the best of evenings holding its minted breath. That's what performers want to do as musicians, to slay the audience, let it snuff itself out with astonishment. Bravo!

The orchestra members take their positions and set up their music, the conductor strides out, clap clap clap. Houselights down, let the show begin.

You wouldn't have noticed her if she hadn't looked right at you. It's the Beatles syndrome, you tell yourself. It's absurd to think one of the performers would pick your orbs out of a crowd of hundreds of beady and bespectacled eyes. What would a virtuoso want with a mere aficionado of music, someone who has to pay to hear live music? But she looks again, fondly it seems, then leans toward the concertmaster in front of her, sharing a joke. For some reason you are affronted.

The orchestra opens with Britten's Simple Symphony, easy for this well-fed audience to digest. It's very stringy, full of violins doing their mournful thing as well as their jigs. You realize you miss music, you should buy a subscription series, you could sit in the last row for chrissakes, if you're so worried about something going wrong.

After the intermission, the orchestra returns, string players talking amongst themselves. The violinist turns to see if you've remained. You have. Then she shares a laugh with her stand partner and swivels again to you. You don't want to smile in case it's not you at all she's looking at. Gaze surreptitiously to your right, your left. Whip around in your seat and you're looking directly up the nostrils of the dowager behind you. Her escort grins at you like a bow tie.

At whom does the violinist smile? Is it her parents? Is there a fiancé in the audience? This thought alarms you. But with the exception of the imperial dowager and her escort, you are surrounded by immeasurably reverent Japanese teenagers, tourists. So it must be you. It is you. You are her focus. Accept it. She is flirting with you. The violinist is flirting with you from the stage. And you can't take your eyes off her. Three Sibelius humoresques and you can't look at anything onstage but her. How does she do that? How does she move you without speaking a word?

You love the intermission, the longing, the sostenuto with its endless hurt. When she returns with the string section, she sits gazing at you, her violin upright in her lap like Cimabue's *Madonna Enthroned.*

Maybe she's a nut job, one of those rare city souls who constantly smile to themselves—even Born Agains aren't that happy. But look closely. She's not exactly smiling. She's practically calling you.

Maybe she simply senses your interest in the music. Maybe she thinks you're a kindred spirit. More than once you've taken sympathy for seduction, right?

Maybe she's a god-awful musician, carrying on like this. Or else she has tremendous concentration.

The conductor's tuxedo returns to the podium, arms flapping.

You haven't heard a word of the concerto, some noisy American composer. You're busy taking down her details like minutes at a meeting. Already you love her. You imagine her legs under that long black skirt, white as plants grown underground. You're ashamed to admit it, but you have pictured her brassiere, its lace, worn, the color of bone. You've already noticed she has lovely feet, walks well in heels, walks in a way that makes your heart drop to your hips, and her hair clips sparkle like a flinty Wisconsin lake. For all her nunnish attire, she has a good-time laugh as resounding as a kettle drum. And by the way, she knows everything you're thinking. Who is she?

Edith Feldsteiner, Concertmaster, she is not. That leaves Ingeborg Ausgelicht, Kerri Clarke, Ruth Ferrar, Michiko Ubayashi, and Paulette Natalia Pierce-Smyth, the only women first violins, according to the program. You hope she is Ruth, Biblical Ruth, Ruth Ferrar, a name that comes in whispers.

She is revealing herself to you. Don't you realize, you dope, her instrument is doing all the talking? It is telling you strange things. That she loves a thick veal chop, which until this moment you dismissed as ruthless. That her kisses spill across your neck like red wine. That you will fall to your knees during her daily practice, an indigent being thrown quarter rests like bread crusts. Look at yourself. How soft and rotten you are with desire.

Oh, how beautiful she is, her broad, pale forehead framed by her dark, dark hair! Oh, how she moves with the grace of a stingray. Oh, how much like a man you feel, lusting after the calf of a woman boarding a bus.

The orchestra takes its final bow. There's no question she's looking directly at you, bewitchingly, beseechingly. You give in. You'll meet her at the stage door. The guard won't let you through the dressing room; he senses you're an imposter. But loosening her bow and wiping down her violin, she'll see you waiting there, she'll recognize your voice, she'll wave to you. The guard will let you pass.

You're on your way to her, you can't be stopped. There are music stands all around the room, winter coats draped like mourners over chairs. You push the chairs aside. You drop your program as your arms open. She closes her violin case, she closes you in her embrace. She smells like tea, vanilla wafers, freshly ground pepper. She whispers in your ear, it excites you, whispers what you've wanted to hear your whole life, whispers on even after you've become so weak she has to help you to a chair. She speaks in a lowered voice while you regain your strength. You watch as notes black as pupils fly out of her mouth, whole notes, quarter notes, half rests. Tremolos like a family of blackbirds flutter off her tongue. Chords peek from her teeth like corpses in coffins in horror flicks.

She winds her scarf around your neck, tucks her music under her arm. She says her goodbye to her colleagues and takes your arm. The whole notes shimmer under the street-light as she explains she is taking you home.

Where is home? Your childhood house? Land of the first Homo sapiens? Her hotel room? Wherever it is, that is where you're going.

She opens the hotel door. The bed has been turned down; it looks humble. You decide before you make love you will bless her, make magic signs on her body. You'll begin with the part in her hair, then down the knobs in her back, to the moist place between her unnatural toes.

"Did you enjoy yourself?" your partner asks as she reaches for your hand in the dark taxi. You're speechless. You feel the weight of lead on your chest. The program lies coiled in your lap. You can't summon any sensible words. You think you've had a stroke. It wasn't a stroke. It was the Sibelius.

contributors

←——————————————→

Harlyn Aizley is the author of *Buying Dad: One Woman's Search for the Perfect Sperm Donor* (Alyson Books, 2003). Her writing has appeared in journals, magazines, and anthologies, including *Boston Magazine, Mangrove,* and *The South Carolina Review.* Harlyn challenges her own vegetarianism each year with a pastrami sandwich from Katz's Deli.

Kathryn Ann's short fiction has appeared in the Canadian literary magazines *Prairie Fire, Room of One's Own, and Fireweed,* and in the anthologies *Dykewords II, Tide Lines,* and *Best Lesbian Love Stories 2003.* She has also published a book of short stories, *Snakes and Ladders.* Her work as a writer for *The Journal: Addictions News for Professionals,* published by the Addiction Research Foundation of Toronto, has inspired and informed her upcoming collection of stories about lesbians, alcohol addiction, and recovery.

Sally Bellerose is working on a second novel about a jaded nurse, a developmentally challenged man, and a griefstricken mother. She received a fellowship from the National

Endowment for the Arts for her first novel, *The GirlsClub*. The novel has found an agent and will hopefully find a publisher in the near future.

Lucy Jane Bledsoe is the author of the novels *This Wild Silence* and *Working Parts* (winner of the American Library Association Gay/Lesbian/Bisexual Award for literature), as well as *Sweat: Stories and a Novella*, a Lambda Literary Award finalist. She received a 2002 California Arts Council Individual Artists Fellowship as well as a National Science Foundation Artists & Writers in Antarctica Fellowships. Her work has been widely published in anthologies and periodicals such as *Ms.* magazine, *Newsday, Fictional International*, and *Northwest Literary Forum*.

Cheyenne Blue writes travel guides and erotica. Her erotica has appeared in *Best Women's Erotica, Playgirl, Mammoth Best New Erotica, Best Lesbian Erotica*, and on various Web sites. Her travel guides have been jammed into many glove boxes across the U.S. To see more of her work, log onto www.cheyenneblue.com.

Orly Brownstein lives in Los Angeles, where she writes and edits fiction and nonfiction, and spends too much time watching all the variations of *Law & Order*.

Lisa E. Davis lives in Greenwich Village and has no children, but she admires those who accept such an enormous responsibility. She is the author of a novel *Under the Mink* (Alyson Books, 2001), about gay and lesbian entertainers in Mafia-owned Village nightclubs in the 1940s. Find out more at www.underthemink.com.

Zsa Zsa Gershick is the author of the award-winning oral history *Gay Old Girls* (Alyson Books, 1998) and the forthcoming *Secret Service*, a collection of interviews with lesbians who have served in the military. Reach her at gershick@hotmail.com.

Tzivia Gover is the author of *Mindful Moments for Stressful Days* (Storey Books, 2002). Her prose and poetry have appeared in anthologies and journals such as *Testimonies, Love Shook My Heart* (volumes 1 and 2), and *Home Fronts*. She has holds an MFA in writing from Columbia University.

Carol Guess is the author of *Seeing Dell, Switch*, and *Gaslight*. She teaches at Western Washington University and lives in Seattle.

Jane Eaton Hamilton is the award-winning author of six books, most recently a collection of short stories, *Hunger*, a finalist for the Ferro-Grumley Award for Lesbian Fiction. She is also a two-time first-place winner of the Prism International short story contest ("Goombay Smash, 1998"; "Sperm King," 2003). Her stories have appeared in the *Journey Prize* anthologies, *Best Canadian Short Stories, Best American Short Stories*, and the Pushcart Prize series. She is working on a novel, *Wild Mare*. For more information, visit www.janeeatonhamilton.com.

Amy Hassinger is a graduate of the Iowa Writer's Workshop. She has worked as an English teacher, a freelance writer, an educational consultant, and a technical editor. She has published a Maine studies textbook for middle and secondary school students (*Finding Katahdin: An Exploration of Maine's Past*, University of Maine Press, 2001), as well as a novel, *Nina: Adolescence* (Putnam, 2003). Amy lives in Michigan, where she's working on her second novel.

Karin Kallmaker is best known for having published more than a dozen lesbian romance novels, from *In Every Port* to

One Degree of Separation. In addition, she has a half-dozen science fiction, fantasy, and supernatural lesbian novels in print under the pen name Laura Adams, including *Seeds of Fire.* Her novel-length works, including "After Dark" erotica, can be found at www.BellaBooks.com. Karin and her partner have been together for more than a quarter of a century, and are Mom and Moogie to two children.

Andi Mathis is a muscle-bound union shop steward waiting for a picket line. She has distant ties to Mississippi. "Lessons" is her second published story.

Lesléa Newman is an author and editor whose forty books include *Good Enough to Eat; She Loves Me, She Loves Me Not; The Best Short Stories of Lesléa Newman;* and the classic children's book *Heather Has Two Mommies.* Her literary awards include fellowships from the National Endowment for the Arts and the Massachusetts Artists Foundation. Nine of her books have been Lambda Literary Award finalists. A native New Yorker, she lives in western Massachusetts. Find out more at www.lesleanewman.com.

Achy Obejas is a widely published and award-winning poet, fiction writer, and journalist. She is the author of the short-story collection *We Came All the Way From Cuba So You Could Dress Like This?,* and the novels *Memory Mambo* and *Days of Awe,* a Los Angeles Times Best Book of the Year and winner of the Lambda Literary Award for Lesbian Fiction.

S. O'Briant spent several years as an executive recruiter, but she quit the headhunting business to return to her original ambition of writing a novel. An excerpt from that book, *The Sandoval Chronicles: The Secret of Old Blood,* was published in *La Herencia.* Her work has appeared in *Whistling Shade, AIM Magazine,* and *Ink Pot.*

Jenie Pak received her MFA in Poetry from Cornell University and has writing published or forthcoming in *Alligator Juniper, Asianweek, The Asian Pacific American Journal, Blithe House Quarterly, Dangerous Families, Five Fingers Review, Love Shook My Heart 2, Many Mountains Moving, The Oakland Review,* and *Watchword Press.*

Shelly Rafferty is a writer, activist, and parent living in upstate New York. Her fiction has been published in more than twenty anthologies and journals. She is working on her dissertation, "The Necessary Secret: Ambivalence, Silence, Disclosure, and Knowledge in the Personal Writings of Teachers, 1905-1935." When she's finished, she plans to drink more beer.

Gina Schien's short fiction has been published in anthologies in Australia and the U.S. She is the author of the novel *Timing the Heart* and the play *Relative Comfort*, which was produced in Sydney and in Chicago as part of the Pride 2000 season. She has been a resident at the MacDowell Colony in New Hampshire and lives in Sydney's inner west with her girlfriend.

A creator of lesbian songs and stories, **Anne Seale** has performed on many gay stages, including the Lesbian National Conference, where she sang tunes from her tape *Sex for Breakfast*. Her stories have appeared in many anthologies and journals, including *Set in Stone, Dykes With Baggage, Wilma Loves Betty*, and *Harrington Lesbian Fiction Quarterly*. Her first novel, a comic mystery called *Packing Mrs. Phipps*, is due out from Alyson Books later this year.

Elizabeth Sims is the author of the noir novels *Holy Hell, Damn Straight*, and the forthcoming *Lucky Stiff*. She holds degrees from Michigan State University and Wayne State University, where she won the Tompkins Award for fiction.

An experienced reporter and bookseller, she has written about the bookselling business for *LOGOS: Journal of the World Book Community* as well as book reviews for the *Detroit Free Press*. Learn more about Elizabeth at www.elizabethsims.com.

Jane Summer is the author of the novel *The Silk Road*, a finalist for the Ferro-Grumley Award for Lesbian Fiction.

A single mother, **Lana Gail Taylor** is an MFA student at the University of Oregon. Her work has appeared in many places, including *Best Women's Erotica 2004*, *Best Gay Erotica 2004*, *Best Bisexual Women's Erotica*, *Slow Trains Literary Journal*, *Element* magazine, and *Blithe House Quarterly*.

Leslie K. Ward lives in Alaska. Her work has been published in *Pillow Talk II* and *Bedroom Eyes*. She used to own a café.

about the editor

stacey halper

Angela Brown is a born-and-raised Midwesterner living in West Hollywood, Calif., where she is an editor, writer, and cartoonist. Her work has appeared on NPR and the Pacifica Radio Network, and in *Out* magazine. Her anthology *Mentsh: On Being Jewish and Queer*, is due out from Alyson Books later this year. Her best friend in the world is a one-eyed dog named Harry Caleb Brown.